DUMAINE STREET

By Evelyn Klebert

Dumaine Street
By Evelyn Klebert

A Cornerstone Book
Published by Cornerstone Book Publishers

Cornerstone Book Publishers
Hot Springs Village, AR
cornerstonepublishers.com

ISBN: 978-1-61342-902-0

This book is dedicated to all of those who have been misunderstood and all of those who have suffered because of hatred, violence, or cruelty.

Table of Contents

DUMAINE STREET

Chapter One

Rebecca Wells

Footsteps, that was the answer, simple answer really, just placing one foot in front of the other and moving slowly, telling yourself to breathe and asking your heart to slow its ridiculously quick pace.

It was no mystery that life had become overwhelming. In fact, she often felt as though she was drowning in its furious maelstrom of activity. She couldn't shut it out, you see. All the clamoring, clawing, in her head — emotions, painful, vicious, draining. Some days it took all her effort to move. To even venture outdoors seemed impossible. There was no doubt. She was collapsing inward.

Doctors would prescribe antidepressants, sedatives, but it wouldn't stop things, certainly not. For a time, she would become numb, distant, and hear those voices more removed, far off. And then, of course, they would encroach again. Sometimes at night, in dreams, she would wake up screaming, shaking. But she lived alone, and there was no one to hear.

She continued to walk onward. She hadn't parked near his house. Walking, she'd thought, would give her time, time to reconsider if she wanted to do so. After all, what did she really know about this man? The lady at The Waxing Moon Bookstore had recommended him as somewhat of a spiritualist. He was a writer, she'd said, of esotericism, who lived quietly in the city, used to be a doctor of some sort. But now was almost a bit of a recluse, or so she thought.

"Why would he see me?" she'd asked.

The lady was a palm reader, one she'd been to on more than one occasion. She'd always been drawn by the supernatural. That was undeniable. And truthfully, she'd wondered and, at times, was convinced that it had caused the increasing problems she was experiencing. It was a question she'd asked her friend, her friend, the palm reader. "It's not quite that black and white. I know you want a simple answer, but it isn't. It truly isn't that simple."

But a week ago, on her last visit, she'd given her his name — a name and a phone number she'd called with great trepidation.

"Hello."

What an awkward moment. Her strongest inclination was to hang up, but with cell phone technology, he could easily call her back or at the least trace her number. That was, of course, if he was inclined to bother.

Deep breath, "Hello, Mr., I mean Dr. Sutton, a friend gave me your number, Louise Dufour from The Waxing Moon bookstore."

There was silence, and just for a moment, she thought perhaps he'd hung up. "I see," the man at the other end of the line responded quietly.

"She thought that maybe I should consult you, but if this isn't a good time—"

"Louise doesn't usually give out my name, except in extreme cases."

"Well," she murmured, at a complete loss as to what to say. Was she supposed to spill it all out to a stranger over the phone? "Maybe this was a mistake," she said, at a loss amidst the awkwardness and uncertainty.

"Would you like to meet?" he said unexpectedly, joltingly. After all, she hadn't told him anything.

"I, um," she hesitated, remembering in a rush that she was desperate, and this was a last-ditch effort. "Would that be possible?" she asked.

"Yes, Miss."

"Rebecca, Rebecca Wells."

Dumaine Street, that was the address, 3226 Dumaine St. *"Becca, what's the matter with you?"*

Back then, it had seemed somewhat manageable. *"I can't explain it. I feel panicked."*

"It's only nerves. That's natural when you're off to school."

But it didn't feel like nerves. How could anyone have this kind of wild, over the top, **"Nerves"** when they weren't thinking about anything at all? It was different, bone-crushing panic.

She walked down Dumaine Street, down the small, uneven sidewalk. It was an older neighborhood in the Faubourg St. John district of New Orleans. Very old, actually, some of the houses dated back to the 1700s. But not on this street. These weren't quite that old, a lovely mixture of well-kept shotguns, doubles, single-family homes, such a lovely landscaped, well-kept, inviting neighborhood. Hadn't she been here on a field trip with her history class? No, that was touring the old Creole Plantation on Moss Street, near the water. They'd picnicked on Bayou St. John, but that was several years back when she could still teach before that too became too much.

She stopped. She hadn't realized she'd traveled so far. Scanning the houses, she spotted it. There it was, a double, but with only one address — 3226 Dumaine St.

"*Becca, what are you doing here?*" she whispered to herself. How could she possibly explain to a stranger the shambles her life had become? She wasn't a candid or a particularly truthful person. She'd learned long ago to cover, cover so many things, but that was before she'd become so desperate.

It was a quiet house. That was how it struck her, serene. Just a few steps backward, there was a busy one, painted dark colors of burgundy and brown, delightfully artful latticework, and a bold slab of stained glass as its front door window. But this house was different. It was predominantly ivory with thin white columns in front and dark green ironwork running across the porch. And, of course, the doors, there were two as was usual in doubles but still the one address with dark green doors that looked like extra-long shutters. It was similar to the old French Quarter houses, those shutters covering up the real doors, folding in on themselves in pursuit of privacy. Is this what Dr. Gabriel Sutton was doing, pursuing privacy?

Again, she hesitated. *What are you doing, Becca?* She asked herself. Was there any way to turn back, step backward, and still survive?

There was some young girl who'd been found not long ago in the water, had driven her car straight into the Bayou St. John. They said she'd been drinking, and it had been late at night. She wondered if that was so or if she was just seized in a moment, a dark moment, and those silent waters felt more welcoming than continuing to go on. Fatigue does that, she supposed, just fatigue.

She looked again at those green shuttered doors at the house on Dumaine St. What were they covering? What would change if she rang that doorbell near one of them?

The one on the right, not the left. No doorbell there, just the one on the right.

She ascended those few white steps without thought. Too much thought would stop her, would make her lie to herself and believe she could return to what had been.

The clock over the stone fireplace chimed three. At night, he turned off its sound. There was a little button in the back. He had acute hearing, always had, very sensitive. He strummed his fingers on the walnut mantle. He'd thought about making himself a cup of tea, but then again, his appointment would be here any second. Perhaps she'd like tea. He bowed his head a bit, listening, concentrating. There was movement outside. He could hear it from where he was sitting, out there on the sidewalk. A change in the air, a rustling, someone's light footsteps on the concrete, but they hesitated. He wondered now if, indeed, there would be an appointment at all.

Louise rarely referred anyone to him for help. It wasn't as if he had any kind of practice anymore, nothing traditional. There was one fellow about four years back. He was now studying in India, still received an email from him now and again. It was more that he tried to help, put people on a new path.

He wondered how long he should wait before making his tea. She wasn't pacing, this lady, exactly. It was more like shuffling, shuffling her feet a bit anxiously on the pavement, clearly very nervous this one. But then he'd gotten that loud and clear on the phone — Rebecca Wells. He turned the name over in his mind just to see how it felt, its textures, its nuances. It felt like mystery, secrets to him.

Now that could be intriguing. He did enjoy a good mystery.

He felt a shift, sort of a slight charge in the air, and then quick determined steps and the doorbell. Well, it seemed he would indeed have company after all.

He wasn't what she'd expected, although she hadn't realized until just that moment that she'd expected anything in particular. He was a youngish man, somewhat, perhaps in his forties, maybe, although she'd never been particularly accurate in age estimation. He was tall with light hair, not blond, not exactly brown, maybe something bordering on both. He had a deep voice, not incredibly deep, and wore casual clothes, blue jeans, and an untucked button-down plaid shirt over them. Not what she'd expected. She'd expected someone, well, maybe someone older, more aloof, less amiable, less accessible. This man, this Gabriel Sutton, seemed far too approachable. Rebecca didn't trust people who were too friendly at the offset. She'd been taken in before.

"Would you like some tea?"

They were inside the house, had stepped right through that shuttered door. She was right. Behind was a sort of glass door with a screen door beyond it. And within was a warm room, a den with a fireplace, though unlit, and walls that were a curious mixture of sheetrock and brick, probably renovated from the original structure. And paintings, there were lots of paintings and old photographs on these walls. She hesitated, "Sorry?" she asked, feeling relatively certain he'd said something.

She was standing still near that front door, still ajar, still time perhaps to make excuses and leave if indeed that was what she chose to do. "I asked if you'd like some tea. I was just going to get myself some."

"Oh," still choice, still moments and fluid instances to shift the path of things to come. "Yes, I suppose."

He was looking at her oddly, or did she simply feel odd? He had strong cheekbones and watchful eyes, a color that she wasn't close enough to glean. "Peppermint, is that all right?"

"Yes, fine."

A smile hesitated across his face, and for an instant, she wondered if perhaps he felt as awkward as she did. "Well, why don't you make yourself comfortable, Rebecca while I get it."

She nodded tentatively and watched him disappear down a hallway. She glanced around again. This was only one side of the double. She recognized its dimensions, but it was one address. With some distraction she wondered what was on the other side.

He put the tea kettle on the stove. He could have used the microwave. It would have been quicker, and he seldom used that bright red tea kettle that his younger sister had bought him as a Christmas present some years before. But he needed a few moments, a few moments to assimilate whatever was happening. He sunk into one of the wooden chairs at the small breakfast table. This was unprecedented. His legs felt wobbly, and his hands. The only way he could describe them was almost trembling.

He closed his eyes, bowing his head a bit to collect himself. He breathed deeply, centering his focus, his energy.

This sensation, this particular sensation he was experiencing was impact. Rebecca Wells' very presence had hit him hard, nearly physically, in a way he had not experienced before.

The tea kettle began its loud whistle, and he opened his eyes. Steam had begun pouring out of its spout — not enough time, not enough time for him to compose himself. He stood up on legs that he demanded hold him up more steadily than they were inclined to do, and he pulled the tea kettle from the heat, flipping the knob below to its off position.

Again, he cleared his mind, demanding internally that he focus as he leaned with his hands against the white cast iron stove.

Perhaps, he should send her away. How could he help her if he wasn't able to function properly?

Steadying himself, he pulled two mugs from a wooden cup tree on the counter. Give up before he even tried? That wasn't his style. He put the tea bags in the mugs and poured the steaming water from the kettle. He had to get hold. He had to figure out exactly what it was about this woman that had elicited this reaction from him.

Chapter Two
Muddy Water

It was insulated here, she thought, continuing to wander around the den of Gabriel Sutton's home — no clamor in her head, as there usually was.

"No, Ms. Wells, there is no evidence of schizophrenia or any other similar psychotic aberration."

Not schizophrenic, not bipolar, not clinical depression, nothing on a psychological radar, and yet she heard them, voices, feelings in her head that simply didn't belong to her.

"Tea's ready," he said from behind her. She hadn't heard him return to the room. She was too deeply caught up in that sticky web that was her thoughts. She turned toward him. He was holding two steaming mugs in his hands.

"Dr. Sutton, I think maybe this is a mistake."

"Gabriel, please call me Gabriel, and at least have a cup of tea with me before you leave." He'd handed her the hot mug, then settled into a recliner near the fireplace. "Please sit down," he indicated a rocking chair not far from his. "Mistakes, I think, are a bit underrated. It's where we learn the most about ourselves."

Rebecca could hear stirrings in the house, stirrings that seemed unattached to where she presently found herself. So, she sat down in the rocking chair, complacent for the moment to make the best of what could be a calamitous error.

Medicine, he'd practiced it for nearly twenty years, initially as an intern and then later as an endocrinologist affiliated with one of the larger hospitals in Texas. Upon reflection, he could see it clearly as a path, a cord tying the events of his life, leading him to where he should be. There was a connectedness within the body to something beyond he'd found. It was truly the only explanation. Colleagues might insist on the randomness of events, but Gabriel, Gabriel Sutton had always been afflicted with a holistic sight. He could see the larger patterns, patients who'd lost their interest and connection to the world, organs one by one going into failure — high emotion causing the body to attack itself almost as though it were punishing itself. And then there were the survivors, given hopeless prospects, who defied any prognosis. Something, a more profound hand, was at work in it all. And it frustrated him, at times, that he seemed to be the only one who could see it.

So, he moved on, seeking to learn in other ways.

He was quiet. With this Rebecca Wells, he was in no hurry to try to force much of anything. "Tea's all right?" he asked.

She glanced up. She had large eyes, large brown eyes with flecks of gold and green, and shoulder-length brown hair, not straight, sort of wavy. "Yes, it's fine." She was slight, on the thin side, small, maybe five-five, and maybe in her thirties mid, late, perhaps. "I suppose you're wondering why I'm here at all."

"Well, Louise sent you. Do you see her often, Louise?"

"Oh," she hesitated, "every few months, more often lately, I find it helpful, her readings."

He responded carefully, "So then you believe in palmistry, psychic intuition."

"Yes, I suppose to an extent. I've read some Edgar Cayce, Jane Roberts."

He nodded, "And has it helped reading them?"

"Helped?"

"Yes, with what you're struggling with."

She didn't answer him, just sipped her tea for a moment and then brought the mug down to a resting place on her knees. She was wearing a skirt, a dark, longish skirt with black boots, and a burgundy-colored sweater. "I suppose, at times."

He wondered if he should push. He was feeling so many levels of protection here — sort of like a wound with layers of scar tissue over it, haphazardly trying to heal but unable to do so properly as the wound is frequently ripped open. "Rebecca," she looked up a bit fearfully. "Tell me what's wrong."

Tears, he could see them, sudden tears just hesitating on the brim of her eyes. "I'm so tired," she whispered.

"I know," he said because he could feel this. "Tell me what's going on."

She hesitated, and he wondered for an instant if she would answer at all. "It feels like pain, pain inside me all the time."

The floor creaked, creaked beneath the long skirt of her cotton nightgown. It was damp at the edges, making it heavier, more cumbersome than it should have been. Even her bare feet made the floor creak. The wood in that long hallway was rotting. It could give way easily beneath the weight of her water-soaked hem.

"Pain?" he said, though it sounded like a murmur.

There was something up front again in that room. She should wake her mother and father, but they were sleeping somewhere, so hard to reach.

"You're feeling pain now?"

"Sounds crazy, I know."

It sounded like a hiss to her, a curious hiss. Maybe it was a nightmare, and her gown was so heavy, so soaked, stained with muddy water at its hem.

"Can you tell where it's coming from, this pain?"

"I-I don't know. It hurts so much. I'm afraid to look."

"Afraid of what, Rebecca?"

"I don't know. That I'll discover something terrible, something I can't live with. There's so much fear."

She hated the voices. They frightened her. All she wanted was to find her mother. She would fix things, make things better.

"It's loneliness, fear, fear engulfing me. And anger, I don't understand it."

"Rebecca, listen to me. I want you to try to focus on the feelings, where they are coming from. I don't believe they are yours."

If only they would leave, leave her house. Then she wouldn't go outside and be lost again, lost inside that cold water.

"It feels like I can't breathe, like drowning."

She felt Gabriel Sutton's hands on her arms. "Try to be calm, focus, focus on being calm."

"It's so cold, so much fear. I can't. I can't!" She rasped, feeling his hands tighten on her.

She stood up, pulling away from his grasp and moving toward the front door. She stared down at the wooden floor. Sometime over the last few moments, she'd spilled her tea and hadn't even been aware of it. "I can't do this. I can't stay," she said shakily.

Gabriel Sutton stared at her with confusion. Then, an unexpected expression crossed his face as though he was a bit pleased. "Well, Rebecca, thank you, I had no idea."

"Thank you? For what?" she said shakily.

"Clearly, I have a ghost. Must be a shy little thing because I had no sense of it."

Her head spun, and she stared at him as though he'd lost his mind. "What did you say?"

The smile that she was relatively certain had lit his face only seconds before dissipated. "I feel pretty certain that's what you're tapping into."

"Tapping into? What does that mean, tapping into?"

"You don't have a clue, do you?" She wasn't sure, not sure at all if he was speaking to her or himself.

A sharp intake of breath, her sharp intake. "I need to go."

"You don't have to be afraid. You're feeling emotions, hearing things, sensing shifts around you, isn't that it?"

She stepped back. How far back did she step? Perhaps her back was against the door, but she wasn't sure. What was he saying? She couldn't make it out. There was this sound in her ears, this roar rising, muffling the rush, rush of cold water. She opened her mouth to speak, to scream, but nothing came out. There was no air, that hot bottled-up feeling of getting no air.

He'd grabbed her arms again, shaking her roughly, shaking her so hard she could feel it rattling through her spine. "You've connected Rebecca," he said. Was he shouting? The water, the rush of cold water into her ears, made it so hard to hear much of anything. "Break it. Break it!" And then he slapped her face, causing a sudden jolt.

She yanked herself out of his grasp. "No!" she screamed.

But he put his arms around her, pulling her securely against him. She thrashed, thrashed, and then fell to her knees.

Her skin felt so cold, so cold. It was warm in the den, but her flesh felt cold against his hands. She was taking deep breaths, gasping as though she were hyperventilating. He still had his arms around her, but he could feel the connection had broken. She was trembling, trembling in his hands. "You struck me," she whispered.

He had. Gabriel Sutton had never hit a woman in his life, but he had this one out of fear, fear that Rebecca Wells might actually drown in front of his eyes, drown from some bizarre empathic connection to a ghost he couldn't see. "I'm sorry," he said softly. They were sitting on his hardwood floor, and he had no idea what to do next. "I didn't know how to stop what was happening."

Her head was bowed, and she was still shaking in his hands. "Am I losing my mind?"

"No," he touched the top of her head. He could still feel the terror coursing through her. This was more than problematic, to say the least.

She looked up at him, eyes filled with panic. "Can you help me?"

He gently touched the side of her face. "I'll certainly do my best."

Becca fought to clear her mind. She was closing tonight, a boutique on the edge of Magazine Street. She breathed in deeply. She needed this job and had graciously been offered the post of assistant manager by a friendly acquaintance a little less than a year ago. That was after she'd determined that she couldn't teach anymore.

It was a nice shop, *Nola's Apparels* — sort of a mix of souvenirs, lady's apparel, and a small smattering of jewelry. Not a particularly fulfilling place to work, but it helped pay the bills, although she did have to deal with the public. Luckily, it was not the sort of prolonged exposure that teaching had demanded.

They closed at six, just half an hour away, and she was alone tonight. If she would just concentrate on the menial tasks that were demanded of her, she could get through the evening. Then it would be all right.

"You clearly have some extreme empathic abilities."

"What does that mean?" He had helped her to her feet, and she was sitting in the rocker again, the one she started in not so very long ago.

She blinked, her eyes trying to resituate herself in the present, but it was more than difficult. Yesterday had been a day like few others.

"You need to relax."

"I need to understand."

"Of course," he'd said. He'd been standing near her, nearly over her, one hand leaning against the fireplace's mantle. He wasn't so calm now, not so affable as he'd first seemed when she'd arrived. "Rebecca, maybe you should start by telling me what drove you to come here."

She frowned. She couldn't help it. It had finally subsided, all that calamity in her head. "I thought that was obvious by now."

"I'd still like to hear it," he said with some deliberation.

"Well, I've been to doctors, psychiatrists, because of the things I hear, things I feel, and sometimes—"

"See," he finished her thought.

"Yes, sometimes, I've always tended to be rather emotional, changeable, and for most of my life, I assumed it was a personality quirk. Some people are born less stable, but it's gotten worse over time. And—"

"The other things, the voices."

She nodded, beginning to feel truly ridiculous. After all, it was one thing to say something to yourself and quite another to express it aloud. "Yes, voices like people are talking around me. Most of the time, I hear the sounds, loud murmurings, but have no idea what's being said. It's in a rhythm, a cadence that is undecipherable."

"Foreign?"

"Honestly, I have no idea. But then other times—"

"Other times, you do understand."

She sighed, feeling completely and utterly drained of every ounce of her strength. "Why are you finishing my thoughts?"

There was a slight smile, although he did still seem very grim. "Sorry, seems easy for me to follow their direction, you were saying."

"Yes, sometimes I understand. But they're so often upset, and the emotion rages like waves. It's painful like it was," then she stopped. She hadn't intended to go that far.

"I need you to be open with me about this, Rebecca, if I have any hope of helping at all."

"I used to teach at a private school on Canal St. I taught science and history."

"Used to?"

"Yes, then it got too difficult. It became difficult for me to be around people so much, to engage them. I felt — I don't know how to explain it."

"Their emotions?"

She looked up at him as though he were mad. "But that's not possible."

"Did it happen?"

"I thought I was just becoming unstable."

"I have no doubt you were. But now the question becomes what exactly was making you unstable."

Chapter Three

Navigating Normal

She frowned at the recollection and began straightening a clothing rack in the boutique. It hurt her head to think about this. This was a good day to be at work. A good day on Magazine Street when it wasn't so busy, not so many people, and she could breathe.

They'd talked a bit longer, and then she'd left his house. She didn't ask him what had happened to her there, didn't ask him to explain his reference to a ghost or much of anything else. It was almost as though he understood there were real, tangible, finite limits to what she could absorb. And when she left the house on Dumaine Street, she had more than reached it.

He had told her, however, that he would be in touch. And that was about it. Rebecca really didn't expect much of anything. She simply wanted to go home, disappear into her apartment, and shut the world out. But as it was, that was not to be. Just as she was walking to her car after closing the shop, her cell phone rang.

"I'm glad you could meet me."

She smiled, still slightly surprised to be here at all, but events had escalated quickly. It was a little Italian restaurant, Compagno's, on the corner of St. Charles and Fern. In truth, she'd only been here once before, actually many years ago. "I was surprised that you called. I mean so soon—" her voice drifted off. This was awkward. Her life was awkward, so she supposed it was only par for the course.

"Yesterday, I didn't like where we left things. It felt very unresolved."

She picked up an oversized glass of red wine. The glass was only about a quarter filled, but it felt ridiculously huge. She sipped it, and it was strong, intensely comforting to her just now. "Can things like this be resolved?" she murmured.

He frowned, eying her in a way she found intensely uncomfortable. Then again, she'd found it necessary to shun people for some time, so who was she to say what was "normal" in any regard?

"I realized I don't know much about you, Rebecca."

"Becca," she answered softly, wishing they'd topped off this overly large goblet of wine. "How's your ghost?" she asked, taking another sip. They'd ordered dinner before they'd begun this conversation. It was early enough so that the restaurant was virtually empty except for a couple across the room in a darkened corner that she was more than sure had no interest in their conversation.

"Hiding," he murmured. "I can't sense her at all."

"You're sure it's a she."

"Seemed to be, at least, what I picked up when you made your contact. You know you have quite a gift, Becca, being able to connect with lost spirits at such a level."

She looked at him in dismay. "Gabriel, I mean—"

"No, please, Gabriel is fine."

"Gabriel, I have no idea what you're talking about. Contacting spirits, gifts, I have lived with this, whatever it is, instability of mind for so long. I mean, it's virtually driven me insane. All I want is to get rid of it, be a normal person, and live normally."

He was staring at her intently again, making her uncomfortable, so she did what she could, took another sip of wine. "Does that help?"

She frowned, "What?"

"The wine? Does it help?"

"It doesn't hurt," she said a bit defensively. She was good at defensive.

He nodded, "I can't help you become what you're not, but I might help you learn to cope with what you are."

"That's not really what I had in mind," she said with a tad of disappointment.

"Well, sometimes we have to change course."

And then the waiter arrived with their Caesar salads, effectively slicing the intensity of the moment.

It bothered him, the drinking, mostly because he didn't, not anymore, not for some years. There had been a time, a time a while back when he'd fallen onto that crutch, finding that indeed he had to be careful in that regard. Addictive personality was the technical term.

There were so many layers here. He had to be careful to keep somewhat of a clinical distance. That much he'd learned from being a doctor. It would be difficult to help if one got too emotionally involved.

"Have you been married?"

She glanced up from her salad. "What?" she asked with a bit of surprise.

"Just wondering, that's all."

"No," she said flatly. She'd ordered a refill on the wine, second glass. He was keeping count, couldn't let her drive home if it went beyond this.

"Really? Not close?" he asked.

"Close?" she echoed his question.

The armor was powerful here. "Becca, you have to open up with me a bit if I'm going to help you."

"How could prying into my personal life possibly affect my psychological makeup?"

"I think you just answered your own question."

She seemed to stiffen a bit, then looked off beyond him over his shoulder to some distant place. "This isn't easy for me," she murmured.

"I understand that, but you did come to me."

"Close? I suppose, once," she sighed. "A teacher where I worked, but it just seemed too complicated. I mean, I was too complicated."

"Because of what you were struggling with?"

She nodded, "I had to quit my job. Teaching, I mean. I loved it, but then it began to hurt too much. Being too close to all those people, I could feel so much—"

"Of their pain?"

She shook her head, "I don't understand. Why does it seem so simple to you? Other people — doctors, friends, family — no one can understand this, but to you, it seems so simple."

He shrugged, "I don't know Becca. I guess I've learned to look at life differently."

There was a girl, a teenager, who broke the camel's back, so to speak. Her name was Beth, Beth Wallace. She could still see her in her mind, long blond hair, lovely girl. But there was always something about her that chafed at Becca, but that was before she was in her history class.

She would see her in the school, walking through the halls, and it would happen. She would feel her skin nearly crawl with irritation, so much that, at times, she would feel the need to walk outside just to center herself.

Then that year, that last year she taught at St. Jerome High School, Beth was in her class.

Rebecca felt more than certain that she was losing it. It was torturous not only to be near the girl but even just read anything she'd written. She had the students write a research paper about the founding of Louisiana. It was crazy. She could barely touch it, the paper that girl had written. It felt succinctly as though something was clawing at her chest. So, she stopped and gave it B with just a quick glance.

There was no puzzling it out. On the surface, there was nothing particular about the girl. She laughed. She smiled, and she eyed Miss Wells oddly, with curiosity. That summer, after the school year, Rebecca found out Beth had died of a drug overdose. The news made her physically ill for two days, and then she resigned. She didn't understand what had happened, only that whatever it was, it had become intolerable for her.

She and Gabriel Sutton were walking down St. Charles Avenue. They'd finished eating, and he'd suggested the diversion. And along the stroll, he'd asked her why she'd stopped teaching. So, she told him the story or rather what she considered the non-story of Beth Wallace.

He'd been silent during her recitation, but now he asked. "And you never really understood what the problem was with the girl?"

"Other than the fact that she overdosed on drugs? No, that's all I know."

"But these feelings you had of her, you felt that maybe you should have understood something."

"Your words, not mine," she quipped. "I never felt responsible for what happened to her, if that's what you mean."

"I wasn't suggesting that you should, but something made you stop teaching."

"Yes, I couldn't bear it, those feelings and then what happened. The thought that there might be more like that was intolerable. I didn't understand it. I—" she stopped. Why had she told him this? It didn't make sense to her. How could it make sense to anyone else?

"I'm sorry, Becca. Sorry you went through that, but it's clear the only way is forward."

"I don't know what that means," she said slowly.

"You will," he replied quietly.

After Gabriel Sutton brought Rebecca to her car and saw her off, he continued to walk for a while. It was January and getting dark much earlier, so he remained aware but found himself deep in thought. St. Charles Avenue was still very active. The streetcar continued to run down its long stretch. And people, mostly young people, milled around. He breathed deeply, not knowing exactly when he'd passed through the pale and had become "not young."

He'd come to think it had less to do with age than events. Somewhere around the time that his marriage fell apart, during his mid-thirties, he'd felt that shift. Undeniably, the emotional toll, the feeling of utter defeat, of failure, because, as a young man, he was more fixed on goals and results than assessing growth during the journey.

But life, as he'd realized, was humbling and enlightening. In some ways, it was enviable to return to that time before, when vision felt so clear, although he knew now that it was limited. There was a comfort in youth, believing the world was indeed how we perceived it and therefore malleable to one's persistence.

But these days, as the eyes of Rebecca Wells floated through his mind, he'd adopted a stance more akin to surrender than activism. By surrender, he certainly didn't mean defeat but instead opening oneself rather than trying to control the intricacies and mysteries of the world around him.

Gabriel Sutton didn't consider himself a psychic per se. He had worked hard to increase his sensitivities and awareness, but he knew there were those out there who were more infinitely gifted in this realm. There were others he'd spent time with, learning their subtleties, learning the signs. In some ways, he supposed he might be considered a psychic counselor, someone adept at navigating the gifted ones through the perils of their abilities. And at times, he'd seen these perils in the extreme. So, Rebecca Wells sent up red flags, but disturbingly, a multitude of red flags. Unfortunately, he'd noted in many cases that such powerful, suppressed gifts easily mutated into destructive personal demons.

She felt dizzy, but she managed to make it home anyway. Perhaps, it was the wine at dinner, but she doubted it. It wasn't that kind of dizzy. It was him, that man who made her feel so strange. The first time they'd met, it was the same, but she was so nervous, so ridiculously out of her skin, anxious about the meeting in the first place that she assumed this was the cause. But it wasn't. It was him. He made her think about things, look at things differently. He was unnerving and comforting in the same space.

She walked into the darkened apartment and flicked on the lights. The figure was standing by the patio doors, long blond hair, pale skin, eyes filled with dread. One would wonder why Rebecca didn't scream. But then again, this wasn't exactly an unusual occurrence. Until recently, she had assumed it was a product of an insanity that had taken root within her. Now she wondered differently. The girl stared at her for a moment in that silent, intense manner that had begun the first autumn after her death, then turned her head to stare out the back glass doors of Rebecca's townhouse.

She wondered with distraction for perhaps the first time what Beth Wallace wanted with her. But she wasn't strong enough to ask, not yet.

There were things she hadn't told Gabriel Sutton, so many things.

Chapter Four
The Blond Girl

He had spent the early morning hours working on a chapter in his new book on meditation, using techniques he'd learned the past summer studying in Peru. And what was left of the early morning hours he'd spent gardening in a small plot of land just off his back patio that he'd cultivated for just that purpose. Here, he had an array of winter vegetables that were thriving. But then again, any winter in this city was mild compared to elsewhere. The whole endeavor was serene and relaxing, except that he was feeling an extraneous element — an element that seemed to be getting braver since Rebecca Wells had darkened his doorstep.

He was sitting on a plastic stool, weeding around the plants, but he whispered under his breath. "You know, it's all right," he murmured. It was subtle, so subtle that it had gone, or should he rather say, she had gone undetected for so long. "I'm not going to hurt you," he said softly, not stopping what he was doing.

Some people, with their very presence, just tended to open doors. Their particular energy caused a domino effect of events, whether intentional or not. In the case of Rebecca Wells, he was more than certain that it was unintentional. He couldn't say he'd ever met someone like her, so wildly out of touch with who she was. Again, a shift in the air, as though someone had brushed past him. He didn't look up. He had to be patient, patient to let things unfold as they should.

She was lying down on the futon sofa when her cell phone rang. She was expecting the store. She'd left a message that she was sick today, not coming in, but it wasn't them.

"Hello."

"Becca," Gabriel Sutton, this she hadn't expected. "I was thinking about you this morning, wondering if you got home all right last night."

"Oh yes, thanks," she murmured hesitantly.

"Are you all right?" he asked, way too perceptively.

"Yeah, I mean, I was feeling a little sick this morning, mostly tired, so I decided to stay home and rest."

There was silence for a moment, and she wondered if he was still there. "Well, listen, I know a lovely little restaurant around the corner from me that makes an incredible vegetable soup. Why don't you let me bring you some for lunch? I've been thinking about some things I'd like to talk to you about." She sat up on the couch, rubbing her head a bit. It was throbbing from lack of sleep last night.

"Alright, I guess. I won't be much company, though."

"No problem, I'll take care of you a bit. All I need is an address."

Rebecca lived in Metairie, a suburb of New Orleans proper. It was a small brick townhouse in a cul-de-sac of similar townhouses. Gabriel was familiar with the area, although he had always lived around the Faubourg St. John section of New Orleans. He parked on the street, not unusual for any place in the city where parking always seemed a scarce and in-demand commodity. As he exited his black jeep, with a bag of take-out soup in hand, he was overcome with a heavy feeling. He breathed in deeply. He'd learned over the years that every place had its energy — every building, structure, sort of like its own distinctive coat of paint. It was mostly absorbed from the sort of living that had taken place in it previously. And as he walked closer to Rebecca's front door, he could feel a distinctive oppressive quality, like an atmosphere that was physically more difficult to walk through. Certainly, it must be challenging for her to live here, someone of such a sensitive nature.

She was pale. That was the first thing he noticed when she answered the door. She smiled, but it was forced. Maybe he shouldn't have pushed this meeting with her now, but he had a feeling that it was needed. And he wasn't one to ignore intuition.

The physical dwelling within was pleasant enough, though rather sparsely decorated. "How are you doing?" he asked, following her through the foyer into a den. The house seemed warm, but as he walked toward a small table near the back patio doors, he hesitated. He glanced around the room but simply saw Rebecca standing near the sofa, staring at him oddly.

"What's wrong?" she asked slowly.

He stepped back into the warmer air. Clearly, she'd had the heater running. "You have a cold spot here," he said, looking at her and recognizing that she didn't seem surprised.

"What does that mean?"

"Usually? Either you have a very ineffective heating system, or there is supernatural activity."

She frowned at him, staring not at him but just to the side of him where he'd felt the cold spot. It dawned on him, not slowly, but quickly like the falling of an ax hammer. "Oh, but then you already knew that, didn't you, Becca?"

"Yes," she said with a measure of fatigue, "yes, I did."

Here they were, standing in her townhouse, she, Gabriel Sutton, and Beth Wallace watching both of them with that wide-eyed glazed look that she so often had. What exactly was she supposed to say about all of this?

He was looking at her intently, then turning, his eyes passing over the spot where Beth was standing. But it was more than clear that he didn't see the blond girl.

"Is someone here with us, Becca?" he said, entirely too calmly for her.

"Depends on what you mean by someone," she said slowly.

"Do you see someone else here?" he asked, a touch more sternly.

She sighed deeply. "Will my answer land me in a lunatic asylum?" she replied pointedly because it was a real concern or, should she say, a tangible fear of hers.

"Of course not. Spirits exist and what you would call ghosts as well."

She clasped her hands in front of her, horribly afraid. These visions that she had, she'd always kept to herself, always more than terrified people would judge her for them. So, to open that door, answer truthfully was not short of jumping off a cliff. She bowed her head. "I can't be sure it isn't some sort of hallucination."

"It's all right," he said in that comforting tone.

"It's Beth," she murmured.

"The girl that died at your school?"

"Yes," she said quietly, still gazing at the hardwood floor. She didn't want to look at him, didn't want to see his eyes judging her.

"How long have you been seeing her?"

"For a while, it started the first autumn after she died. I got up during the night, and she was here, here in the shadows of the den. Then every few days after that, I would see her in the hall, my bedroom upstairs, even outside on the patio."

She glanced up. But he wasn't looking at her at all, just at the very spot where Beth was. Clearly, he wasn't seeing her, but she felt as though he should, the way he was looking at her. "Has she ever spoken?"

"No, I mean, I haven't encouraged it. I've just asked her to leave, but she hasn't. She just keeps coming back."

"There must be some reason she needs to be here."

"I-I didn't think she was real. I thought I was going crazy."

"That's why you never told anyone."

"Yes, am I being haunted? Have I done something terrible for her to be here?"

He finally looked at her, more than a bit puzzled. "Of course not. What would make you think that? She's here because she needs something and knows she could reach you."

It was too much. She started to cry, and she wasn't sure why it began, only perhaps that it was a release. For so long, she believed something was wrong with her — something terribly wrong. She bent her head weeping, and then she felt his arms go around her. "It's all right," he murmured.

She put her head on Gabriel Sutton's shoulder and began to sob because there was no way for her to stop it.

He paced the den of Rebecca's townhouse, back and forth, pausing from time to time in front of the patio doors, still somewhat wary of passing through the cold spot identified as the apparition of Beth Wallace. Rebecca was silently eating the soup that he'd brought at her small dinette table near the kitchen. He'd bought enough for the both of them, but the food was the furthest thing from his mind. Gabriel had come to the grim conclusion that he would soon be dragging Becca, kicking and screaming, into the role of a medium. There seemed no help for it. Whatever vision she'd had of the parameters of her life, it was clear some greater power had different plans for her.

He paused again, just in front of that unidentifiable cold spot, staring intently, even squinting his eyes a bit, but there was no perceptible shift in his vision. This was not for him to see.

He moved his gaze across the room. Rebecca had stopped eating and was staring at him intently. "She's still here?" he asked.

She nodded slowly in a silent affirmation.

"We need to find out why she's here. Find out what she wants."

"How are we going to do that?" she asked in a rather quiet voice because he could tell by her tone that she already knew the answer.

"You're going to have to talk to her," he said, perhaps a bit too pointedly. He had to remember that this woman was fragile and, as she'd described herself, a bit unstable.

And he knew at once that perhaps he'd gone too far as she abruptly stood up, practically glaring at him. "You want me to what?"

He took a breath. Calm was the only way to handle this. "What I meant to say is that you're going to have to try to talk to her. You are the one she is drawn to for some reason Becca." Her eyes glanced over again to that space in front of the patio. "What is it? What is she doing?"

She shook her head, "I can't do this."

"Listen, just listen to my voice right now. I can walk you through this."

She looked at him with what was now unmistakably fear. "She's staring at me with those eyes — eyes that look like they've seen something horrible."

"Is that what you feel from her, that she's afraid?"

Becca had crossed her arms in front of her. "I feel like," she hesitated, "that I'm so cold."

"Is that what she's feeling?"

"So tired and so cold," she whispered, rambling on.

"Ask her what she wants."

"I can't feel any light, anything warm. It's all been dragged out of me."

He walked to Rebecca, but she wasn't looking at him, nor that spot where he believed Beth stood. She'd seemed to have been drawn somewhere else. "Becca, listen to me," he said, grasping her arms. But she still wasn't looking at him. "You need to remain separate from this."

"I—" she murmured, but then there was a hesitation before she collapsed into his arms.

Chapter Five
Pressure

There was always pressure, a pressure that she was feeling, but she didn't know why. It was just the sensation that things and people were crowding in on her, agitating her, making her feel *unhappy*.

She couldn't understand it. What did she have to feel unhappy about? She was young. She was smart. She was *popular* and had a handsome boyfriend. But still, there was that pressure, annoying, disturbing.

The halls at St. Jerome High were congested, filled with students. Every morning she'd take the time to meticulously blow out and straighten her long blond hair. She knew she was pretty. Her friends told her so, her boyfriend, and then her heart fell a bit. She didn't know if he was still her boyfriend. She'd told him to delete all those pictures he'd taken of her.

"No one will see them," he promised. "You're so beautiful," he'd said. That's how he'd gotten her to take them. They'd been drinking, and his parents weren't home. "Come on, baby, you're so beautiful." And she'd let him. After all, what was the harm? Celebrities take nude pictures all the time.

But then, she'd had that dream about them, about the pictures and these horrible ugly birds, like vultures, picking at them, pecking away at her body. And she was bleeding, bleeding all over the place in the photos. So, she'd told him to get rid of them, but he wasn't happy. "It's like you don't trust me."

"Just do it," she insisted. She was crying, and she didn't know why.

She should be happy. She would graduate next year. She stopped in the hallway down a few classrooms, where she saw that dark-haired teacher. Her history teacher Miss Wells, stared at her, such a strange woman. She would smile her brightest smile at everyone, and they would smile back. But not her. She would just look at her oddly, like something was wrong. Someone passed by her, then put their arm around her. "Hey baby,'" he whispered in her ear, but she didn't feel good. She felt pressure, felt like someone had sapped the breath out of her.

The next few nights, she was dreaming again, dreaming about the birds pecking at her skin, so she took a few sleeping pills her mother had in the medicine cabinet.

And the next night took more.

Becca opened her eyes slowly to the dim light of the den. She was sitting upright on the futon sofa, having no idea how she got there. "Are you all right?"

Gabriel was standing in front of her, looking more than a bit concerned. "What happened?" she murmured, trying to clear away the cobwebs of Beth's memories that only a moment before felt as though they were her thoughts.

"I think you blacked out. I'm not sure. It seemed as though you slipped into some altered state. You weren't responding to anything I said, and then for a few moments. You lost consciousness."

"Beth," she murmured. It was drifting away, this connection they'd had.

But those feelings, those intense feelings of confusion, anxiety, were still clinging to her.

He sat beside her, taking her hand in his and then slipping his fingers around her wrist to take her pulse. "It's rapid, and you feel a little feverish," he said. "You need to relax."

"I felt," she was trying to puzzle it out somehow. "I felt like I was her, that I'd stepped into her skin. Before," she was still trying to piece it together in her mind, "before she died."

He nodded, "Did it help? I mean to explain why she's here."

She shook her head. "I don't know. She seemed troubled and perplexed as to why."

Slowly, he stood up. "Let me get you something cold to drink. Then we'll talk about this more."

Rebecca nodded, closing her eyes but then opening them again, recognizing that Beth wasn't in the room with them anymore.

"So, I don't understand what the significance of the pictures are. I mean clearly, it didn't show good judgment, but why did it seem to impact her so negatively?"

Gabriel was sipping a bottle of water, one of two that he'd retrieved out of the refrigerator for them. Becca seemed to be a bit calmer and in better spirits. But even he, with his limited psychic abilities, could feel that she'd been deeply drained of energy by the whole event, which she'd described to him in great detail. She was still sitting on the futon, feet tucked beneath her, and a dark green chenille throw blanket wrapped around her shoulders.

"It's complicated," he said. "By what you described as Beth's mental state, anxiety, depression, it sounds like extremely low energy, possibly somehow facilitated by those pictures."

"The pictures? I still don't get it. The internet is flooded with nude pictures. Our society is proliferated with them."

"I know it seems odd to you, but it has more to do with how energy, spiritual energy is lost and gained. The fact is that our Western culture is painfully devoid of information concerning spiritual health."

She pulled the throw more tightly around her. For some reason, she was freezing. "When you say spiritual? Do you mean like religious teaching?"

"No, not at all, really. I'm talking about the spirit, the divine energy we all possess. The eternal essence that reincarnates lifetime through lifetime in different bodies in pursuit of growth."

Her eyes widened a bit. "Reincarnation? So, you're saying that all of that is real?"

"To get rudimentary, we're all comprised of three parts — the body, the soul, and the spirit. The body is more or less the instrument you work through during your time on Earth. The soul is the new clean sheet or personality, if you will, that connects the body and the spirit. Then there is the spirit, that divine part of oneself connected to God."

She leaned back on the sofa, looking at him with curious eyes. "I don't know Gabriel. I've always considered myself a bit of an atheist, unsure if I ever really believed in God."

"And yet, you have been drawn to esotericism."

"That doesn't seem like the same thing."

"Well, certainly not dogmatically religious, but it is in some ways a field that studies the spirit."

"You know, I don't see how any of this links to Beth?"

He took a sip of his water, pausing for a moment. Currently, he was perched on a wooden counter stool that sat near the border of her kitchen and den. "Well, what I was trying to say is that a spirit choosing to incarnate on the Earth, clothes itself in the physical and thus is always taking risks, making itself vulnerable. That's where spiritual health comes in, something most largely ignore. Certain things, symbols, experiences, rituals deeply affect the spirit. Some of these things could greatly aid it, while others could damage it."

She frowned a bit, looking at him with question. "You're not saying those nude pictures."

"It depends, really depends. Exposing the heart area could cause someone to greatly gain energy, but on the other hand, it could make someone vulnerable to energy being taken. It seems those pictures and whatever was done with them possibly made Beth susceptible to particular types of spiritual attacks, mostly draining I would assume."

"Draining?" she echoed.

"Yes, draining of her energy by spiritual vampires."

She looked at him with more than a measure of disbelief, and he wondered for not the first time if all of this was too much too soon. "Did you say spiritual vampires?"

He smiled a bit, standing, then sitting next to her on the futon. "It does sound a bit macabre, but it is an apt description. There are people and other types of entities that drain the spiritual energy out of people like parasites or at least those who are vulnerable to it."

She was studying him closely, desperately trying to understand what he was saying. "Vulnerable, how?"

He shrugged, "Again, that's complicated. There are many ways you can make yourself vulnerable and more open to spiritual attacks. Some people simply are because of the cycle of evolution their spirit is in. Others have done things to damage their spiritual health."

"And the pictures?"

"The pictures seemed to have made Beth vulnerable, and severe enough draining could cause wounds to the spirit."

She sighed deeply, "Again, you're losing me, Gabriel."

"Wounds to the spirit, wounds that can make someone open to other kinds of attacks."

She stared at him intently, "I don't know, Gabriel, all of this—"

"Seems like something I made up," he said, looking at her with a curious smile. "Well, you were the one who saw the picture, the bleeding picture, the birds attacking her. What do you think it means?"

She shook her head slowly. "I don't know. All I know is all the pain and upset I felt."

"Also indicative of someone very low on energy."

"Yes," she said softly, considering his words, "yes, I suppose."

Her head was spinning, trying to absorb what he was telling her, and more than that, she hurt. Her skin actually hurt. "I'm not feeling well."

He nodded. "It's clear you've tapped into what she was and probably still is experiencing. It's difficult. She's confused, still clinging to the pain of her former life. It's something she'll simply need to release if she's to move on."

She frowned again. Her head was still throbbing. "Gabriel, all of this is so alien to how I've been living. I have no idea what I'm supposed to do here."

He could feel that, and he'd never claimed to be any sort of empath. But it was written all over Becca's face. She was drowning here, washed over by Beth's aggressive emotions and fragile in her own right. "Well, it would be good if we tried to help her."

"She's dead," she whispered harshly. "Seems as though any help will be of a limited variety."

Such contrasts, for being such a sensitive, he was beginning to note that Rebecca Wells, in certain arenas, wasn't very sensitive at all. "At this point, it would be best to coax her over to the other side where she can get some real help. Trapped here, she's just likely to continue to hang around you and sap your energy."

"My energy!" she snapped.

"Sssshhhhhh," he said, lightly patting her hand. He was working very hard to be patient here. "We'll get to that later, first, Beth."

"Okay, okay," but then she glanced around again, noting that they were still alone. "But she's gone. Maybe she won't come back."

His blue eyes steeled just a bit. "Is that what you feel? She's connected to you in some way, Becca."

She leaned back in the chair, trying to clear her mind. She could feel tuggings here and there, things pulling at her. "I'm not sure," she murmured.

"See if you can find her."

She closed her eyes, concentrating. Then, after a few minutes, it felt like movement, like she was moving somewhere, a turn, a twist, and then she was standing at night on the banks of Bayou St. John, and a young girl in a long nightgown was standing there, so near the water. "It's someone else," she whispered.

"Focus now," he coaxed. "Focus now on Beth."

She turned from the young girl and tried to keep a mental picture of Beth in her mind — Beth as she remembered her in school, so bright, lovely. And again, there was a tug, but this time it was a violent one.

Suddenly, she was in a bedroom, a darkened bedroom, and Beth was there. She was just the same as she'd been at Becca's apartment but standing over someone's bed, a boy, or rather a young man, asleep. "What are you doing?" she slowly asked her.

"I can see into his dreams. Sometimes he sees me there. It frightens him." And then Beth turned to her. "He feels guilty, sometimes, and when he's afraid—" she stopped.

"When he's afraid?" Becca pushed.

"I feel better, stronger," she murmured. Something akin to dread turned over in Becca's stomach. This wasn't good, not at all.

"Beth," she said softly, "let's leave this place. It isn't good here."

"Nowhere is good," Beth answered.

"No, no, come back with me. I need to talk to you." The girl suddenly looked up at her with fear, and then Becca opened her eyes. Gabriel was standing in front of her. Across the room, Beth was standing there again, near the patio door, looking terrified. "All right, she's back. What do we do now?"

Chapter Six
Expediency

Expediency, they had to deal with this quickly. Becca, beside him, seemed shaky, pale, and from what he could gather, extremely weak. In the best of circumstances, he'd like to do more to help Beth Wallace, but the truth of the matter was that she didn't belong on this plane of existence. All he could do now was get her to move along.

"Is she listening to you?" he asked curtly.

Becca's focus changed from him to the cold spot in front of the patio doors. "Beth," she said slowly, then nodded in affirmation.

"Ask her if she knows that she's died." Becca's eyes flew back to him in surprise. "Ask her," he said firmly.

Becca felt terrible, frightened, sick to her stomach, and tired, so incredibly tired. And the girl in front of her looked so terrified, so lost. She braced herself, understanding on a level what Gabriel was doing but also realizing how it would devastate the pathetic little thing in front of her.

"Beth," she began, not knowing at all how she could deliver this news. "Beth, do you realize that, that you've died?"

The blue eyes widened, so huge, so frightened. "No," her voice so small, "No, I'm here."

Becca shook her head, "Beth, you're lost, but you have died."

"Tell her it's time for her to move on." Becca stared at Gabriel. His face was set stonily, not the compassionate expression he usually wore. "Tell her that her loved ones are waiting for her and will help her once she moves on."

"Beth, listen to me," she murmured. "This isn't where you belong. It's time to move on. There are people who love you, are waiting for you."

The blond girl was trembling, and Becca could feel it inside her, shaking her violently. "You have to step back, Becca," Gabriel said, grasping her arm. "She's drawing energy from the link you have with her."

"Link? What do you mean?"

He squeezed her arm, "Focus on stepping away from her, Becca, concentrate." In her mind, she tried to step away from Beth, from the wild emotions that were coursing through her. "Tell her to move into the light. She'll find peace there."

"Beth," she whispered out loud and in her mind. "You need to move on. You need to move into the light and find peace." So much fear, terror ripping at her, but she forced herself to step back. In her mind, she had to pry the girl's grasping hands off of her skin. They had held so tight that it tore. Wounds were there, bleeding now, but she moved further away from her. "Beth, you must move on," she said firmly. And in her vision, she forcefully thrust her away.

She didn't realize she'd physically stepped backward as well. Stumbling, she felt Gabriel's arms go around her, and she felt it, the last tearing yank, as she sunk to her knees. Her eyes were tearing over, but except for her and Gabriel, the room was now empty.

"I feel sick."

His hand was on her hair, her head, sort of stroking it with comfort. "It will pass."

She was sitting on the carpet of her townhouse, trembling all over. It was chills wracking her body, although she knew it wasn't particularly cold in the room. He quietly draped a throw around her that had been on the rocking chair. "I can't stop shaking."

"It's a reaction from the loss of energy." She wanted to answer, but her teeth were nearly chattering.

"She's not here anymore."

"The link was broken."

She shook her head, realizing her face was moist from tears. Was she having some sort of breakdown? "What link?" she mumbled.

"You'd achieved some sort of empathic link with Beth, but it was draining you greatly of energy."

"I don't understand."

"I know," he said calmly. "It's not something I entirely understand either, but it's clear it's been severed."

"But did she move on?" Quite suddenly, she realized he was sitting next to her on the carpet. His face seemed a bit grim. "I don't know, Becca, honestly. I'm more concerned about you right now. This took a lot out of you."

She nodded, not disagreeing. She felt like she'd been hit by a truck. "Maybe I need a doctor," she murmured.

"I am a doctor," he replied softly. "And I do have a plan."

It felt physical. No matter how much Gabriel told her this was a spiritual phenomenon, she felt physically ill. Her skin hurt, ached as though she had a fever. Her stomach was in a nauseated tumult, and she was dizzy. It was torturous to pull together a few days of clothes in her overnight bag. "I have to go to work tomorrow," she'd insisted weakly, having no idea if she'd be in any physical shape to do so.

"Don't worry. If you go, I'll drive you," he comforted gently, or was he indulging her? She had no idea. The only thing she wanted was more aspirin and sleep, but they weren't staying at her townhouse. He was driving her to his home on Dumaine Street.

"Is this necessary?"

"It will be easier for me to take care of you there."

"That girl," she'd protested.

"We'll handle it."

Of course, she would probably be handling it because he hadn't even realized he had a ghost. It was amazing how quickly things had shifted beneath her feet. Only hours earlier, she'd believed all this stuff was in her head and that she was demented. And now, she'd readily seized upon the idea that she was indeed not only seeing but somehow linking empathically to ghosts.

And all of it because Dr. Gabriel Sutton had told her this was so. It seemed rather foolish now not to believe him because it did feel right. Somehow the pieces had fallen in quite neatly to a puzzle that had been confounding her pretty much all her life. But in the grand scheme of things, what did all of this mean? And what kind of life could she lead by accepting these truths?

Truths that were now drowned out pitifully in the swirl of her discomfort.

"I'm so tired," she murmured.

"Close your eyes. You can rest when we get to the house."

She did try, closing her eyes, but nausea continued to swell up in her. "Why do I feel so sick?"

"It is a reaction to everything that happened. It will pass. Be patient, Becca."

"That's easy for you to say."

And she thought she might have heard him laugh a bit but couldn't be sure. Her eyes were still closed.

There was a spare bedroom that he had set up in his house. It was a room that had been used occasionally by visiting family, once in a while, a friend, but primarily left untouched. After the divorce, several years after, he'd settled in the house on Dumaine Street. It was largely a solitary enterprise. He hadn't meant to shut out the opportunity for relationships, but something inside him shunned the prospect. The failed marriage, and in those days, he had categorized it as a failure, had burned him, burned his interest in the prospect of sharing his life with someone. Instead, he'd thrown himself into study and had forged other types of relationships focused primarily on his evolution as a human being. In this regard, he found it possible to look at his past with Cynthia differently as a learning plateau. Painful feelings aside, the emotional unraveling and disintegration of the life he'd expected had taught him valuable lessons and guided his life in a particular direction. It left him with a thirst for understanding and wounds that could only be healed in a spiritual venue.

In essence, he became a bit of a monk. But now, Rebecca Wells would be staying in his house, and he had no idea how he felt about that.

He opened the door to the back bedroom carrying her bag inside. "This is where you'll be."

She stood in the doorway, completely oblivious to her surroundings. Of that, he was certain. "I'm so tired," she murmured. He placed the bag on the bench at the foot of the bed and pulled back the quilt he'd brought back from a trip to the Appalachians.

"You need to sleep a while, Becca."

She nodded but didn't move from her spot in the doorway. "I just keep seeing her eyes in my mind. She was so terrified."

"Well, the unknown is often terrifying, but it will be all right." he said lightly, grabbing her arm and guiding her to the double bed. She sat on the edge of the mattress, still seeming completely out of it.

"I don't know Gabriel."

"You need to rest," he murmured, smoothly reaching down and pulling off her black leather loafers.

"I am tired," she whispered.

"Lay down," he said, and he was grateful she complied with no further resistance.

It hit him as he quietly pulled the wooden door in the guest bedroom — exhaustion, pure, bone-draining exhaustion. He supposed he should have expected it. As much energy as Becca had lost and given on her quest to aid Beth Wallace, he had simultaneously poured energy, his energy, into her to keep her functioning.

He sluggishly made his way into the den and lay down on the sofa. He didn't want to be isolated in his bedroom in case Becca woke up disoriented. The only thing he knew for certain was that he had no earthly idea what to expect next.

Dreams, she found, were rarely pleasant. She seldom awoke rested after sleep because the world she visited when she dreamed was not a calming place.

She wore sunglasses and walked down the warm pavement of Harrison Avenue. It was dusk, the light just beginning to eek away. Sometimes she knew when she was within the confines of a dream, but not this time, clearly not this time. Just now, it all felt too real.

The street was not deserted but not overly populated either. There were restaurants along the well-traveled sidewalk, restaurants with black wrought iron furniture on its curbs for patrons, although there were few of those this night. She continued to meander down the street, an occasional car passing by. It felt as though she moved through the air with effort, painful effort, as though the atmosphere was thick with humidity, although she knew it wasn't.

But it wasn't warm, just a thick day, as though it had rained recently, but that too there was no sign of. She continued to walk, albeit slowly, wondering why again she needed the sunglasses. It was nearly night now. She didn't notice him sitting there, the man. But he stood up suddenly, and she was startled by his intrusion. He stood up, grabbing her arm forcefully, and it jolted her. "I'm looking for someone," he rasped.

She saw clearly that he didn't recognize her and was befuddled by it. "What?" she whispered. His face was the one she remembered, pudgy, flaccid cheeks, small brown eyes looking a bit evolutionarily challenged. Again harshly, "I'm trying to find someone," but no recognition. She sat up in the bed, feeling her head swirl. It wasn't her bedroom. It wasn't familiar. Then she remembered — Gabriel, Gabriel Sutton. She leaned back again amongst the pillows. Her body felt soaked and sticky from her sweat. She needed a shower, but she didn't want to get up, not yet. So instead, she stared at the ceiling.

Chapter Seven

The Houseguest

Cynthia had long black hair and high cheekbones with pale skin — a bit exotic next to his fairer looks. Maybe that was what had drawn him, the lure of adventure. He had no idea what had drawn her. Gabriel didn't want to belittle her, but dismally, he suspected perhaps it had been the lure of a doctor's salary. That was something, however, that had lured him as well, accumulation — the lovely, beguiling temptress that assures with material accumulation comes happiness as well.

But there were only so many vacations, so many new gadgets, so many things that one person could get, or rather two people could get. Cynthia sold real estate, and there had been the house. It was a huge house uptown for which she worked hard to finagle financing. That house had broken them, not financially, but spiritually. They'd placed all their hopes on it, all their hopes for happiness in the future. And then they'd lost it, outbid, and it fell apart. Silly, really. After all, they could get another house, but they couldn't get another symbol quite like that of what they should be. So much emptiness, so much hollowness, came crashing down. It's quite something to be in love with a dream and not recognize it.

He pushed these thoughts aside. It was the low energy. He was certain of it. It allowed negative thoughts to gain access more easily. He couldn't afford to dwell. He should meditate to recharge a bit, maybe after, after he slept.

She silently tiptoed out of the bedroom. Her bare feet hit the cool wooden floor, but it was oddly soothing to her, something that her townhouse had not been for some time. There was always a weight on her there, anxiety, fatigue, a whole manner of things. But not here, in this cozy little house where Gabriel Sutton lived. She tiptoed past the door of another closed room that she believed was his bedroom. He was probably in there now, resting, as she was supposed to be doing. She'd had a disorienting kind of sleep. Her head still felt in a strange sort of swirl, a swirl that told her definitively that she'd rather be home, anxiety and all. She'd spent her whole life dealing with her abrupt mood swings and anxiousness. And she'd rather deal with it privately, not under the steady gaze of someone else.

She would sneak out of the house and maybe call a cab from somewhere. She gazed down at her feet as she headed into his front den. Shoes, now where were her shoes? Probably back in the bedroom, and then she stopped short. There he was, stretched out on the small white sofa against the brick wall of his den. Why was he there?

Just as the thought entered her mind, he began to shift, then his eyes opened. He stared at her oddly. "I thought you were sleeping," he murmured.

"I-I think I need to go home." Then he sat up, his feet swinging over to touch the floor.

"What's wrong?" he asked, rubbing his eyes a bit. She glanced at the window. Drapes closed but parted enough that she could see it was dark outside. It hit her suddenly. She had no idea what time it was or how long she'd been asleep.

"I just, I feel terrible, and it would be easier for me to deal with it privately."

He straightened a bit, not getting up from the sofa. This, all of this, felt so alien to her. "That's why I brought you here, to rest and sort things out."

"That's not how I usually deal with things," she mumbled with restrained irritation.

He leaned back on the couch, still eying her groggily. "How do you usually deal with them? Hide out until you feel normal again?"

She rubbed her arms a bit, feeling oddly vulnerable. "Maybe, I do whatever I need to cope."

He nodded, "And how's that working out for you?"

"You know, I have no idea why you think you can help me."

And then he stood up, crossing over to her. "Would you like to borrow a robe?"

She frowned. "I don't know, maybe."

Then he reached out, softly touching her arm. "Becca, how about you take a shower while I fix us something to eat."

"A shower?"

"It will help get rid of some of that negative energy I feel on you."

She answered slowly, not entirely wanting to assimilate what he'd said. "Where—" she began with a bit of trepidation.

"I'll show you," he said calmly.

There was a counter separating the kitchen from a dining room combination. Within was a larger wooden table, but they sat on stools at the counter, eating a salad and light soup he'd put together. Becca had pulled on a nightshirt and pants and, over it, a dark blue robe she'd found lying across the chair in her bedroom once she'd returned from the shower. Her long brown hair was still slightly damp, but she'd twisted it into a loose bun on the back of her head.

She'd noted it was nearly eight at night when she'd checked her phone. Time felt oddly distorted. The whole day had slipped into a strange sort of memory muddle that she'd decided to put off sorting out until the morning.

"This is good," she murmured, relishing the taste of the warm tomato soup on the back of her throat. It was a bit sore, something else she hadn't noticed until just now.

"Feeling any better?" Gabriel asked beside her. He had a warm, gentle sort of smile. She wasn't at all sure if she'd noted that before. Too much intensity too quickly had entered their little bubble of acquaintance.

She shook her head, "I'm still having difficulty wrapping my mind around what happened today with Beth. I mean, did any of it really happen?"

He'd picked up the glass of iced tea in front of him, sipping it. "If I were you, I wouldn't think about it too much tonight. Let things settle a bit."

She smiled briefly, then shifted the subject impulsively, "Have you been married?"

He looked over at her oddly. "Married?"

"Yeah, I just remembered you asked me that, but I don't know if you have."

He nodded slowly, "Fair enough, yes, yes I was."

"Oh, was?"

He smiled, "I guess it's been about four years now."

"Sorry, that must be difficult. I mean divorce, I'm assuming—" she smiled awkwardly. "You know, I don't know what I mean, just feeling incredibly off-balance. I'm still not sure being here is a great idea."

"You don't think I can help you."

"I've no idea and am not sure if that's the point." She averted her eyes, taking a rather large gulp of iced tea lest anything more tangled and conflicted come out of her mouth.

"Isn't it?" she glanced over at him, who was staring at her rather solemnly. He seemed, well, rather unruffled at the moment, and that perplexed her. She'd never felt that way as far back as her memory stretched— unruffled. Hers was a life of constantly dodging, defending, hiding one thing and then the next. She glanced beyond him. In front of the front door was that little girl in the long white nightgown still dripping from her spill into the river, face as pale as her cotton gown — always hiding things.

He touched her arm, and her gaze returned to him. Her heart was beating so quickly, painfully, always in a state of stress, always inexplicable emotions. "What are you seeing?"

She looked at him with real puzzlement. "How can you live here and not feel her?"

He shook his head, "The little girl?" And then he murmured, "She hides."

She frowned, feeling that shakiness overtaking her again. "She's afraid. We're all afraid," she commented sadly.

Then he squeezed her arm, and she felt a warmth pass into her skin. "Maybe we can help her."

She looked at his face, so filled with hope. But she didn't feel hope, just desperation flooding into her from so many places.

It was tabled until the morning. Becca returned to bed and then slept, slept heavily, so much that it was ten minutes until nine when she called in sick for work again. Distracted, she wondered if she was about to lose her job. But luckily, tomorrow was Sunday, one more day to get something sorted out. She dressed in blue jeans and an off-white sweater that she'd hurriedly thrown into her suitcase the day before. She hadn't been thinking much then about ramifications, like her job and life, only that Dr. Gabriel Sutton had thrown her a life raft, and she'd grabbed on with all her might, not considering what that might mean.

She pulled her hair up in a ponytail, not bothering with make-up, and made her way up front. The den was empty. She hesitated, looking around. The couch was also empty, although she felt sure he'd slept there most of the night. And then she heard heavy footsteps behind her and the light pressure of his hand on her shoulder. "Good morning."

She turned around slowly, trying to quell that ridiculous fluttering in her stomach that seemed to encroach whenever he made any kind of physical contact with her. After all, she wasn't a kid anymore, and this, whatever this was between them, wasn't about that.

He was smiling but looking ever so slightly disheveled as though it hadn't been a restful night. "Do you want some coffee?"

"Yes, please."

He headed back across the den to the kitchen area. He was dressed casually this morning, untucked burgundy corduroy shirt over jeans. Vaguely, she wondered what this day would bring and how it would stack up to yesterday.

She sat on the barstool at the counter where they'd eaten the night before.

"Did you manage to get any sleep?" he asked over his shoulder as he poured the coffee.

"Some," she said quietly.

"Cream, sugar?" he asked.

"Everything," she murmured drowsily.

"Are you all right?" And she looked into his very concerned eyes, wondering why he was so concerned about her. They barely knew each other.

"Do you normally take virtual strangers into your home?" she asked lightly. "You know we do live in New Orleans. Being too trusting can be very dangerous."

He placed the mug in front of her, watching her from the other side of the counter. "And not trusting anyone can be damn lonely."

She frowned. "You think I'm lonely?"

"I think you're incredibly unhappy, possibly in a depression."

She shrugged, "I've tried the medicating route."

"Medication won't take care of this. I'm a doctor. I should know."

"It won't?"

"No, neither will fighting against—" Then he stopped abruptly.

"Fighting against? What were you going to say, Gabriel?"

"Fighting against who you really are, Becca. You have gifts. You can't just try to bury them because they don't fit the picture of how you feel life should be."

"You're presuming a lot," she whispered.

"And getting defensive with me isn't going to help either. You have to accept who you are and find some peace with it."

She sipped the coffee he'd given her because she didn't want to talk about this anymore. No more of who and what she thought she should be. "What are we doing today?" she asked, very much signaling she wanted to change the subject.

He placed his mug firmly on the counter, so firmly that it made a loud thud. Her eyes flew up. Evidently, she'd rattled his normally placid personality just a bit. "Okay, well, how about I make some breakfast, then we try to track down my shy little guest."

"I thought I was your shy little guest."

"No, shy isn't at all how I'd describe you. You need to get used to mastering your abilities, and nothing will achieve that like practice, lots and lots of practice."

Chapter Eight

Ellie

"What are you feeling?"

They were sitting on his couch, eyes closed, trying out this searching sort of meditative stance that Gabriel had instigated. "Not much of anything, actually."

He squeezed her hand, and that tingling thing shot right through her skin. She wondered if he felt it at all or if she'd been bereft of male companionship for so long that she was pathetically vulnerable to just about anyone. Oh yes, and of course, they were holding hands so he could serve as an anchor for her, he'd explained. "Really? Nothing?" he murmured.

"No, I don't sense her anywhere."

"No, Becca, that's not how you find her. Try through the emotions. What are you feeling emotionally?"

She sighed inwardly. Her emotions, what a muddle. "I—" she hesitated. "I feel pain, like a stabbing pain right in my heart. But then, that's not all that unusual."

"Unusual? What do you mean?"

She shifted uncomfortably. Being so candid was difficult when she'd ignored or dismissed these wayward feelings for so much of her life. "I mean, it's sort of something I live with. Not all the time, but I've always felt like it was a type of depression, not anything else."

"You are going to have to change the way you think about things. It seems a lot of these dark emotions you struggle with on a daily basis aren't necessarily yours. You seem to tap into others' spiritual pain, those who are living and also those who are not."

"Then why does it feel like mine?" she muttered.

"That's the nature of emotion. It always feels personal. The trick is learning where it is emanating from."

"Why does this seem so simple for you?"

"On the contrary, there is nothing simple about it. Now, I want you to focus on this pain you are feeling just now."

Becca leaned back against his sofa, trying to relax, trying to put a thousand contradictory thoughts out of her mind. It felt like pain, as she'd described, right to the heart but more emotional than physical, although it was decidedly uncomfortable for her.

"Follow the thread of the emotion. Try to trace where it's coming from."

She breathed in deeply. She could feel a fluttering in its consistency — a breathless quality to it. "I don't know how to follow it."

"You must relax and not attach any judgments to the feeling. Don't get in your own way. Just allow your mind to be cleared of everything except that feeling."

"It's so delicate," she murmured, "so slight," and then a crashing sensation flooded over her that jarred her to open her eyes. "Oh God," she said aloud.

"What is it?" he said, eying her with concern.

"I don't know, something strong, intense sort of—" Then she stopped.

"Sort of what?"

She looked at him with confusion. "Pushed back."

Gabriel stared at her momentarily, seeming to want to process what she'd said. Then his handsome face broke into a smile. "Looks like someone doesn't want to be found."

She frowned in direct contrast to his expression. "How is that a good thing?"

"I don't know if it's good, but intriguing, undeniably intriguing."

Trying again.

She walked along the darkened shores of the water, hearing movement even within the stillness, a cloudy sky. The fear hadn't come yet. Her mind was drawn elsewhere, shrouded within the fog of a dream.

She struggled against it. Why hadn't they taken precautions, putting up obstacles so she couldn't leave the house?

"I-I," she whispered roughly.

"It's all right," his voice soothed.

She could feel the wet mud slipping beneath her feet, sliding into the impossibly cold water — such horror, wrenching her out of the fog into terrifying panic and fear.

Breathe, no breath as she thrashed.

She sat up, gasping for air as though she was hyperventilating.

Strong arms went around her, shaking her out of the connection.

"It's all right, Becca," he repeated calmly.

"She was sleepwalking. She walked right out of the house into the water," she managed to get out, although still feeling as though she couldn't get any air into her lungs.

He squeezed her arms more firmly, rubbing soothingly. "You're all right."

"So scared," she rasped.

"How young?" he murmured into her hair. She hadn't realized he'd pulled her against his side, continuing to rub her arms.

She squeezed her eyes shut, trying to feel again, to feel the trembling girl. She wasn't in the water now, but still so cold, still terrified, as though she could not escape that watery torment, trapped within those last moments of life. "Young," she said, "maybe twelve, maybe thirteen."

"That's why they didn't take safeguards. She was older."

She shook her head. "They should have. They should have taken more care with her."

"Some things can't be prevented," he said, his voice low and thoughtful.

"Why, why doesn't she move on?"

"There may be another purpose at work here."

"What does that mean, purpose?" she asked. She should move away from him, from the close embrace, but she was still trembling — still feeling covered by the girl's terror. And his body, his warmth, was the only reason she was holding it together.

"Maybe she's a teacher."

"Teacher?"

"For you, Becca, a teacher to help you control your gifts."

She squeezed her eyes shut. "I feel like I'm losing my mind. I can't handle this kind of pain."

"It will get easier. I promise you," he said softly.

They took a break and took a long walk down Dumaine Street around the Faubourg St. John area. "Do you want to go by the water?" he asked.

Just the thought of going anywhere near the Bayou St. John made her insides clench in apprehension. It was so strange. She'd never felt that way about that body of water in the past. But now, it was as though all the girl's fear had soaked right into her, had become her fear. "I can't," she answered.

He nodded, not verbally responding. He hadn't said much to her since they'd left the house. They just continued to walk in silence. And then, finally, as they turned down another street, he asked. "Did you pick up a name?"

"A name?"

"The little girl. It would be easier to soothe her if we had a name."

"I, I don't know. I'll try to focus on it."

"Not now, later," he said as they continued to move. "You need a break from this. There's a coffee shop on Esplanade if you feel up to the walk."

She was pale and deeply shaken. That much was easy to see. It was what was unseen that bothered him more deeply. Gabriel had worked with psychics before, some as teachers, some in collaborations, and some as his students. Many had been deeply gifted, but never, never in all his experience had he seen anyone who connected so completely and irrevocably with the spirit world as Rebecca Wells did. It seemed alarmingly unconscious the way she sank so completely into the experiences and emotions of those who had departed from this plane of existence. To say it was dangerous for her was a wild understatement. He was more than convinced she had spent much of her life walking along the fringes of insanity.

Her lack of awareness was deeply perilous and had clearly already taken quite a toll on her life. His mind had sunk deeply into the mode of evaluating and analyzing the best way to proceed. The little girl that was haunting his house needed help, but much more than that the woman that was sipping coffee right across from him also needed help, help of a critical nature.

"Is it that bad?"

He glanced up from his very strong cafe mocha. "Sorry? What?" he asked, being pulled abruptly from his contemplations. Becca's dark eyes were watching him with what he could only describe as curiosity.

"You look like the patient died."

He put his coffee cup slowly back down to the table. He wasn't even aware he'd been holding it to his lips. They sat outside at a wrought iron patio table in front of the Nola's Brew coffee shop. "I'm sorry, Becca. I'm just trying to sort through what's happened."

"You don't look very happy about it."

"Honestly, it concerns me the toll this takes on you," he said, maybe a shade too grimly.

And evidently, his mood wasn't lost on her, "Well, maybe we should stop, I mean, all this experimentation."

"Yes, honestly, if I thought that would solve your problems, we would."

"But it won't," she said softly.

"No, unfortunately, your talents won't just go away. You will continue to link with the emotional trauma of the living and the dead. And it will continue to take its toll on you unless—"

"Unless I learn to control it."

He smiled. "You know, you're developing a habit of finishing my thoughts."

"I'm sorry. You tend to repeat yourself a bit. I mean, you've said as much before." She glanced away, looking out onto Esplanade Avenue.

"Sorry, I can see how that could get irritating."

She shook her head. "It's not, not really. Ella or Ellie, it feels like something like that."

"Well, that's something."

"I just wish, I wish she'd move on. She must have been afraid for so long."

"It's not the same time, I mean. Where they are, for her, it might have been a very short time. "

"Do you think we can help Gabriel?" she asked, focusing in on him again.

"I'm convinced of it." And then she stared at him a bit oddly. "What?" he asked in confusion.

She looked down nervously, he thought, swirling her coffee mug a bit. "I-I don't know. I'm just not used to people like you."

"Okay, you need to clarify. People like me?"

She glanced up, almost shyly, and he found it so compelling. "People who really believe in things, optimistic, I guess. My family, people I've known, haven't been like that. They're so busy with themselves, with the moment, their moment, they don't believe in much of anything. You'd be amazed at how much apathy there is in the world. Even for people who go to church, it's still about them, how it all affects them. But you honestly seem concerned about other people."

He took a moment, trying to let her words soak in. "I understand what you mean. I used to — well, be more like that. But then things shifted, shifted inside me. There is no experience like really helping people. There is no greater high than that particular feeling I've found."

She laughed, "So, it's not so entirely unselfish."

"Let's just say it's a nice byproduct. Do you want to walk some more?"

"Yeah, but you know, unfortunately, I will have to get back to my real life at some point."

"Lives change, Becca. Believe me. It's not a bad thing."

She drew him rather profoundly. He wasn't a young man, nor an inexperienced one. He'd been through an ultimately disastrous marriage. And nothing could quite strip away one's innocence, one's idealism, quite like that. So, it wasn't hard for him to see what a complicated woman Rebecca Wells was, see the dark places within her that seemed to dominate at times who she was. But knowing all of this and the potential traps and quagmires that moving closer to her might present didn't change anything. She drew him, her energy, her physicality, her mind, her essence like an intriguing mystery.

They walked in silence, meandering around the Faubourg St. John neighborhood, slowly making their way back to his home. She wasn't talking, just seemed deep in thought. He wasn't sure reopening communication with the young girl was a good idea. It had seemed to sap so much out of Becca. But then again, sometimes hard work was just that, hard. He had to get her to a new plateau where she could gain some control of what she was feeling. That step he knew was essential.

"Do you like living here? I mean, in this area?" She asked, surprising him.

"Well, yes, I do. I like the energy of it."

She nodded, "I can see that. It's very old."

"Yes, some of it goes back to even before the founding of New Orleans."

She smiled, remembering fleetingly teaching her history class. "Parts of it feels soothing, and others, well, like Ellie."

"So, you've settled on Ellie?"

"I think so. I can feel people calling her Ellie. It might be a nickname, though," she said hesitantly.

"Don't ignore your impressions. It's important to encourage them."

"It's hard to separate them from my imagination."

"Don't try to sort everything out. Just open the doors and allow everything to flow."

Another smile, but she turned away from him, looking off into the distance as though it was uncomfortable to meet his eyes directly. "I've spent a lifetime trying to suppress things."

"Well, then, we have our work cut out for us."

"Yes, I suppose we do," she answered quietly.

Chapter Nine

Skittish

Becca closed her eyes once again, trying to focus on the little girl seemingly haunting Gabriel Sutton's house. She really didn't want to. She was finding this whole process somewhat excruciating. The only thing dragging her through this experiment was the man seated on the sofa beside her and his unfailing determination.

"Once more, then we'll have a lovely dinner to reward ourselves."

"It better be one heck of a dinner."

"Just hang in there. I know you don't feel as though you're making any progress, but you are."

And she acquiesced because she simply didn't know what else to do. Somehow, in the last few days, she'd moved beyond the life she'd been so uncomfortably comfortable within. Things had and she had changed somehow. And there was simply no path to returning, no place to go but forward now.

"Clear your mind and feel," he coaxed, as was their routine.

She followed his voice, relaxing and allowing the barriers, because she now recognized them as barriers, slip down. Calmness, she was surrounded by calmness. All except, and then she felt it, that thin thread of agitation — so delicate, just a gentle tremor that she now concentrated her focus on.

"Can you feel her?"

"I think so. It's slight."

"Try to trace it now, Becca."

Again, she allowed herself to open a bit more and feel that discordant thread. *"Ellie,"* she reached out with her mind. It was painful, that painful plaintive place that tugged at her heart. A child's confusion, so pure, so innocent, and unfair, she remembered —

"Keep focused on her." He said, strangely in response to her thoughts. How was it that he could be so in tune with what she was feeling?

Again, *"Ellie,"* a whisper without speaking it. The pain in her heart flamed up for just a moment and then diminished. *"Where are you?"* She asked, but then it stopped, strangely snuffed out. And she could not find that thread again.

"I don't know what happened," she repeated with distress.

He squeezed her hand reassuringly. They were sitting outside on his patio. Gabriel had made them some iced tea. "It's like anything. Sometimes you have success, and sometimes you have to—"

"If you say try again, I might scream."

He nodded, "I know you're frustrated. But some things won't happen conveniently or on a schedule."

She frowned, feeling a bit as though she'd just been insulted. "Am I sensing a criticism there?"

"No, not at all. I've just found modern culture seems to insist that we have more control over life than we actually do. It's important to allow things to unfold at their own pace. It causes a lot less stress."

"I have to work tomorrow."

"All right, we can pick up again when you're finished."

She looked at him oddly. "Are you saying I should continue to stay here with you?"

His eyes swept over her briefly, couching an unreadable expression. "For the time being, you might need to pick up some more things from your place in the morning."

"Yes, I'm sure I will."

Rebecca wasn't comfortable here. He knew that as he watched her move around his house. But what he didn't know and dearly wanted to know was why exactly. He supposed it might have been Ellie, the little girl ghost, whose name they'd sort of settled on by just referring to her with it. "How old do you think Ellie is?" or "Can you feel Ellie anywhere around here?"

As he continued to type on his laptop on a paper he was writing for a journal, Gabriel assumed this was the case. But it didn't exactly settle well with him. He allowed his mind to wander over to the woman resting in his guest room. He didn't consider himself a psychic, not at all, but then again, he did have feelings, intuitive, perceptive feelings. He leaned back in his office chair, closing his eyes and allowing his mind to clear.

He could feel her distinctly down the hall. She possessed a sort of kinetic energy, not at rest by any means, but driven, uncomfortable, almost too active for the body she inhabited. He allowed himself to be drawn in her direction.

Psychologists and psychiatrists he'd known over the years always insisted that every personality quirk could be traced to some life experience. In other words, every person was explainable in earthly terms. Perhaps that was what had driven him to seek and learn elsewhere. It simply wasn't true. Some people were created with dilemmas that simply could not be explained or 'fixed" by conventional measures. And then again, some simply could not be fixed.

He could feel Rebecca, and therefore a visual manifestation of her came to his mind. She was asleep, but it was a tortured one, caught in erratic energies that seemed to be preying on her vulnerabilities — no protection or guard for her. It bothered him immensely. How, he wondered, did she become so vulnerable to such parasitic attacks that normal people seemed immune to?

He imagined her wrapped in a blanket of pure white energy, acting as a buffer between her and the base attacks. In sending the energy out, he felt an acute pressure in his chest. They had to work on building more energy somehow. He opened his eyes, and his fingers lightly tapped on the desk. Things were beginning to coalesce in his mind.

She was sitting at the foot of the bed, curled up, staring at her with wide eyes. Becca watched her for a while in the semi-darkness, wondering why she was here and, more than that, what she should do about it. She used to have a cat, a small skittish gray tabby that would curl up on the foot of her bed when she was a child. From experience, she knew if she moved too quickly or even just rocked the mattress slightly, that cat would spring up and flee her bed quicker than she would have her next thought.

And she suspected, with no real evidence, that the same would be true of the little girl curled up on her bed, the little girl she knew had probably died close to a century ago.

She sighed deeply and considered simply going back to sleep. It was true she was so tired it would be easy, easy to doze off and write the whole thing off as a dream. But the rapid-fire experiences of the last few days had taught her rather quickly that all these extraordinary occurrences were far from just imaginings.

She closed her eyes for a moment and considered what Gabriel would do. He was calm, the anchor on the wild seas she was sailing upon. She cleared her mind trying to fill herself with calmness. Slowly, she opened her eyes and saw that the young girl was still watching her, but it was different now, just a little less fearful.

"I saw her last night."

He turned around with surprise. He'd been pouring them morning coffee. He planned to drive her back to her apartment and then to work. Why exactly he felt it was necessary to stick so close to Becca just now, he couldn't quite explain. Only that somewhere in his skin, he felt she was in some sort of transition and quite vulnerable.

"Ellie?" he asked.

She sighed, somewhat audibly, "Yes, I saw her last night sitting at the foot of my bed."

"Well, it's clear she's become attached to you."

"She seemed, I don't know, so skittish. But I tried to stay calm, and she stayed. But was gone this morning, of course."

"Did you feel anything?"

She shrugged, "I don't know Gabriel. Honestly, so much is happening. I'm just feeling overwhelmed."

"Well, that's understandable. Let's have some coffee. Then we can get going. I know a nice little bakery on the way where we can pick up something to eat."

"So, exactly how long will I be staying here?" she said slowly.

"I don't know. I suppose as long as it takes."

She was too tired. He could feel that acutely from her. Something or someone was draining energy out of her. Perhaps an energy bond formed somewhere along the way. It was true that the less energy you had, the more susceptible you were to draining. They'd taken a few moments at the pastry shop to drink some coffee. "Why don't you call in sick?"

She glanced up at him with a frown. "I can't. I need the money. I don't want to dip into my savings. Since I stopped teaching, things have been more than shaky."

He nodded, sipping his coffee slowly. There was no point in elaborating, and after all, trying to figure things out would entail a lot more disclosures about her life. Already, it felt as though he was constantly prying.

But there was the energy problem. Energy bonds were curious things. Most people had no idea how or when they were creating them — and more than that, how they could come to tax their very existence. "When you get home, you need to rest. You're expending too much energy."

"All right, Gabriel, but your house isn't my home, you know."

"I know," he murmured. "Are you ready?"

She smiled, and he thought not for the first time that Becca smiling made an amazing difference in her appearance.

She didn't want to go to work. Why exactly? She had no idea except to say that it would be like stepping out of a delightful cocoon into a harsher world. She was being foolish, about him, possibly about everything. The air felt heavy on Magazine Street today, and it felt odd, as though she'd been away from this for a thousand years. Hannah Wilder, the manager of Nola's Apparels, was there in the morning but told Rebecca succinctly that she would be leaving after lunch. It was up to her to steer the ship until closing. In some ways, that suited her better, as Monday afternoons weren't notoriously busy, but in other ways — Well, suffice to say, she was out of sorts, a bit destabilized by Gabriel Sutton's prominent role in her life over the past few days and all the strange happenings he'd brought in tow.

Or had she brought the strange happenings, and he'd just begun sorting them out for her? It seemed to be the latter, as fantastical as that sounded. He'd insisted that she return to his house to stay for a short duration longer until they could figure out how to go forward.

And she'd agreed. She felt safer there, in some ways safer from herself.

She glanced up at the clock. Almost three, just two hours more, then she could get out of here.

She heard the chiming of the front door and glanced up from the counter where she was laying out a new shipment of jewelry. But then her eyes froze at what she saw. It was a girl in her twenties, she thought, but she was completely covered in flies — flies all over her, buzzing around her. At that moment, Becca felt purely as though she'd been violently kicked in the stomach. She bent over the counter and shut her eyes, then slowly, cautiously opened them again.

The small brunette was still there, sifting through one of the round clothing racks, but now quite ordinary looking. She swallowed on a dry throat. She wanted to say, "Can I help you?" but the words remained soundlessly stuck somewhere.

Irritation was all over her skin. She was feeling it intensely. She closed her eyes and tried to focus, mentally stepping away from the sensation. Of course, it wasn't her at all. She was sure of it. The girl in the store, the one covered in the insects. This was her irritation. White light, that was what Gabriel had said. Imagine yourself surrounded by white light and then breathing it in, filling you up inside.

"Can I try these on?" The light, soft voice slammed into her. She opened her eyes. There she was, standing right in front of her, looking quite normal now.

"Yes, of course," she murmured. "Just in the back," gesturing to the white door toward the back of the shop labeled boldly— dressing room. "It's open."

The girl smiled at her slightly, then turned on her heel heading in that direction with garments in hand. Twenties, she'd estimate, early to mid. Older than Beth had been, but slight, so thin. She could see that clearly though she had been wearing a sweater. It sort of hung on her like those emaciated models you so often see on fashion runways.

She took a deep breath, and it felt painful in her chest, as though something had been pulled out of her. The girl was clearly sick in some way, but it didn't feel like conventional sickness. She glanced at the time, not too much more to go. Gabriel had driven her to work today, which she was somewhat grateful for now. The dressing room door flew open, and the girl sauntered out, looking strangely in better spirits than when she'd entered the boutique.

Becca hadn't moved from behind the counter. It was almost as though her feet were somehow cemented in place. "These didn't work, but I think I'll come back tomorrow when I have more time. Can I leave them with you?" she said of the mound of rejected dresses she held in her arms.

Becca nodded, quickly taking the garments in her hand while slightly brushing the girl's arm in the process. It chilled her, touching her. She knew she didn't want her to return, and she also knew that she felt trapped, truly trapped, somehow.

Chapter Ten

The Water

"Did you know her?"

"No," Becca shook her head. She put down the cup of tea she held in her hands because she'd suddenly noticed some of it trickling down the sides of the cup. Her hands were trembling, and she hadn't even been aware. What had happened at work with the girl had hit her much harder than she'd even realized.

"Are you sure? Could she have been one of your students?"

She frowned, overwhelmed again by what had occurred and more so by her reaction to it. She couldn't keep riding this roller coaster they'd been on for the last few days. Things had to settle down. It was too jarring. And Gabriel's relentless interrogation wasn't helping at the moment. "No, not as far as I remember." Just getting back from the store had been no easy task. When she'd walked outside to Gabriel's jeep after closing the shop, she'd felt physically ill — dizzy, nauseous. Immediately, he'd picked up on what was going on, while all she wanted to do was collapse in on herself.

She slumped down on the sofa. All she wanted to do was sleep. Sitting down next to her, he took her hand. "You might need a shower. This feels like a lot of bad energy."

"I'm too tired. I can barely keep my eyes open."

"It's clear you've lost a lot of energy."

"How is that even possible?"

He squeezed her hand. "It is. Becca, you're going to have to trust me."

She looked up into his very concerned eyes. "This can't be what my life has become now. It's too exhausting."

"Give it time. You're evolving."

She sighed deeply. "Okay, fine, shower first."

He nodded, smiling, but there was so much else behind that smile. She could feel it acutely without him even saying a word.

Gabriel paced the den of his Dumaine Street address. This was like patching a sinking boat, one hole fixed, and another springs a leak. What was more than clear to him was that he was going about this the wrong way. This wasn't working to address each psychic situation that Becca was being besieged with. Instead, he needed somehow to make her stronger.

He stopped amid his pacing and focused. He could sense her in the shower, steam surrounding her, water dancing off her skin. He breathed in deeply, trying to feel, trying to connect to what might be helpful. Initially, he'd thought cocooning her here away from disruptive energies would help, but that wasn't possible. There were always disruptive energies, especially in a neighborhood as old as the one he lived in. Maybe it had been foolish to do this so quickly, to get so involved. She was so different, sensitive, yet so defensive. Different, he thought, sinking into a nearby lounge chair, and he was undeniably, complicatedly drawn to her. Their partnership felt easy, and natural, and it had only intensified during the brief yet intense span of time they'd spent together.

He breathed in deeply, considering. That was one way to build energy, intimacy with a naturally kindred soul.

But to do so seemed like taking advantage of a woman who was in a precariously vulnerable state — one he was undeniably beginning to care for, was extremely attracted to, and had even had passing thoughts of building a relationship with. But what did she want, and was she really in any state of mind to consider such things?

Becca's life was falling apart. She had no idea what to do or where to turn. She was now clinging to a job that she could barely tolerate with her fingernails because already she'd given up her career as a teacher. And now, now she didn't even know if she could keep her retail job. She rubbed her damp hair with a towel frowning at herself in the steam-filled mirror. How could things have gotten this bad? She pulled on a dark blue pullover sweater and a pair of blue jeans, brushing out her long brown hair. She felt a little better, though extremely exhausted. And she thought about Gabriel — strong, enigmatic Gabriel, who seemed to be the only solid thing in her life right now. She didn't understand it, but he seemed determined, intent on sticking with her through all of this.

She dried her hair slightly, struck by the fact that it felt as though there was no energy or strength in her arm holding the dryer. She breathed deeply, lightly dropping the mini-hair dryer she'd brought from her house.

There was a light knock on the door, then Gabriel's voice. "How about some coffee?"

"Okay," she answered, brushing her hair, then pulling it back into a ponytail. She walked out of the bathroom and then down the hall where it connected to the kitchen. Waiting in the doorway, she silently watched him as he finished making the coffee, then turned around to acknowledge her. When he finally was facing her, she said quietly. "I'm wondering if I need something."

"Something?" he echoed with a rather solemn expression on his face.

"I feel like I'm losing it."

"This isn't a psychological issue. Medication will only numb the problem, not solve it."

"She was covered in flies, swarming all over her. Then in the next second, they were gone. What was that?"

He hadn't moved from his position in front of the coffee pot, just intensely answered her. "It was a spiritual manifestation. You have the power to glimpse what is really there. Her spirit was wounded, damaged, and like an untreated wound was being attacked by parasites."

"That's crazy," she murmured, feeling hysterical tears begin to eke out of her eyes.

"Becca, stop labeling everything, judging everything. You must unlearn all those judgments society places on things."

"I can't live this way, Gabriel."

And at that moment, he did walk forward, now holding her arms with his hands. "You have to learn to accept what's happening, Becca. Stop fighting. Just accept who you are now." Lightly he brushed the tears with his fingertips. "This is not a curse. This is a gift. You are exceptional."

And then he folded her into his arms deeply. She put her head on his shoulder and then relaxed, just letting all the bad stuff quietly flow out of her. What was it about him that soothed her so much?

"Let's go for a drive, then we can get something for dinner," he whispered into her hair.

"I thought we were having coffee."

"Later."

It was approaching six, and nighttime was already beginning to set in, but the water along the Lakefront felt so calming. Gabriel had insisted they get out and walk along the concrete paved sidewalk next to Lake Pontchartrain. There was a slight breeze, and the waves from the lake softly crashed up against the concrete layer of steps leading up to the walkway.

"Try to clear your mind and soak up the energy."

"Energy?" she asked.

"Water is a huge conductor of energy, and if you allow yourself to be peaceful, you can benefit from it."

They stared at the rhythmic waves in the distance, and she understood. Becca hadn't spent much time here at the Lakefront, but she did occasionally travel to the Gulf Coast. For her, walking along the beach had always been a place to relax and soothe her frayed nerves. He took her hand in his and guided her to one of the concrete benches facing the water.

She didn't think about the familiarity that seemed to be growing between them. Somewhere along the wild ride of the past several days, she'd come to trust Gabriel Sutton. Whatever was to come, she felt that without question, he had her best interests at heart, and that was saying a lot because Rebecca's nature was instinctively to be mistrustful.

He squeezed her hand to signal that she depart from these dizzying internal reflections. "Now I want you to close your eyes, Becca, and allow yourself to feel the water."

She breathed out deeply and did as he asked. Gabriel continued to hold her hand as she attempted to clear her mind. It was difficult. In the distance, she could feel pulls, strange, disconnected emotions trying to draw her elsewhere. "No, anchor yourself here, Becca, here by the water. Feel the energy all around you and let yourself become a part of it." It was difficult. It wasn't her way to be so calm, so centered. "Focus on breathing, breathing in the calm, peaceful energy around you and breathing out the upsetting emotions."

Again, he squeezed her hand, and she felt the strength from the contact. "Breathe in and out," he repeated.

She did as he asked and began to feel a calmness seeping into her. The fear and franticness of the day began to slowly leave as she saw a soft light blue energy filling her inner vision. "Just be calm," he murmured. "Let it permeate and drive away all the anxiety."

His voice was close but distant, as well as she finally began to relax.

They picked up some shrimp po'boys from the Blue Harbor restaurant and picnicked in his car along the Lakefront. Gabriel was reluctant to leave the area as the energy felt particularly strong tonight, and Becca seemed to be benefitting from it. The energy wasn't always good here.

The water as a conductor didn't mean it always reflected positive energy. Everything, including weather, he'd found, had its personality, energy, if you will. A storm could bring in great amounts of positive energy or carry a massive store of negative energy. It just so happened that, fortunately, the balance of the energy on the lake tonight was positive.

And Becca decidedly seemed stronger than she was at the house earlier. And he was glad but also concerned that just as quickly things could flip again. Her abilities were evolving through their work together and undeniably through their association. He could feel it just being around her was sparking feelings, ideas, and impulses within him as well.

Ostensibly, she'd turned his very quiet existence upside down a bit, and upon reflection, that wasn't a bad thing. He hadn't realized that he'd closed himself off so much and was becoming mired down in his routine. Helping her was bringing him back to the land of the living, making him reflect on where he wanted his life to go.

"Are you feeling better?" he asked, lightly patting her hand.

She turned to him, her eyes seeming quite luminous in the dim light of the car. "Yes, thank you, Gabriel, this helped, and the food wasn't bad either."

He smiled and took a breath. She was so beautiful at the moment, and if they were together under different circumstances, he would have kissed her. But in some respects, he felt like her doctor and definitely her guide, trying to lead her out of a dark forest. And he didn't want to take advantage of her.

She stared at him for a moment, then looked away, leaving him with the distinct impression that she knew exactly what he was thinking.

The rest of the evening was quiet. After they got back, he talked to Becca a bit about spiritual protection, placing a white light of protection around herself visually whenever she went out. For some, that might seem extreme, but he knew that Becca was particularly vulnerable right now. Situations that might on the surface seem benign at the offset could turn difficult very quickly, like the girl with the flies. He'd noticed how quiet she seemed after their time at the lake.

"Are you feeling okay?"

She smiled, "Yeah, just sorting things out, I guess."

He nodded, "Well, don't spend too much time with that. You need some quiet, recovery time, nothing too intense." And then a thought occurred to him, "Do you like cards?"

"You mean like Poker?"

"Maybe, or something else. I'll get a deck, and we can play for a little while."

Chapter Eleven

The Seer of the Lost Ones

The night had been quiet. She'd been exhausted, so Becca had slept a heavy deep sleep though she'd awoken still tired. But no dreams, and at this point, she'd considered that a win. As she dragged herself out of bed, she grabbed her cell phone from the nightstand. There was a text from Hannah Wilder at the store. "Business has been slow the past few days. Why don't you take the day off? And we'll talk tomorrow." She stared blankly at the screen. What did that mean? Was she slowly losing her job? She took a quick breath and wondered how she really felt about that. She'd been thinking for some time this wasn't a good fit for her, the retail business. Maybe she could find a way to get back into teaching, tutoring or some kind of work from home.

She picked up the heavy blue velour robe from a nearby wooden chair. She had a robe at home, but once Gabriel had lent this one to her, she'd gotten into the habit of using it. It felt comfortable, like him, soothing to her jagged nerves.

This work thing, Becca knew she should be concerned and upset, but at the moment, all she felt was a bit relieved. Down on Magazine Street, it seemed vulnerable, a place where anyone could walk in. Any stranger with all their baggage could get near her, and she had to stay put because it was her job.

She took off the robe and decided to get dressed, pulling some blue jeans out of her suitcase and a red mock turtleneck. She brushed out her hair, swirling it into a loose bun that she contained with a hairband. Taking a quick look at her appearance, she decided she was presentable. Today, she would take hold of things again. She glanced over to the corner of the room where Ellie stood quietly watching her with virtually no expression. Becca had seen her when she woke up, but in truth she was getting used to her presence, rather more accepting.

She would have to ask Gabriel what he thought they should do, if anything, about the lost one. She sighed. Yes, that's what she was — the seer of the lost ones. She headed with some purpose out the door to find Gabriel.

"Is that unusual?"

She sipped her coffee. They were sitting out on his patio at a small two-chair wrought iron table. It was breezy today but certainly not too cold to enjoy a leisurely breakfast —a cup of coffee and a bagel. "A little, I know business has slowed down recently, but honestly, I wasn't paying attention, just trying to navigate moment by moment." He looked at her with concern just for an instant, then stared off somewhere beyond the perimeter of his small yard. "What?" she asked, perhaps a little too abrasively.

He returned his gaze to her with a questioning expression. "You want to be more specific?"

"You obviously have something to say, and I don't like it when you hold back."

He shrugged a little, picking up his coffee and clearly contemplating if, indeed, he was going to tell her what was on his mind. "I have been thinking."

"Clearly," she murmured.

"The job, it's—"

She frowned, "I know. It's not ideal."

"Yes, but more than that. Right now, it could be detrimental."

She looked down, tapping her fingers lightly on her bagel, which in a matter of seconds, had lost its appeal to her. "Detrimental, bad as all that."

"You wanted to know."

"Yes, I did, I suppose. I just would like some good news for a change."

He reached out and touched her hand, spurring her to look up. "Becca, we're figuring out how to manage things. That's all. I believe you're in a transition phase, making you particularly vulnerable right now."

She nodded, "I know. Truthfully, the idea of potentially leaving this job made me feel relieved, except, of course, the problem of having no money coming in."

He removed his hand and picked up his coffee cup again. He wasn't finished, had more to say. She could feel it acutely. "I had a thought, a temporary one. I could pay you."

"For what?" she asked a bit dubiously.

"I'm a writer, you know, outside of this. I'm working on a few projects, and a book is one of them. I could use help organizing things, light editing. I mean, just until you figure out what you want to do if that would appeal to you."

"So, you mean I'd stay here."

"For a while, we'd continue to work on mastering your abilities as well as the other work. And you wouldn't have to worry about constantly being exposed to disturbing psychic phenomena."

"So, I'd just stay in this cocoon until we see what kind of creature emerges."

Now it was his turn to frown. "You know, there is a power in thought. If you expect negativity, you will draw it to you. Thoughts are energy. A positive attitude here could benefit you."

"You find me negative?"

"I find you battered and, yes, somewhat pessimistic at times."

It was her turn to stare off, at anything, away from his gaze. He wasn't wrong. Nonetheless, she didn't like the truth so abruptly put in her face. She'd been on the defensive for so long that it had become a habit. "You know, this isn't a perfect cocoon, Gabriel. Ellie is making a habit of visiting me, particularly at night, though I did see her this morning."

"Well, I need you to tell me these things, Becca."

She turned back to him. "I just did. I didn't think you wanted me to wake you up every time I see something."

He tapped his fingers on the table and hadn't touched his bagel for several minutes as well. Apparently, she wasn't the only one rattled by this conversation. "Okay, how about this? I want you to start journaling every time you see something or feel something unusual that doesn't seem directly connected to your feelings. And also, anytime you have a particularly strange or disturbing dream."

"That's a lot of journaling," she murmured.

"It's time to get scientific about this. We might be able to start mapping out patterns that could be helpful."

She nodded slowly, "So, the job. I mean the one I have now. You're saying I should leave it."

"Yes, yes, for the time being, we need to try to control your external stimuli as much as possible. I don't want you encountering things like—"

"Like the girl with the flies."

"Yes, you know people do have free will. You can't help everyone."

"Now, who's being pessimistic."

He shook his head, "No, I call that realism. Let's stick with what we can do. Maybe help the little girl ensconced in my house."

Quite abruptly, a quick image traveled across her mind of a dream she'd had and the disturbing man she'd encountered in it. But she swept it away, best to deal with manageable things. She looked again at Gabriel and noticed him watching her closely. She knew he couldn't read her mind, but she couldn't help feeling that he was in tune with her, somehow aware of shifts in her mood. And at what point they'd become so connected, she wasn't entirely sure.

He was uneasy, as his former wife had always said, *"You can't help but be waiting for the other shoe to drop."* Maybe Becca was right. Maybe he was a pessimist, just disguising himself as a realist.

But he didn't believe that. Something was bothering him, something in the ether. He remembered a former teacher contradicting his assessment of himself. *"You don't lack in psychic abilities, Gabe. You're extraordinarily intuitive."*

He'd heard of this instructor through a network of acquaintances and traveled to Northern Arkansas for intense instruction on meditation and other related sessions. This particular teacher worked out of a metaphysical center and was in her early sixties. After his divorce, he'd begun to pursue this esoteric interest in a bit of a shotgun manner, not sure what he'd hoped to gain or accomplish, just following an intangible thread that seemed to be leading him from experience to experience.

He was still practicing medicine back then and had taken a short leave of absence from his job to ostensibly try to get his head together.

He remembered how astonishing he thought it was when his teacher, Jean Rampart, had told him she was originally from New Orleans.

"What brought you up here?" he'd asked.

And she'd looked at him oddly. "I was led here, my path, you see."

He remembered thinking at that moment that he was out of his depth, path? What could that mean? Life was just a series of random choices with no particular pattern or path.

At that first meeting, Jean was dressed in a sort of loose purple caftan, and they were sitting in a comfortable room on a sofa with large pillows and a soft light blue rug on the floor. Several mats were placed about the room where no doubt, yoga or some other meditative exercises might be performed. "Is there such a thing?" he murmured.

She smiled at him softly, "Why are you here, Gabe?" she asked.

Funny, he hadn't asked her to call him that, but most of his casual acquaintances and his family did. He laughed a bit at the question, wondering. "Impulse, I suppose. I've started reading, studying esoterics since—" Then he stopped. What exactly was he going to say? How much of the chaos of his life was he going to open up to this stranger?

Jean Rampart was a slight woman with dark hair streaked heavily with gray, pulled up into a bun. But she waited, waited patiently for him to complete his thought.

"I've gone through a divorce recently. It wasn't easy," he said haltingly. It was unnatural for him to share personal feelings like this. But what the heck, he figured, he'd probably never see this woman again after these sessions. What did he have to lose? "It shook me up quite a bit, made me question, well, just everything that I believed, everything that I thought was important. So, I suppose I've been searching."

She had dark brown eyes, he recalled, very intense, watching him closely, not just listening to what he said. "And it was because of that divorce, the breakdown of your marriage, that you began searching for understanding, for meaning."

He remembered that moment clearly, crystal clear, because it was pivotal, like the lost scrambled puzzle pieces suddenly snapping together. "Yes," he said quietly.

"Gabe, don't you see. You are on a path. Events in your life have led you here to learn, and they will also lead you elsewhere."

Then, at that very instant, he'd started listening, really listening, because that made sense to him. What happened with Cynthia had changed him, rewrote him, and now he was ready to find out what was next.

He'd planned only to stay a week but stayed several months instead, learning from his new teacher. He found his mind so hungry, perhaps starving, for the information she imparted. And after that, there were other teachers, some even out of the country. But he'd always held her in high regard and remembered her last call to him. He'd always believed he lacked psychic abilities, but she'd told him they manifest differently in everyone. "Gabe, you are deeply intuitive and will be a powerful guide to others. But never dismiss your feelings. I've found them to be largely infallible."

A month later, he'd received correspondence from another counselor at the Ozark Metaphysics Research Center. Jean had passed away from leukemia. He hadn't known she was ill when they last spoke, but he'd never forgotten her guidance, so he was determined to follow this uneasy thread. As openly candid as they'd been with each other, he couldn't help but feel that there was still something important that Becca wasn't telling him, something that could potentially have significant bearing on everything.

Chapter Twelve

Family

"So, I know it's short notice, but I will be in town for a few days."

He glanced up with distraction from the pile of papers he'd been sifting through at his desk. "What?" he said a little abruptly into the cell phone.

"Gabe, are you listening to me?"

His younger sister Anna had called him this morning, just as he was enmeshed in researching a chapter in his new book. "Yeah, sort of. Sorry, I was in the middle of something. What did you say?"

"I'm attending the APA convention. It's in New Orleans this year. Didn't I mention this?"

"No," he shook his head with distraction as he tried to reassemble the convoluted mass of loose documents before him. "At least, I don't remember."

"Well, maybe I didn't. No, that's right. I wasn't sure if Peter could get time off to watch the baby."

He stopped and leaned back in his chair. "And he did?"

"Yeah, last minute, so he said go. Take a break, do something with your mind."

He smiled. Anna had taken off time from work after the birth of their second child, Nina, and he knew how antsy she was to do something other than entertain the toddler and the newborn. Peter was right to tell her to go. "So, how long?"

"The week, I'm staying at the Hilton near the convention center. But I did want to come to visit my big brother while I was in town. How about dinner tonight? We could go to one of those restaurants on the Lakefront."

"Yeah, yeah, we could do that." And then it hit him, Becca. "Well, actually, I'm not really on my own right now."

There was quiet, which was a bit unusual for Anna. He'd always considered her the chatty type. "Really?"

"Yes, someone is living here with me right now."

"What kind of someone?"

"Her name is Rebecca Wells, Becca," he murmured.

"Is this a girlfriend?"

"No, no, someone I've been trying to help with some issues she's having. So, we decided it was best if she moved in for a while. She's sort of working for me now as well, trying to get my new book organized. My research is all over the place."

"Yeah, yeah, I'm sure you need help with that. So, how long—"

"Not long, but that shouldn't interfere with any plans—"

"Well, ask her to come to dinner."

"I will. But I don't know what she'll say."

"Yeah, okay, Becca, that's pretty. I'll come by around six. I have a rental car."

"Okay, Anna, it will be good to see you."

The morning had already been chaotic. She'd spoken to Hannah early. Unexpectedly, she seemed a bit relieved when Becca first told her that she'd be leaving her position at the store but bookended it with, "There's always a place for you here if you change your mind," which she couldn't help but think was simply being gracious rather than realistic. She was even more suspicious now, given the reception at her resignation, that the store was struggling more than she'd ever suspected.

By the time she'd found Gabriel puttering around the kitchen, she was having second, third, and fourth thoughts about giving up her job and going all in on their peculiar arrangement.

"So, I did it," she said abruptly as she entered the room.

He looked a bit befuddled at her comment, which did nothing to quell her mutinous misgivings. "Did what?"

"I quit my job. Remember, we had a conversation about —oh my God, did I make a mistake? I thought that—"

He put up his hand to cease her mounting panic. "No, no, that's good. I'm glad you did. I'm just a little scrambled this morning."

As he sat down at the counter, silently stirring his coffee, she waited for elaboration. But there was none. "So, Hannah took it well. In fact, she seemed a little happy about it. Maybe I did her a favor."

"Maybe," he murmured, taking a sip.

She frowned, "Okay, well, I think I need to pick up some more clothes from my place. Are you sure you want to do this, Gabriel? You seem very preoccupied this morning."

He glanced up at her with a bit of a distracted look in his eyes that only bolstered her assessment. "I'm sorry, Becca. This has nothing to do with you. You did exactly what you should have. I just got a phone call from my sister this morning. She's in town and wants to see me."

Quietly, she sat down on the chair next to his. "Okay, isn't that a good thing?"

He nodded, "Sure," placing his coffee cup on the counter. "I haven't seen her for a while. She's in town from Missouri for a conference. She and her husband live there. They have a young family," he sort of rambled on disconnectedly.

She was feeling things from him, unusual things. Gabriel was always calm, determined, focused, but right now, he seemed different, strangely vulnerable somehow. "You seem bothered about this."

He stared off in front of him. "It's complicated."

"So, is she the only family you have?"

"No, my parents live up in Maryland. But we don't talk much."

She smiled softly. Pain, she was feeling pain from him. "Family can make you crazy sometimes. I know."

He focused on her at that comment. "Is that how your family is?"

She shrugged. How she didn't want to open up this can of worms. "I suppose. My parents relocated to Tennessee once they retired to be near my sister. And I have a brother in Texas. We don't talk much, none of us. My Mom and Dad never really understood my problems, so I just stopped telling them. It was easier that way."

"I'm sorry. After my divorce, I cut myself off a bit. And then, I began to pursue arenas that, well, let's just say most of my family wouldn't be open to."

"What about your sister?"

"Anna? She's a bit different, I suppose. She's a psychologist, but there are limits. And as you said, it's easier for some people not to talk about it."

"I don't know if it's easier. It hurts being so distant and unable to share things with people who profess to care about you."

"Profess?"

She smiled grimly, "Well, there's love, and then there's love with conditions, you know."

"I suppose. Anyway, the problem comes with—"

"Me, why I'm here." She said flatly.

"I do like the way you get to the point."

"You told her about me?"

"I did. Well, I told her you were staying here. I was helping you with some issues, and you were working for me, helping with my book."

"Hmm, what did she say?"

"She asked if you were my girlfriend."

She laughed a bit impulsively, "Yeah, that would be an obvious jump. I guess. What did you say?"

"That you weren't."

"Well, your story is a bit thin. She'll probably want more details. But that shouldn't be too difficult to fill in. I'm a master fabricator. It's been a lifestyle with me."

"That sounds difficult."

She brushed his comment aside. Even given the closeness they'd developed over the past several days, she was still uncomfortable sharing all the painful little niches of her existence. "When are you seeing her?"

"Tonight, for dinner, you're invited, by the way."

She smiled, "Thanks, but I think I'll just let you go and catch up with baby sister. We'll have plenty of opportunity to fill in your story if you want to ahead of time. Don't worry."

"You know, I'm not entirely comfortable with this. I want you to get away from having to live this way, in secret."

"It's not my secrets we're dealing with. It's yours. Any coffee left in the pot?"

"Yeah, there's some. Help yourself."

Gabriel didn't like it. He felt as though he was leading Becca back to a place of shadows, a place she'd lived too long.

"Thoughts have power, you know. They contain energy and can even manifest on another plane of existence."

It was a conversation he'd had with Jean Rampart on one of his trips to Arkansas.

"I'm not sure I follow what you mean by manifest on another plane of existence."

"There are many other planes of existence other than just the physical one that we actively perceive. I'm sure you've noted in dreams many occurrences and landscapes that seem rather alien to our daily life in the physical plane."

"Yes, of course, but dreams are something people disregard — a sort of wish fulfillment that the brain indulges in."

He remembered she'd smiled at him almost as though he was spouting nonsense. "Is that what your dreams do for you, Gabe? Fulfill your wishes?"

He took a moment to reassess because these sessions with his mentor were certainly not a time for self-deception. There was no place for it here and, more than that, no gain for him in doing so. "Actually, most of the time, I find my dreams frustrating and confusing."

"Yes, it is very hard for our physical eyes, physical brains, to interpret in a reasonable manner what we experience on the astral plane."

"The astral plane?"

"Yes, most often we visit there in dreams. That is the nearest plane of reality to our own. And it's where the energy of our thoughts manifest, usually in a temporary fashion but sometimes not. That's why it's important to gain mastery over your thinking. Do not dwell in negative places. It will only yield unpleasantness."

He felt acutely that Becca had been caught up in a somewhat self-inflicted depression that complicated her ability to manage her sensitivities. It was so easy to get caught up in other people's expectations, society's expectations of what you should be, and how you should live, and to just put a toe out of that box can meet with disapproval — others and your own. All of this was difficult to manage for ordinary people, much less someone who was extremely empathic.

And the last, very last thing he wanted to do was make her feel as though the work they were doing together needed to be hidden, needed to be secret because he had a difficult relationship with his birth family.

And yet, on the other side of the coin, right now, the last thing they needed was outside complications.

"Stop worrying."

He'd been sitting in front of his computer staring at the screen for some time, unseeing, just caught up in his concerns. Becca was leaning against the door frame of his study, looking at him with, he had to admit, a bit of a light-hearted expression. "I'm not."

The smile grew on her face, and he was reminded of how lovely she was. "You're a bad liar."

He sighed, "That's not what I hear."

"Honestly, Gabriel, this is not a big deal. It's not lying if you just don't choose to share everything with some people."

"You know you're the only person who calls me Gabriel. Everyone else usually calls me Gabe."

She looked a bit surprised. "Oh, I'm sorry. Do you want me to—"

"No, no, I like it. I mean, it seems right, if that makes any sense."

She nodded slowly, "Yeah, well, it feels natural to me. Anyway, you shouldn't worry so much about this."

"You know, I tried to talk to Anna, I mean, about spiritualism, what I've learned over the years, and she just seemed as though there was a limitation to what she wanted to hear. I believe she knows my life is different but doesn't want hers to be. Maybe it's Peter, her husband, or maybe it's just her."

"Well, if things weren't this way with me, the sensitivities, the craziness, maybe I wouldn't want to hear it either. I don't know. I really don't."

"Everything in its time," he said quietly.

She smiled softly at him. "I suppose. You know, just tell her I lost my job and am transitioning, so we're helping each other out."

"Yeah, something like that."

"Or you could tell her we're madly in love. Would that be more believable?"

He hesitated momentarily as a strange feeling of déjà vu fluttered across his mind and then was gone as quickly as it had arrived. "If you give me a few minutes to finish up, I can drive you to your place to get some more of your things."

"Okay, maybe we can talk about how I can help you with your book on the way."

"Maybe so," he answered, unwilling to address the rather large pink elephant that had just arrived at his doorstep on Dumaine Street.

Chapter Thirteen

A Shift

Anna Michaels, Gabriel's sister, was nervous, and Becca wasn't at all sure why. She was a striking but approachable woman, a little taller than her, with dark blue eyes and short curly blond hair. The resemblance between her and Gabriel was unmistakable, similar coloring, and bone structure, though his hair was sandy brown and his eyes not as purely blue as hers, being more of a grayish-blue mix, unmistakably siblings, however.

"Are you sure you don't want to come to dinner with us, Becca?" she asked with evident interest.

It felt awkward at that moment. In fact, the whole encounter felt awkward, as though there was something unsaid lingering in the air. But Becca also knew she was way too sensitive to nuances. That was something she wanted to talk to Gabriel about. She desperately needed to find a way not to be so thin-skinned.

"No, you two need to catch up, and I have about a million things to do around here."

The blond sister had smiled speculatively. She wanted her to come with them. She wanted — then she stopped, such odd emotions but strong. She felt worry from Anna, clearly worry about her brother, and hope also—clearly, she hoped Becca might be the key to helping.

Gabriel was quiet during the exchange, less gregarious than he was usually with her. "Well, let's get going." He smiled at Becca, "See you later."

"Okay," she nodded, stepping back as they left. She took a deep breath, realizing strangely that this was her first time alone in this house.

They'd settled on Bailey's on the Lakefront and had requested seating near a scenic window overlooking Lake Pontchartrain. "Too bad Becca didn't want to come along," Anna murmured.

Gabriel barely glanced up from his menu. "She's just a friend."

"She's really pretty, not your usual type. I mean, not like Cynthia."

He sighed, "Really?"

"No, no, you used to go more for obvious beauty. Becca's different, subtly exotic, I'd say. Are you sure—"

He closed the menu and set it down. "Look, she's got a lot going on in her life, and I'm just trying to help right now. Nothing complicated."

She smiled, "Too bad, I'd like to see you with someone. Since the divorce, you just don't seem interested in a relationship."

He looked at her, now understanding. Lightly, he patted her hand, "Don't worry, Anna, I'm fine. If I get involved again, it will be for the right reasons with hopefully the right person."

"Yeah, I hope so. You deserve to be happy. You're a good guy."

She decided to take a walk before dusk settled in on the city. For some reason, tonight she was drawn to the water, to the Bayou St. John, which she had avoided since they discovered what had happened to Ellie. So strange, it had felt like a tangible fear, but not tonight. Tonight she felt drawn, so she followed the inclination and began to walk along the shore where there was a walking path. A slight breeze flowed across the glistening water, causing a ruffling of its placid surface. "It's all right," she murmured. Not at all sure if Ellie was near, as she wasn't feeling her, wasn't feeling anything but quiet at the moment.

She tried to clear her mind and simply soak up the energy of the water, just as Gabriel had told her to do when they were on the Lakefront. She breathed in deeply, then out slowly, trying to feel calmness throughout her, and then suddenly, she had a vision of him in her mind, sitting silently at a table with his sister.

It was uncanny how strongly she could sense him, his emotions, his thoughts, as though he was right in front of her. He was calm, and then he glanced forward. "*Becca*," she heard in her mind, then stepped back. She stood rooted to the spot on the banks of the Bayou St. John. It was real. She'd heard his voice distinctly in her mind. How in the world was that possible?

A chill swept over her, and a quick surge of fear and then panic set in. "All right, Ellie," she whispered as she turned around and began to head back.

"So, I'll be tied up for the next few days, but maybe dinner Friday night. I fly out Saturday."

"Yeah, or you can come to the house, and I'll fix something."

"Would that be all right with Becca?"

"I'm sure," he murmured. Anna had insisted on driving, and they were heading back to his house in the darkness. Something was bothering him, pulling him elsewhere, and it had been so all evening, even though Anna had largely commandeered his attention with stories of her small children.

"Don't you want kids?" she'd asked.

"Maybe, I don't know. I suppose if it happens, fine, but if it doesn't, then that's all right, too."

"You know, you've changed so much. You used to be, well, I don't know."

"Driven?" he murmured, picking up his iced tea.

"I was going to say more of. I don't know—"

"A jerk?"

She smiled tentatively, "At times, I think."

"Well, I used to believe I could control everything."

She laughed, "And you finally realized that you can't?"

"Life made me realize that I couldn't."

She hesitated as though she was almost afraid to respond. "I'm sorry, Gabe. I didn't realize that things got so hard for you. I just figured you would handle it. You know, we just didn't talk that way about what was going on in our lives. And, well, to be honest, Peter and I were going through a rough patch. We almost broke up after Josh was born." She voiced this so matter-of-factly that for a moment, he wasn't sure if he'd heard correctly.

"I didn't know that, Anna."

"Yeah, nobody in the family did. We weren't taught to share personal things, stiff upper lip and all. Anyway, we got through it with a little therapy and later decided to have another baby. Things are much better now."

"And you're happy?"

She shrugged, "Well, I'm not always happy. Raising kids is hard, but I'm more peaceful now and happy most of the time. But I kind of wonder if happiness is a choice, not just something we wait to happen to us."

He nodded, so unusual seeing this new side of his sister. "Yeah, maybe. I'm glad things are better for you, and I hope, well, I hope we can be closer."

"I'd like that," she said softly, and then the food came, and they gravitated back to a more superficial setting, which he'd always found was their family's fallback.

It was close to nine when she heard the front door open and close. She was still awake, though in a nightshirt and shorts, flipping through one of Gabriel's books by Edgar Cayce. She didn't get up to greet him, though she was more than curious about how the evening had progressed, especially after she'd felt she'd somehow heard him communicating with her. It didn't make sense, not any sense, but she could no more deny it happened than deny anything that had occurred since they'd met.

She tried to focus on the pages before her but found she couldn't. And then she heard a light tap on her door. "Yes," she said softly.

Gabriel partially opened the door, staring at her with a tentative expression. She smiled, "How'd it go?"

"Okay, do you feel like some tea?" he asked.

"Sure," she answered.

"Good, I'll make some. I'd like to talk for a while."

"What's wrong with you, Becky?"

She'd pulled away from his grasp. It was high school, after the senior prom, and she'd just received her first kiss and found herself completely, profoundly repelled, body and soul. "I don't know. I just don't want to." The truth was that there wasn't anything particularly wrong with the fellow. He was a good-looking, athlete type, blond-haired, tall. But the closeness, the feel of his breath, his body heat next to hers only made her want to run for the hills. She pulled away from the embrace that had happened on her front doorstep. She hadn't expected to feel this way, but the feelings had come over her in a wave.

Steve Jacobs left, of course, in a kind of huff, then never called her again. Over the years, there were a few other brief entanglements that culminated in an engagement just out of college. This one she'd actually slept with, but it had felt nearly devastating to her, and it was difficult to hide. So, not long after, the whole thing dissolved. A girlfriend of hers had suggested that maybe she was simply more attracted to her own gender, but she also knew deep down that was not the case. There was simply something, something intrinsically wrong with her. And no matter how drawn she felt to Gabriel Sutton, she was afraid, afraid it would simply be the same with him as with all the others.

She donned the plush robe she'd been using since she had begun staying with Gabriel and headed to the kitchen. As she made her way down the hallway, she heard the rumblings of the tea kettle on the small gas stove in his kitchen. Was he making her tea like that first day, three or four days, or was it a week ago? It seemed like so long now. Sometimes time crept by immeasurably slowly, with such little life lived in its intervals. And at other times, it was so jam-packed with events that it felt as it did now, as though eras had passed.

His back was to her, and she felt oddly nervous now about disturbing him. There was intensity emanating from him, intense reflection, as though his very spirit was not here in these close quarters that they found themselves in.

"Mint all right?" he asked.

The sound of his voice so startled her that she almost jumped. "Yeah, sounds good," she answered a little shakily. Something, something unpredictable was happening now, right now, in the small kitchen of Gabriel's house on Dumaine Street. Something important, though the two inhabitants had barely spoken. "Um, Gabriel, if you'd rather be alone, I can go back to my room and give you some space."

At that, he turned around, looking at her with a rather questioning expression. Perhaps, she was wrong, and it was in her mind, all in her mind, as so many things had always been. "Why did you ask that?" he said calmly.

The phrasing, not — *"What do you mean?"; "What are you talking about?"* The way he always spoke to her was gentle, respectful, inquisitive, comforting — nothing abrasive, nothing condescending ever. "I don't know. I just feel," she struggled — how, how to put the amorphous into real words.

"Go ahead," he said quietly. "You feel—"

"I feel that you have a lot on your mind, that maybe—"
He smiled, "Maybe?"

"You're making me feel self-conscious," she murmured.

"You know, you don't have to. You can just tell me what you're feeling, thinking. I'm not going to judge you for it."

"I know, but it's elusive like something is happening. I don't know what it is. But I feel like there are things you need to figure out. I'm sorry if that seems silly."

"Of course, it doesn't, and I suppose I do. Tonight, just talking with Anna jarred something in me. Things I guess I've suppressed or maybe just didn't want to deal with. She opened up a bit, but there is so much I can't tell her, share with her. In fact, it feels like the only person I can share just about everything with is you. Does that sound strange?"

She leaned against a counter, feeling like she needed the support at the moment. "I guess it does on paper. We haven't known each other very long. But I would be disingenuous if I said I didn't know what you meant. I've never felt as accepted by anyone as by you, Gabriel, flaws and all. And I don't understand it. It's been so short a time. But I-I don't know."

She heard the tea kettle suddenly whistle behind him. He hesitated momentarily, then spun around and turned off the burner on the stove. And in the smoothest motion, less than an instant, he turned around again, then took her in his arms, pulling her in a comforting embrace against his chest. "Gabriel," she whispered. But then he bent down and began to kiss her softly in a way that pushed all reasonable thought aside.

Chapter Fourteen

At the Moment

She knew

Her eyes traveled through a misty space, thick, foggy.

The sounds were undeniable, disturbing, yet she was so young. She didn't understand.

"The girl, she killed herself. She was a child, only thirteen. Why would she do that?" She stared at the ceiling of her bedroom and watched it melt away in a fog.

"Come here, Becky," his voice was thick and ponderous. But she ran, ran past him through the doorway because, because she knew. But then his hand reached out, out of the fog, surrounding her, clamping down hard on her slight arm, and she screamed with terror.

"Becca, Becca, it's all right."

His arms went around her. For a moment, she struggled against him, still caught up in the horror of the dream. Then she stilled. It was Gabriel, Gabriel, who pulled her against him, against his chest.

"It's all right," he whispered to her softly. "It was a dream."

Her heart was racing as a cacophony of colliding images swept through her mind, not the least of which was that she was in Gabriel's bed with no clothes on. But then, she remembered last night, a passionate, unprecedented night they'd spent together after he'd begun kissing her in the middle of his kitchen.

She had to admit her first reaction had been a bit of shock. She knew they were caught up in a rather intimate confessional moment where she was ostensibly telling him how much she trusted him, and he was telling her essentially the same. But then, well, Gabriel, controlled, measured, and yes, she'd have to say careful, Gabriel just went ahead and crossed that line.

She'd pulled back initially, not expecting this at all. Her hands were on his chest, his arms around her, and her mind was not thinking coherently at all. "Gabriel," she whispered. "What are you doing?"

She remembered he'd smiled at that, and upon reflection, it was an awkwardly phrased inquiry. "I'm kissing you, Becca. Do you want me to stop?" he asked.

Another awkward question, well, maybe not awkward, maybe too direct. "I-I don't know," she answered softly because that was honest. She hadn't thought this through. Throwing caution to the wind wasn't her strong suit.

And then he leaned in and softly kissed her neck, sending more of those crazy sensations cascading through her body. "I'll just do this while you make up your mind."

She felt breathless, still trying to piece together coherency. "Are you sure this is a good idea? I mean, won't it change things?"

He stopped again momentarily, then pulled away a bit, looking at her. "Would you like to sit down and talk about this?"

Would she? Is that what she wanted to do? No idea, no earthly idea, "I guess," she murmured. And then he took her hand and led her into the den, where they sat down rather close to each other on the sofa.

"I don't want to push you into anything," he said calmly, well, somewhat calmly. She had to admit he sounded a bit breathless as well.

"I-I never thought that. I just was surprised. I mean, you caught me off guard, you know."

He was still holding her hand, and he touched it to his lips, kissing it softly. "I care about you. You know that."

"Yeah, I do. But I-um." Was she really going to talk about this at this moment? "This is difficult for me."

He squeezed the hand he was holding. "Tell me," he murmured.

Her mouth was dry with nervousness. "You see, involvements, relationships, intimacies, I guess. They don't go very well for me."

And then he stopped and seemed to focus intently on what she was saying. "You're very sensitive, Becca. That's really not all that surprising."

"Um, what?" She was a little confused once she sifted through what he'd said.

"I don't know if this is the time to go into all of this," he murmured.

"You might have to."

"Okay," he said, seeming to struggle to collect his thoughts. "Well, you know, we've talked about how the spirit, when it clothes itself in flesh, is very vulnerable and must take special care."

He had put his arm around her, and she was pressed closely against the side of his body, making concentrating on what he was saying a little tricky. "Yes, I remember. You talked about that in regard to Beth."

"Yes, the acts of intimacy are very profound to the spirit and powerful. If the proper partner who is spiritually

110

connected to you is not chosen, then the spirit can be compromised, wounded if you will."

"What does that have to do with me?"

"You're so sensitive to psychic phenomena that I'm sure you could sense that the individuals you were involved with were not a good spiritual match. That involvement with them could potentially be harmful to your spirit."

"You're saying that it wasn't a bad thing that I couldn't, well, I couldn't respond to them."

He nodded. "Yes, I would go as far as saying it was a protection for you."

Her head was whirling. That possibility had never occurred to her, only the pervasive feeling she'd struggled with all her life that something must be wrong with her. "And if it's a good match?"

He pulled her even closer, whispering into her hair. "Then it will be extremely positive for both people involved."

"But how, how do you know that we're a good match," she murmured, distractedly, because he was kissing her neck again.

"I knew the first time we met Becca. I felt it, a powerful connection between us. Couldn't you feel it?"

She hesitated, remembering the intense draw she'd had to Gabriel right at the beginning. "Yes, I felt it," she whispered. And then she turned to him before she bent in to kiss him softly. She pulled back, but his arms were around her. And she simply let herself melt into his embrace.

She leaned against him, trembling uncontrollably in the aftermath of the dream. It had been so vivid and so damnably familiar.

"Becca, are you all right? You're shaking." Gabriel murmured as he softly stroked her arms, trying to calm her.

"Yeah, just a really bad dream," she whispered.

"Do you want to talk about it?"

"Not now," she said, "just hold me."

His arms tightened around her, and she felt safe. Safe? She had no idea what a profound feeling that would be for her as she had lived without it for so long.

Becca decided at that moment that one of her favorite things in the world was having breakfast with Gabriel in his cozy kitchen on Dumaine Street. He'd fixed her coffee and was now working on an omelet for her packed with fresh vegetables from his patio garden. Of course, this would probably qualify as more of a brunch than a breakfast. The truth was that they'd postponed officially starting their day and had a leisurely morning in bed exploring the many plateaus of this new facet of their relationship.

She couldn't help but smile as she sipped her morning coffee, more than happy to bask in his affection.

"Ms. Wells, I've noticed a lot of smiles on your lovely face this morning. Any chance I had something to do with that?"

"Be quiet and cook. You're going to make me blush."

He returned to his pan, expertly folding the homemade concoction into its proper presentation. "I've seen you blush. I have to admit I'm rather fond of it."

She sipped her coffee because she didn't know how to respond. This was new territory for her. All the fears she brought with her last night had dissipated. It was more than clear that there was no problem with her responding to Gabriel's caresses. In fact, she felt that she'd been starving for them all her life. The intensity, the joy, the real happiness they'd experienced scared her. It scared her how easy it was. And the thought of returning to the desert of a life she'd been living also scared her. But now, this morning, she was determined to put all those fears at bay and simply enjoy the moment.

He put the plate unceremoniously down in front of her. "Wow, that looks great. Where's yours?"

He sat beside her on a barstool at the counter. "I'll get it in a minute."

"Let's split this one, then you can do another later, and we'll split that one too."

"Okay," he murmured. But he was looking at her a little intently. And it bothered her. She suddenly felt a pesky fly in their paradise, just buzzing around.

"What's the matter?" she murmured.

"Last night, that dream you had seemed very upsetting to you."

She sighed, "Do you want to get another plate?"

"Yeah, then, do you want to talk about it?"

She smiled, "Not now, maybe later. I just want to be happy right now."

He nodded, "Okay, happy it is. And I'll take half of that omelet."

"You know, I may have changed my mind. We'll just have to see," she said, laughing.

"Always watch the energy, where it goes, where it's strongest, where it vanishes. Spiritual energy is an essential component of life that goes largely ignored. But you, Gabe, can't afford to ignore it."

Words of advice from his mentor were now ringing about in his mind.

He would like to ignore things and sink into an oblivion of passion with Becca, but things around him were shifting. He could feel it. Ever since they'd bonded or rather became lovers the night before — energy had begun shifting, stronger in some respects, and he was becoming more aware.

Just standing in the kitchen cooking breakfast, he could feel bands of energy reverberating between the two of them. "Acts of intimacy create bonds, energy bonds." Knowing it and feeling it were two different things. He had never professed himself to be psychic but rather a psychic counselor of sorts. But what he was feeling was different, direct.

"Gabriel, are you all right?"

He glanced down at the pan in front of him, that he quickly took off the heat. He'd almost burned the second omelet. "Yeah, just not concentrating." He flipped the omelet over, luckily salvaging the meal. "You still hungry?"

She smiled at him, and he decided that Rebecca Wells smiling at him like that might just be one of the best things he'd ever experienced. "It was great, but I'm kind of full."

He moved it over to a plate. "Yeah, me too. I'll put it in the icebox until later. So, what do you want to do today?"

"Um, shouldn't we be working on your book so I can earn my keep?"

He moved over to her, "Yep, but maybe that can keep a little while longer."

"Why? What do you have in mind?"

"Spending a lazy afternoon with a breathtakingly beautiful woman."

She put down the coffee cup she'd been holding on the counter. "Really? What's her name?"

He smiled at the teasing but felt something beneath the surface. She didn't know, really didn't know how beautiful she was to him. Softly, he touched the side of her face. "You, Becca, you are exquisite," and then he kissed her again to punctuate just how sincere he was.

Chapter Fifteen

Just Quiet

It wasn't a problem to take time off, especially when life was going well. So, for the balance of the week, they did just that. They spent a little time doing a soft organization of his research materials, and Gabriel, with little focus, managed to finish a chapter of his book, though he knew there were heavy rewrites in the future. Between romantic walks, dinners, drives, and other enjoyable activities, Becca also seemed to be doing a lot of reading. Often, he'd find her curled up on the sofa reading a volume of Edgar Cayce or Annie Besant she'd taken from his shelves.

He'd asked once or was it twice during these leisurely days about Ellie.

"Have you seen her?"

She'd glanced up, almost a little befuddled, "No, not really." And he'd nodded, not voicing the elusive idea that not seeing Ellie was in itself strange. Because everything, even Becca's troubled dreams at night, had seemed to stop or rather had taken a pause as they had.

At first, Gabriel didn't think about it, and then he began to think it was curious.

"How are you feeling?" he asked.

She glanced up from her book on Dream Interpretation by Edgar Cayce. "I'm feeling good," she smiled.

"No odd emotions or upset?"

She shook her head slowly, "Not really, not since," and then she hesitated, considering. "Not since the bad dream the other night, nothing, just quiet."

He smiled, lightly touching her dark hair with his hand. "Good," he said before he leaned down to kiss her. He was doing that a lot, kissing her, touching her affectionately, and she as well. Just contact seemed so comforting between them. And the lack of psychic activity couldn't be a bad thing. After all, she'd been through so much. Maybe their connection and the energy they were obviously creating was building this lovely cocoon around them.

Surely, it wasn't a bad thing. After all, his goal had been for Becca to achieve more control over her gifts. But then he hesitated, wondering. But was this control or just a sort of buffer until—until what exactly?

"You're always waiting for the other shoe to drop."

Cynthia's diatribe about him, of course, they'd never reached this level of contentment, even in their happiest moments.

But it was accurate. He had a suspicious thread to his nature, and the cold hard truth was that the other shoe usually did drop and, unfortunately, at the most inopportune of moments.

"You didn't tell me you'd invited your sister for dinner. Do you want me to go out?"

"Of course not," he said, kissing her softly, "she'd like to get to know you."

She pulled back with a look of alarm, "Why? What did you tell her about me? About us?"

He had to consider for a moment. A lot had happened. The last time they'd spoken was at dinner that night before, well, before he and Becca had taken things to the next level. "Actually, nothing. The last time we spoke, there wasn't anything to tell. Things have escalated kind of quickly. She still thinks we're just roommates."

She nodded, "Okay, well, let's leave it that way. It's too soon. Everything is too new for, you know, questions."

He sat down next to her on the sofa, taking her hand. "Yeah, I guess there will be questions. But I also don't want you to think this is casual for me."

"I never thought that," she said softly. "I just like it right now as it is, me and you, no outside world." He nodded, wondering distractedly how long that would be tenable.

"So, what do you do, Becca?" Anna Michaels asked amiably after taking a huge bite of a cheeseburger that Gabriel had barbequed out on his patio a short time earlier.

Becca smiled at the willowy blond from across Gabriel's den. They were having a makeshift dinner on his coffee table as the only dinette table he had in the house seemed too snug for three. She and Gabriel were on the sofa, and Anna was in an armchair across from them. Becca took a substantial bite out of her cheeseburger to delay her answer, if only by seconds. "Oh, this is good," she murmured lightly. "I didn't know you could barbeque."

"Yeah, I don't do it often," Gabriel answered. Barbeque hamburgers, not the most elegant of meals, but she had to admit she liked this side of her new—boyfriend? lover? Wow, none of that seemed to fit well, whatever they were at the moment.

She glanced up, noticing Anna's eyes were still on her expectantly. Oh yeah, the questions. "Um, yes, well, I was a teacher for many years, primarily a high school history and science teacher."

Her blue eyes widened just a notch. "Really? That must have been demanding."

Anna was a bit unusual, delicate in features, pleasant enough, but Becca could feel a fierce protectiveness emanating from her regarding her older brother. The problem was that Becca and the third degree did not mesh well. "It was, at times."

"But you're not still teaching?"

"Ladies, either of you want another burger?" Gabriel cut in.

"No, Gabe," Anna answered distractedly, clearly still focused on eliciting valuable information from the strange woman staying in her brother's house. "I'm good, though it is delicious. I don't know if I can finish this one."

Becca glanced down at her half-eaten burger. Well, she was finishing hers. She couldn't remember the last time she'd eaten one. "Thanks, I think this one will be enough," she said, taking another bite. Again, she glanced up, soft blue eyes that didn't look so soft at the moment staring at her intently. She didn't have to be psychic to know that Anna here was on to them. She wasn't buying the "*we're just roommates*" cover.

"No, no, I stopped teaching a little over a year ago, I guess. I worked for a while in retail and am in between right now. Helping Gabriel with his—"

"Yes, that's what Gabe said, helping him with his book."

Gabriel smiled broadly. He didn't like this. She could feel it just oozing out of him. "That's the plan."

"And so, you two have known each other for a while?" Anna continued to query passive-aggressively, though not so passive, evidently a little thick about picking up on signals.

Gabriel stood up, "We've known each other long enough. I have a cheesecake in the fridge. Anna, why don't you help me with it?"

She looked at him, a little stunned at first at the abruptness of his tone, then answered, "Yeah, okay," standing up a little awkwardly, then following Gabriel to the kitchen. Becca smiled, wondering if baby sister would get a dressing down.

She leaned back on the sofa, taking a deep breath. She hadn't been aware of how tense she was, but then again social situations had never been her strong suit. The truth was that she would feel too much from other people. That was why she'd given up on teaching. Too much was seeping in.

She glanced over to the doorway leading to the hall and almost jumped out of her seat. Ellie was standing there, nightgown dripping from her fall into the Bayou St. John, just staring at her with that pale face and drawn blank expression. It practically made her heart stop. For a while, just a little while, she'd forgotten that all this was still happening to her.

"You want to lay off a little bit?"

"Lay off of what?" Anna said blankly, genuinely confused about what he was talking about.

"The inquisition of Becca," he said, perhaps too intensely. "She's been through a lot, and I don't want her upset."

She hesitated as though confused, then crossed her arms in front of her, staring at him a bit dismissively. Now where had he seen that stance before? Oh yeah, his mom, evidently Anna had appropriated it. "Do you think I was upsetting her?"

He stopped, wondering indeed what the real answer to that question was. "I don't know. I just would like to keep things light."

And then her eyes narrowed. Yeah, he remembered that expression as well from childhood. "What's really going on here, Gabe? You two, well, there's clearly more here than meets the eye."

He shook his head, realizing he hadn't taken the cheesecake out of the refrigerator nor put on the tea kettle or coffee pot or whatever the hell they were going to drink with dessert. He took a quick breath. He had to get a grip. He was overreacting, and that would not do. "She's vulnerable right now, and I don't want her feeling uncomfortable. Is that so hard to understand?"

After a moment, "No," she replied softly, acquiescing or so he hoped, "and you think my questions are making her uncomfortable."

He looked at her directly, "Maybe, I don't know."

She nodded, "Okay, no more questions, but I want you to know I can see clearly how protective you are of her. I hope she knows how lucky she is."

He turned to the icebox to find the cheesecake, wondering distractedly if that did really make her lucky?"

Becca waited inside as Gabriel walked his sister out to her car. She was unsettled, although the visit had relaxed somewhat once the two siblings came out of the kitchen. Anna seemed to mellow a bit, talking about her life back in Missouri, during which Becca began getting a collage of mixed images as she spoke. Beneath the surface, she sensed some tension between Anna and her husband that seemed to have reached an apex, then settled down, both recommitting to their family and each other. And there now seemed to be a real sense of peace in her. How lovely it was when people actually amicably survived their most intense trials during life and returned from the edge stronger. It was possible, though she had to admit in her former circle, she hadn't seen it very often. Oh, that was right, her pessimistic fallback position rearing its ugly head, which she was determined to quell. The past few days with Gabriel had been too lovely to smother in old emotional habits.

And then, when she was leaving, Anna had stopped and hugged Becca, a genuine hug through which she felt hope, hope that maybe down the line they could be friends — such a comforting thought that there might be a down the line. For herself, she couldn't project too far into the future. There had been too much, too much upheaval for too long to try to predict what life without that could be.

She waited silently in the den for Gabriel to return. She didn't sit down because she couldn't.

Despite the pleasant evening, despite things seemingly going well, something had begun again.

He walked through the doorway, closing the door behind him and latching it.

She smiled, "Did she leave?"

"Yes," he said quietly. "Now tell me, what's wrong."

She wasn't planning to because it had been a nice evening and a nice time with them, just the two of them, and for a little while, she thought that all the bad stuff was gone. That their being together had somehow driven it out of her, but she knew, knew deep down, that this was not the case.

And it was also clear that she wouldn't be able to hide that fact from him. So silently, she moved into his arms, and he pulled her into a strong embrace. It comforted her and gave her the strength to handle whatever was coming next.

Chapter Sixteen

The Gray

"What do you see?"

She breathed in deeply, quietly trying to focus. It was just after dinner. They'd spent a lovely day together primarily working after she'd returned from the pharmacy to pick up the pills she'd had her gynecologist call in for her. Given that she and Gabriel were "living together" now in every sense of the term, it seemed more than prudent.

But once she got back, Becca had implemented a filing system to get Gabriel more organized in terms of research, online and off. There was a wealth of information he'd accumulated in the course of his paranormal studies, for lack of a better description, quite a bit that she was more than willing to just pause and read through carefully. In some ways, it was very helpful to read accounts of other people dealing with the phenomena she'd just written off as her psychological quirks for most of her life.

There were so many other people also hearing voices, feeling disconnected mood swings and emotions, and of course, the visions as well, glimpsing into what was often termed as other planes of existence. And here it wasn't just written off as psychological illness, as she and those around her had most of her life.

But now, she and Gabriel were resuming their exploration of her psychic traumas, though she knew Gabriel wouldn't term it as such. But for Becca, it had always felt like trauma, the frantic quest to somehow be in control of her existence.

To say the least, she was uneasy about uncorking this bottle again, as the past week had shown her how lovely life could be apart from her "episodes."

"Anything?" he murmured.

A guided meditation was what they were endeavoring to achieve this evening. Gabriel would be the directing voice, walking her through this particular exploration.

He'd moved the furniture to the sides of the room in his den and unrolled a small oriental rug that he'd apparently closeted in his study. At its first appearance, she had commented gleefully, "I was just hoping you were planning to take me on a magic carpet ride."

And then he'd smiled engagingly in that way that sort of made her melt a bit inside. "Well, I suppose from a point of view, you could call it that."

And then he'd explained all about this guided meditation, and her heart had sunk a bit. "That wasn't exactly what I had in mind."

He nodded, "I know. But I don't want us to lose ground."

"Lose ground?" she murmured.

"You've come a long way since you first came to me for help. But it's important to keep working. I want you to be able to live comfortably with your gifts, not to just—" And he'd stopped midsentence.

It was an awkward pause. "Not to just what, Gabriel?"

He frowned and, somewhat reluctantly, it seemed, said softly, "To suppress them."

At this, she felt almost stunned. She knew it wasn't his intent, but she couldn't help but feel a little attacked. "You think I'm suppressing my—" she couldn't get the word gifts out. She knew he supportively would refer to them as "gifts," but for her, it had never been the case. It had always been a sort of instability of mind, more like an anchor around her neck, making her different, separate from the world. "You think I've been suppressing?"

He was watching her quietly, though more than cognizant, she suspected, of her change in mood. "I think it's possible," he said a little too stoically for her taste.

And then she'd flopped down on the sofa and asked pointedly, "Why, exactly?"

"I'm not attacking you, Becca."

"You're not?" she said abruptly. "It sounded as though you'd inferred I was deliberately suppressing my psychic — whatever the hell you want to call them."

At this, he'd let the carpet drop quite abruptly from his hands onto the wooden floor with a distinct thump. "I never said it was deliberate, and you don't have to do this."

"Do what?" she snapped out, knowing exactly what he was referring to.

"Become so defensive with me. If you don't want to do what I'm suggesting, we won't."

She breathed in deeply. Ramifications, ramifications, life had been different when she'd been alone, having no one calling her on her own BS, holding up the mirror to her face, not letting her hide when, well, when she was just scared. "I just—" Then she stopped.

But Gabriel sat beside her, taking her hand and murmuring, "You better finish that."

She breathed deeply, so much emotion just under the surface. "I—I haven't been a very happy person most of my life. And these past few days with you, I've been happy, really happy, in a way I didn't know was possible."

He squeezed her hand gently, "I have too, Becca, very happy."

"And the thought of slipping back into that dark place again, where all of this always seems to lead, scares the hell out of me."

The same hand he was holding, he'd picked up and softly kissed. "I know you're scared. I understand. But I'm with you, next to you now. I'm here to help you face whatever comes."

She nodded, feeling some rebellious tears beginning to travel down her cheeks. "Okay," she murmured.

"It's just that suppressing things doesn't make them go away, Becca." And then she focused on him, feeling a new concern rise with the gravity of his voice. "It often makes them just erupt at inopportune times in unpredictable ways."

"What do you see?" His voice was strong and different somehow, not the Gabriel of the past few days — comforting, intimate, jovial — but rather more intense, focused.

She was sitting across from him on the oriental rug, legs crossed comfortably, dressed in a white t-shirt and light-colored jogging pants. "Colors are important for this," he'd explained. "Lights colors are best, and the clothing needs to be comfortable, not distracting during the meditation."

"So, you've done this a lot?"

"A number of times," he murmured, "under the direction of different teachers."

"And what did you see?"

"Later," he commented, somewhat dismissively. "Let's focus on you right now, Becca," He believed she was deliberately delaying, but she really wasn't. She was curious about him, where he'd been, who he'd been before, before all this.

He sat across from her, though not touching her, in a similar pose. He wore an off-white t-shirt and some old, well-worn blue jeans that she assumed he considered comfortable.

She closed her eyes again, knowing the drill. "Now try to relax and just feel your breathing, like we did at the Lakefront Becca." She did as he asked, attempting just to let go, concentrating on the fundamental action of breathing in and then exhaling. "Try to let go of thought and all concerns. Let yourself drop down to a very basic level of just being in the moment."

She breathed deeply, then exhaled, allowing tension to leave her body. "Just listen now to the sound of my voice."

As she did so, a calmness began to seep over her. "Feel me with you, Becca." She breathed in and began to feel a strange fluttering in her body, skimming all over her skin, and then, she began to see. She could see Gabriel sitting across from her, although she had not opened her eyes. In her vision, his form was not still but fluctuating as though it were not solid, moving beyond the outlines of the image of his body.

"What are you seeing, Becca?" he asked calmly.

"I see you," she murmured. "But there's movement all around you, as though the air is fluttering."

"Don't worry, just relax. You're seeing my aura, my energy. Do you see colors?"

She tried to focus further. "Yes, I am now. All around you, I'm seeing blues and golds and splashes of green."

"Good, that's good. Now, try to expand your sight."

She breathed in again deeply, then let the breath softly expel. Beyond her closed eyes, the remainder of the room came into sight. Against the wall were the sofa, the rocker, two tables, and pictures on the wall, but all of it was different, reverberating, not the same as Gabriel but still fluctuating with their own — energy, it seemed.

"Everything seems alive," she murmured, almost in disbelief.

"Everything does have its level of consciousness. Even inanimate objects have energy within them. Just relax. Don't judge what you see. Let things unfold."

"This is very different from how I've seen before."

"You're tapping into a new source of sight, Becca."

Her body on the rug was not moving, but she felt movement within her, the fluttering, fluctuating, now gradually being directed by her. She slowly canvassed the room, seeing cascades of colors emanating from things everywhere she looked. Even the ceiling above was not solid but rather reverberating overhead, as were the floor and room, sometimes contracting, sometimes expanding. "I don't understand what I'm seeing."

"You are seeing the true nature of things. It will aid you in understanding your abilities."

"I feel different, so light."

"Your astral body is poised to travel, but you must take things slowly."

"My astral body?"

"It is a spiritual form. It exists without the need for the physical body. But take things slowly." She understood what he was saying. She felt herself drawn, wanting to see beyond this space. "Can you see anything else here? In this room?"

She tried to remain where she was, concentrating, focusing, but feeling the buoyancy of the energy permeating her being. She continued to look around her, seeing the colors cascading everywhere. It was such a unique, almost intoxicating feeling.

And then, just as suddenly, she felt a shift, a wave of something else pass over her. "What is it?" he asked.

He knew. Somehow, Gabriel was connected to her emotions within this state. "I don't know," she murmured.

She could see it, though not understanding, like a dark layer of a murky grayish color slicing across all the vibrant energy waves dancing throughout the room. "It's different," she said, almost whispering to herself. And then she felt it in her heart like a punch — sadness, confusion, upset.

"It hurts," she muttered.

"It's all right," Gabriel said calmly. "Don't let it rock you. Stay in the moment, Becca."

She hung onto his voice, his calm, steadying voice. She pulled herself back just a notch, allowing herself to see what was happening without being pulled into it. The grayness moved like a heavy, creeping shadow across the room, then spread out in a thick pool of liquid. "It's gray and heavy, so different from everything else."

It was true whatever it was felt detached from the energy in the rest of the room. "It's operating on a different vibrational level," he explained.

"Vibration?"

"Yes, energy is like sound. It operates on different frequencies. The lower, the less positive."

It was getting difficult, so difficult, to maintain her distance. "It's cold."

"Can you see anything?"

All she could see was the mass of gray growing wider and spreading upward, now into a fog, a confusing fog, heavy that made her limbs feel weighted, sapping all the lightness she'd felt moments before. "I can't see here."

"Try to focus, Becca. Concentrate on understanding."

She tried, but what she was feeling was so disturbing and only made worse by the fact that she'd been feeling so wonderful moments before. Her head was pounding, and a strange achy feeling spread throughout her body. "It's dreadful."

"Try to hold on." She couldn't help it, couldn't stop it. Now she was within, within the center of the gray. When she breathed, it felt like confusion, a thick, muddling of thought. The atmosphere was so thick. "It's a very negative space of energy, a very low vibration."

"I hate this."

"I know, just a few moments more."

She tried to look around, but it was so difficult to see, and then distantly, she felt something tugging on her. She looked down and saw the top of her head. The little girl then tilted it, staring up at her with eyes wide with terror. "Oh," she murmured with a bit of a gasp.

"You're with Ellie."

"Yes."

"Okay," he said softly, "let's see if we can help her now."

Chapter Seventeen

Small Hells

"So, I understand there is a distinction between a ghost and a spirit."

"There are a lot of distinctions, fine-tuned distinctions between many stages of existence. But yes, if you want to get basic, a spirit is that eternal entity that we are a part of that reincarnates from lifetime to lifetime as well as exists on many plateaus of reality learning and evolving."

"And that's not the same thing as a ghost?"

"No, if you're referring to a ghost as it's traditionally known, it could be many things. Some are just energy imprints or sort of spiritual movies leftover from strong energy events that people encounter, or some are just the astral shell of a person that has not entirely dissipated for a myriad of reasons after death. Some might be an energy projection sent out consciously or unconsciously with strong emotion by an individual, and some may be confused or lost souls, clinging to the physical life, who haven't yet seen their way clear to cross over to another plane."

Gabriel remembered feeling a bit on overload after having heard this rather complex answer from his teacher, Jean Rampart. Of course, there were many times during his education with her when he felt more than a bit over his head. It was a daunting thing to have your entire vision of reality broken down and then remade, even if the new version was a fascinating and inspiring model. "So, what would cause that? For someone to be lost, not move on as they should after death?"

She shrugged, "There are as many reasons as the stars, Gabe. Some don't want to let go of the flesh. Some are afraid to, some have gone through a violent or upsetting death. Some are suicides, and some may have chosen that path."

"Chosen it?"

"There are all kinds of paths to learning, all kinds of unpredictable ones. And spirits often do things, not for their own evolution but to help someone else."

"Such a selfless act?"

And then she'd smiled, "It does exist out there, Gabe, selflessness and kindness. You just need to know where to look."

It was different, nothing like any meditation he'd ever been involved with before. Not only could he sense and at times, feel what Becca was feeling, but he was also getting clearer and clearer visions of what she was seeing. Perhaps it was the close emotional and spiritual bonds they'd forged in the new intimacy of their relationship, perhaps the significant amount of energy they'd been able to create being together. He really had no idea. Maybe all of it, or maybe it was just the timing of things. Jean had always told him, *"Be patient. Don't try to force things. Let them unfold in their way."* He was honest enough to admit working with many gifted psychics, he'd wondered why he couldn't tap into his own abilities to a greater extent, and on some level had decided that he had a particular role to play and nothing beyond. And he hadn't been patient, as had been his wonderful mentor's advice, but rather had accepted things at face value.

But now, today, this moment was different. He could see the gray, murky fog that Ellie had existed in and that Becca now found herself trapped in. He could see it and hopefully be both an anchor and a guide that could help them both escape.

"Becca, follow my voice." He said firmly, but he could feel how mired down she was becoming where she was. The negative energy permeated everything, making her feel sluggish and slow to respond.

With concentration, he tried to focus his energy directly into her, into her heart area, to help clear the fog. "Becca, listen to me. Becca," he repeated firmly.

He could feel her, movement within her. "Can you hear me?"

"Yes," barely a whisper.

"I know this is difficult, but you must hang on."

"Where am I?" she sent back. It was so difficult for her. She was so sensitive. She was absorbing too much of the atmosphere around her.

"You're still here with me in the room. You're just on a different plane, the one where Ellie is caught. It's difficult there. After her accident, she became trapped for some reason. You need to lead her out."

"I-I can't think." He could see her clearly, caught in that gray fog. It would be so easy for him to reach out to her, to pull her back, but then Ellie would remain lost. They had a chance here if he could just get Becca to control things, just pull back and regain control.

"What do you see?"

She stared at the candle in front of her. Was this like the inkblots? She had to pull something coherent out of nothing. "A candle burning?"

"Nothing else?"

She stared at it, a large pillar candle but malformed by the heat. Already the sides of it were splitting, collapsing in on itself unnaturally. Before very long, the wax would be caving in, streaming down the sides before it had a chance to properly burn.

"No," she whispered. She didn't want to tell the psychiatrist what she really saw because it would make her sound crazy. She didn't want to tell him she saw monsters in his inkblots because, again — crazy.

Her mood swings and unpredictable behavior had landed her here, but she couldn't tell him about the dreams, about the voices, about the hallucinations. He would lock her up somewhere and throw away the key.

She looked down, finding herself in another place. The little girl was trembling, clinging to her for dear life but shaking.

"Becca," it was such a distant whisper, and all the phantoms were reaching out for her, trying to strangle her. Again, small hands dug into her legs, grasping frantically. She didn't deserve to be here. No one deserved to be here.

She reached down and touched her hair. It was damp, damp from the fall into the Bayou St. John. "It's all right," she murmured.

"Becca, listen to me."

She heard but more than that could feel his voice warming her. "Gabriel, get us out of here."

"Take her hand, Becca." She reached down again to find the small cold hand, so chilled. She had to pry it away from her legs that Ellie had affixed herself to.

"It's all right," she murmured, forcing the little hand into hers and pulling her to her feet.

"Help us," she whispered.

"You're going to have to lead her out of there."

"How can I do that? I can barely move an inch myself."

"Do you trust me?"

"Of course."

"Then you will."

"Have you ever talked a lost spirit over?"

"You mean to cross over to where they belong?"

"Yes, that's what I mean."

Jean hesitated as though she was considering whether or not to answer. "Yes, once I did when I was in deep meditation. I was able to access the astral plane, the spiritual plateau closest to our earthly one, and I was able to talk a lost soul into the light, the doorway, if you like to their next plane of existence. There were those, loved ones on the other side who helped in the process. That time was a success, but I can't tell you how many failures there were. I've lost count."

"Why do you think they resisted?"

"So many reasons Gabe. Timing is important and, of course, the most consistent reason, free will. We have all been gifted with free will. If we didn't have it, we wouldn't be able to learn. Without the component of choice, there is no growth. And that goes for everyone and everything.

Even if that choice sometimes does not seem the best, it is sacred."

"But what happens if they choose badly?"

"Then they must deal with the consequences. Every choice brings its consequences. You can't have one without the other."

"Miss Wells, your parents feel as though you are struggling. That you need some help."

She sat on the other side of a large wooden desk, a very dark wood that seemed nearly black to her at the time. The man was old, older than her father, and cold. She remembered how cold he felt to her and how frightened she was. All she had to do was be quiet and be normal, and possibly she might escape this unscathed. All she had to do was lie about everything.

"Do you believe you are ill?"

Her throat felt dry, painfully dry. Where was her mother? Why didn't she come with her? "I don't know," she whispered.

"Are you telling me the truth, Rebecca?" She wanted to scream, but she bit down on it. All she had to do was get through this. Then she could go home and pretend that nothing was wrong, nothing, nothing, nothing—

"Becca!" his voice ripped her out of that dark place. It was so easy here, so easy to slip into all those little hells.

"Gabriel, I can't last much longer."

"I know. Please try to hang on. Now do you remember Beth?"

Her mind was so cloudy. Beth, who was, and then the vision rose in her mind. Oh yes, the blond girl. "I remember."

"Good," It felt like warmth. Whenever he spoke to her, it felt like warmth wrapping around her. "You remember how you tried to convince her to cross over."

"I-I think so. But she didn't. I don't know what happened—"

"That's okay. You need to try to talk to Ellie now."

She glanced down at the girl who was now clinging to her arm. "She's so afraid."

"I know, but you need to tell her that her family is waiting for her. Her mother wants to see her."

"Does she?"

"I hope so."

"Gabriel—"

"You need to try. We need to get her out of that place."

"I don't understand why—"

"It doesn't matter right now. You need to focus on what needs to be done. Try to get control and talk to her."

"Miss Wells, I cannot let you leave unless you tell me the truth. MISS WELLS," the voice was booming in her head.

"Step back, Becca. You have to get control of this," she could feel strength coming from Gabriel. She willed herself forcibly to step away from the painful memory. The painful memory felt as though it had her by the jugular and wouldn't let go. In her mind, she stepped back away from it, outside its ugly reach. In the distance, she could still hear the echo, *"Miss Wells, Miss Wells, did you hear me?"*

"Shut up!" she rasped.

Then Gabriel answered, "What?"

"Not you," she said softly.

She looked down. Even though Ellie was clinging to her arm, she still held her hand. She squeezed it, trying to focus her energy into her. The frightened eyes looked up as Becca knelt next to her. "Now listen to me, Ellie. It's time for you to go home, but you have to trust me. I'm going to get you to your mother."

Her pale, trembling mouth formed the unmistakable words, although there was no audible sound, "Mama."

"Yes, baby, we're going to find your Mama."

Then she straightened up, "Okay, we're ready, Gabriel. What now?" She waited for his response, but there was only silence.

Chapter Eighteen

What the World Believes

"You don't think I know what this is about."

He was dumbfounded. How in the world could someone of his experience, education, and general knowledge be so completely blindsided?

"What are you talking about?"

Cynthia, lovely, intelligent, and at times perilously superficial Cynthia stared back at him as though he was a stranger. How could someone look at him like that? Someone he'd spent the last six years of his life in close proximity with look at him as though she didn't know him at all. "

"You want someone else? Not me."

He stared at her blankly and felt an emptiness, actual hollowness inside him. "Why would you say that?"

"I can see it when you look at me or maybe look past me. It's like you're not even interested in me anymore, Gabe. You're going through the motions."

It hit him hard, but that was something the truth often did. It slew you at times. And all the glasshouses you build and all the illusions you construct, it levels them because they were nothing, nothing that you propped up precariously with hot air.

"No," he said with little force because it was a lie. And he was used to lying because not lying was far too scary to deal with.

Her face was puffy from emotion, and her eyes filled with unshed tears. He wondered if he was being horribly unfair, but he couldn't bear it, not yet. "Are you sure, Gabe?" she asked.

And he regretted with all his being that he hadn't admitted at that point that she was right. Whatever had been between them had dissipated, vanished in the hard light of reality. But he wasn't strong enough to admit defeat yet. Perhaps if he held on, perhaps if they continued, things would change, and the truth would buckle under the sheer force of his will.

Selfish — the words permeated his essence.

And he nodded.

Two months later, they separated. Two months of pain and discord that he might have spared them, but he wasn't ready, wasn't ready to let go and embrace what he knew he needed to do. And they both paid the price for it.

The memories swirled up like a swarm of insects gnawing at him. *"Negative energy will attack you where you're the most vulnerable. You have to be on guard, Gabe. Know yourself. Know where you are weak."*

He had to pull back. He was being inundated by toxic energy, recollections yanking him away from the present.

"Gabriel."

He could hear Becca's voice distantly. "Gabriel, please, help us."

His head was throbbing, and he could still hear Cynthia's voice in his mind. "Why? Why couldn't you love me? What did I do that was so wrong?"

The guilt swirled around him. Perhaps that's why he stayed, the guilt, sense of obligation. He had to step back. It was done and yet so toxic.

"Becca," he whispered.

"Gabriel, what do we do?"

Her voice was stronger. He knew her physical body was just an arm's reach away from him, but she was so much further away in that horrible fog, trapped with little Ellie.

"I hear you," he sent out. "Just be calm."

"Remember, you must send out contact to the next plateau if you want to help a lost spirit move on." Jean's voice from the past, or so he thought.

He remembered. He was the anchor, the guiding force. He concentrated. "Help us open the gateway to receive this child. Help us guide her to the light."

He could feel it, energy mounting, energy traveling. And then, behind his closed eyes, he began to see the bright light, a doorway opening.

"Becca, can you see it?" he asked, but there was no answer.

He focused more intently, sending his message in the energy of pure thought that was now possible in this state they were both existing in now. "Becca, focus on the white light."

There was quiet, but then faintly, he heard, "Yes, I see it."

"You can suppress these things, Rebecca. It's important that you be like everyone else."

It pained her to think of her mother for just that reason. She thought it was a help to Becca, this kind of advice.

"I know you think you're different, but life will be much easier if you can pretend you're not. That you're just as everyone expects you to be."

She was a little girl, so it was very hard to resist the instruction. Eight, nine, and she'd just escaped the clutches of the psychiatrist's office. "A little on the dramatic side, but all I prescribe at present are tranquilizers, but bring her back in if the symptoms continue," was his recommendation.

"You see, I do understand, but if you want to get along in the world, you have to be what it expects you to be."

She remembered her voice and her very sad eyes. Somewhere deep down, she knew she wasn't doing the best she could for her daughter. But she was giving her a get-out-of-jail-free card. "Just Pretend" was the mantra. Bear down until your sweet little knuckles bled.

And then, everything will be fine.

The wind whipped around her, and her head spun in disorientating dizziness.

"Becca," his voice distantly but still connecting.

"I'm in a storm."

"I know how hard it is but hang on. The light, the door is opening for Ellie."

She tried to look around, but the fog was so heavy, that thick gray fog that felt as though it was collecting in her lungs. "I can't see it."

The thoughts crept in like slithering little serpents, crawling up her arms. "You're going to fail," they hissed in her ears. "You're nothing. You never have been."

"I-I," she could barely breathe. It was too painful. And then she felt that firm tug on her arm and looked down into the face of the little girl, so frightened. This wasn't her fault. Why did she have to pay like this?

She breathed deeply, painfully pulling strength from that place deep within that had always left a reservoir for her when nothing else was left. The light, the warm light, she concentrated. It continued to feel like things were all over her, unseen things, crawling and digging into her skin and demanding that she stop.

"The light," she whispered, like a holy mantra, "guide us to the light," she continued to claw and hang onto it tenaciously. She wouldn't stop. Whatever horrible things these were wouldn't stop her.

"It's there, Becca. Feel it."

It was the lightest breath, the softest touch, alive though the darkness raged around them. Warmth began to cascade lightly across her skin. "Feel it, Ellie," she whispered.

She could feel the child's hands tighten on her arm because she couldn't speak. She'd lived in this dark place too long to have words. "Please, please," she whispered outward from her mind.

And the warmth began to spread. She couldn't see it because she was in darkness, blindness, but she could feel it. And she, she began to pull them both toward the warmth.

"Good," she heard his voice with her, near her. "Keep going, Becca."

How impossible to describe how it felt dragging herself and the girl through that fog. It was as though her limbs, which she could feel acutely, were scraping along granite painfully, excruciatingly. But she couldn't stop because if she did, she would never be able to start again.

The warmth reached out to her the closer she got. It touched. It healed, and it beckoned. She wondered what was on the other side. Would it be easier if she just left now, let go of the pain of the world she lived within? She breathed deeply as the fog ripped away from her. It felt so familiar, like home where she could rest.

"Becca," she heard distantly.

She stopped, still blind but operating entirely on feeling.

The child still clung to her desperately. She was so afraid and so resistant to venturing onward without her. She could feel so much. Others around her were not physical but bright, brilliant spirits reaching out. Again, she bent down, whispering to the child. "Ellie, your Mama is here. You need to go with her."

She felt the trembling girl against her. For so long, she'd known fear. How could she trust again?

"Focus, Becca. She can feel what you feel." She could hear Gabriel's voice so close to her.

She centered herself and pictured Ellie's mother in her mind, though she had nothing concrete to base it on. But she conveyed the feelings into the image of her mother wrapping her arms around her and holding her. "She's waiting for you, Ellie," she whispered.

And with her mind, she placed the image into the child.

It felt like forever but also only moments. She felt her when she let go, and she felt her when she crossed over. A warmth of gratitude filled her heart from within and from those on the outside, extending their thankfulness to her. And she felt the softest kiss on her cheek, a goodbye as Ellie left and the doorway closed.

She took a deep breath and reached outward before all fell to darkness.

And when she awoke, she was in Gabriel's arms, looking up into his eyes.

Chapter Nineteen

Opening Doors

When he touched her skin, it was hot, feverish, and she seemed still disconnected, even though her expedition into that other plane where she could free Ellie had ended. They were back, but it was clear it had taken its toll on Becca.

He scooped her up into his arms, carrying her into his bedroom. "Becca, it's all right," he whispered, but her eyes remained closed, flickering strangely as though she was caught in some troubling dream.

Gently, he laid her on the bed. Her arms still felt warm to him. It might have been too much for her. He might have pushed her too hard. He scooped her up against him, laying her against his chest and focusing energy into her. "Becca," he whispered. "Please, come back to me."

She was almost trembling, but he also felt something else distinctly. Her spirit was traveling somewhere, somewhere else.

For a moment, she'd opened her eyes to find herself in Gabriel's arms, and then in the very next, she was somewhere else.

It wasn't the same as before, not that gray space where she'd been with Ellie. This was very different, more concrete. Becca recognized this immediately simply because it was familiar.

Her head spun with dizziness as she looked around. Where was she? It was distorted, convoluted, warped, but she knew it — her childhood bedroom.

Staring at the walls of this not terribly large room, she could see they were unstable, fluctuating, almost as though the sheetrock was taking breaths, changing dimension — larger then smaller, larger then smaller. The small twin bed positioned against the outside wall still had a facsimile of her pale blue satin comforter on it. But it seemed convoluted, moist, even stained somehow. Her hand brushed it, and she felt a sticky substance against her palm, and then visually could see a brown stain beginning to spread across its surface, as though it was expanding from underneath. Her stomach flipped. There was a stench rising everywhere, reaching across the room. Her things, her books, and the pictures on the walls all felt tainted, dirtied by something.

"Rebecca," she could feel it behind her, brushing her hair — something terrible.

"Gabriel, where are you?"

She sent the message outward and felt almost instantly slammed back into her body.

"Becca." It was him, Gabriel, shaking her gently but holding on firmly. She stared into his eyes but felt her body trembling uncontrollably.

"Gabriel," she whispered.

"It's all right," he said softly. "You're safe," and then he pulled her tightly against him.

But she didn't feel safe, not at all. She felt as though something horrible was back there, something horrible that she couldn't begin to understand.

She took a shower at Gabriel's insistence and then took some aspirin with a cup of tea he made for her. He was watching her. She could feel it. In fact, he was watching her like a hawk, and with her brain feeling so completely scrambled, it was a little much to take.

"How are you feeling?"

"Okay, a little tired."

"Do you want something to eat?"

"Not now, maybe later."

He nodded, still watching her thoughtfully as she lay curled up on his sofa with a blanket atop her. "Still cold?"

"A little."

He frowned, "You were running fever after the meditation. Let the aspirin kick in."

"Yeah," she murmured. He sat at the end of the sofa, pulling her feet on his lap.

"You know you were amazing," he murmured.

"I don't feel amazing. I feel like a truck ran over me," she muttered.

"Yeah, well, you lost a lot of energy. We both did, I think. That place where Ellie was seemed very toxic."

"Gabriel, I-I just don't want to think about it right now," she said a bit more forcefully than she had intended. "Can we give it a little time?"

His eyes passed over her face with concern. "Of course, but I'd like to be here with you, even if we don't talk about anything, if that's all right."

She nodded. She was so exhausted but also afraid, afraid to rest, to go to sleep — now tangibly afraid to dream about monsters that she didn't understand. Everything was jarring now, as though there was nothing solid or dependable that she could tether herself to. "Do you want to watch TV? I just feel like doing something mindless."

"Yeah," he nodded. "Let me set it up. I have a flat screen in the back. I have to confess I haven't watched it for a while."

She smiled faintly, "Doesn't surprise me."

As he got up, he leaned over and softly kissed her. "I know you don't want to talk about it, but I'm proud of you, for what that's worth."

"It's worth a lot," she whispered.

She had lost energy, and given what they'd been through, that was to be expected. But so much? It was concerning. Gabriel was feeling more now, seeing more, though his mind was still trying to assimilate exactly what had changed.

As he sat in the den on the sofa with Becca's feet curled up on him, he noted the shift he was feeling within. He looked around the room casually, focusing on a random object, like the tripod wooden floor lamp in the corner. After a few moments of staring, he slowly began to see colors, auras expanding around it, beyond its physical structure. It was even more so with living things, the philodendron on the windowsill near the doorway. As he watched it, he could feel himself relax, then slowly begin to see a clear shape around the plant that moved beyond its natural outline. The more he focused, the more it expanded, actually spreading three to four inches away from the leaves, and then the expanded outline began flickering, moving, and filling in with a slight tinge of blue-green. But once he blinked his eyes and pulled himself out of that tranquil sort of vision, it dissipated.

And he watched Becca closely. She was focused on the flat-screen TV playing old episodes of *Murder She Wrote* just now. And he could feel acutely, just touching her, how tired she was. Her eyes would begin to close, then abruptly, she would prop them open wide in a startling way. It was more than clear she was afraid to sleep.

He squeezed her foot, and she looked over at him. "What's wrong?" Gabriel said softly.

She answered groggily with a bit of confusion. "What do you mean?"

He straightened up, staring at her intently. "I mean, you need to sleep, but you're afraid to. Why?"

He could see it clearly on her face. He didn't have to be any kind of psychic to know that she was frightened of something. She sat up on the sofa, pulling her feet off of him. A bit hesitantly, she said, "I don't know. Something happened after Ellie, something I saw that was confusing. But it felt like an old nightmare I'd forgotten about."

He gently took her hand in his. "How about something to eat? Then we can talk about it."

She nodded, pulling the crocheted beige throw she had over her closer to her face. "Okay, I was just hoping that things would settle down."

"I know," he said, lightly kissing her. "It will."

He set up a TV tray in front of her, which they ended up sharing, two bowls of tomato soup and toasted cheese sandwiches. And he let the TV run mindlessly in the background while they ate. "This is good," she murmured.

"Comfort food, my mom used to make it for me when I came home from school."

She smiled, "Sounds like a nice Mom."

"Yeah, she was, is. I haven't talked to her in a while."

She sipped the iced tea he'd perched on the wooden tray. She tried to be delicate, but it was clear that one false move and this nice, overcrowded lunch could go flying all over the place. "Why?"

"Why, what?"

"Why haven't you talked to your lovely mom, who made you these comforting after-school snacks?"

He eyed her with no expression except that one raised eyebrow thing that he managed to do with little effort. "Is this a dodge so we don't talk about what's happening with you?"

"Absolutely it is, but I'm still interested."

"Yeah, well, let's just say she wasn't overly fond of the mess that ensued after my divorce or actually of my divorce in general."

"Oh, then she liked the Ex."

He intently took a bite of his sandwich and then his soup, making Becca pretty sure he wouldn't be answering her question. Then a few beats later, he did. "Yeah, I don't know. Mom came from a different generation. The *you tough out a bad marriage* one."

"Oh, then, is that what she did?"

Gabriel stopped and looked at her strangely. "What made you ask that?"

She shrugged, wondering indeed why she had said that. "I don't know, just a feeling. My parents came a bit from the same ilk, never seemed as close as married people should ideally be."

"Yeah, honestly, I don't know. As I said, my parents have a bit of a different mindset which makes my changes in vocation—"

"Tough for them to understand," she finished the thought.

Again, he looked at her curiously, "Right."

"I'm sorry," she murmured. "It must be difficult, trying to do what you know you need to but then having family tell you you're wrong."

"Yes, it is," he said with a tone of fatigue that she completely understood. "But you either live your life the way you think you should, or you live it for other people." He then looked at her with that very intense scrutiny. "Your Mom, what was she like?"

"Well, let's see. She took me to a psychiatrist at a very young age and then ultimately told me to act the way other people expected me to. I don't know. I think maybe she thought she was helping."

"And did you?" he asked softly. "Act the way other people expected you to."

So strange how it felt so gut-wrenching talking like this, talking so honestly about deeply painful things, not an endeavor she was remotely comfortable or even familiar with. "I suppose I did, as long as I could. Sometimes it was and is, I suppose, just not possible."

He put his hand over hers, "You know you never have to do that with me."

She nodded, not looking at him. "I know. It's not like you'd let me anyway," she said softly.

And then he took her hand, tugging it so she looked into his eyes. "No, no secrets."

She dragged about, finishing their impromptu meal, but eventually, she had to wrap it up. She waited nervously as Gabriel cleared the dishes. Honestly, it all felt so depressing to her. There wasn't even time to celebrate their success. From all they could see and sense, it seemed Ellie had moved on, out of that dark, gray fog she'd existed in for so long. That was reason enough for them to be happy, for them to pat themselves on the back, maybe break open a bottle of champagne.

But no, this wasn't how things worked. One door opened then seemed to open another and another, more and more upheaval, and then she stopped.

She frowned, if not explicitly, inwardly.

"I know why you're carrying on, Rebecca. It's not about anything you say it is. It's simply that there's something you don't want to do."

Wow, her mother, for all her misplaced intentions, did have her number. She'd call it a *Becca Tantrum*.

Was that what all this was about? Was she simply having a *Becca Tantrum*? A lot of dust kicked up in the air because there was something that she really didn't want to do or, rather, somewhere she didn't want to go back to.

"What is it?"

She looked up. Gabriel stood in the doorway watching her with his *I'm Analyzing You* expression. "What do you mean?"

"You're frowning. And you look a little angry."

How unfortunate. Clearly, it wasn't all internal. "I was just reflecting on how I hate to be pushed."

"Do you think I'm pushing you?"

"I don't know, not really. It feels like everything, the Universe maybe is pushing me to sweep out my dusty old cupboards, and I don't want to."

He sat in a rocking chair across the room. "So dusty is the way you like them."

"Sometimes, maybe, I don't know. I just—I just want things to be quiet."

He nodded, "Calmer shores? I get it, but sometimes you have to go through some rough water to get there."

She leaned back on the sofa and crossed her arms. "Okay, enough with the seafaring analogies."

"Okay, how about this? Eventually, you'll have to go to sleep, and whatever you're afraid of will still be there."

"Wow, great bedside manner you have."

"No, no, I really don't. I just want you to get to that calmer shore. I don't want you in pain."

She looked at his face. He was serious and determined. But she couldn't help but wonder with distraction how it felt, how it felt not to be in pain.

Chapter Twenty

An Evil Man

"Can you tell me about the dream?"

They settled in his study, Gabriel setting up a wooden folding chair and Becca sitting across from him at his desk in his very comfortable office chair. He also lit a white candle and put out water in a clear bowl.

"What's the candle and the water for?" she murmured with distraction.

"The candle promotes peacefulness, and the water absorbs negative energy."

"Does that really work?" she prodded.

And then a quick smile, "Well, it doesn't hurt." And then, of course, not to be thrown off course, Gabriel dove in. Occasionally, she thought of switching it up and just calling him Gabe, but it didn't feel comfortable for her. And the undeniable truth was that she was a creature of habit, much as she might deny it.

"The dream," he repeated, gently steering her back to topic.

"Oh, okay, let's see. This one, after Ellie left, occurred in my old bedroom."

"Bedroom?"

"Yes, back when I was a kid, eleven, twelve, I guess."

"Was this in New Orleans?"

She breathed in deeply. "No, we, my family, lived for a few years on the Gulf Coast, Mississippi. It was a little town, Waveland."

"Why did you move there?" She looked at him. He didn't have much expression, just calmly and smoothly interrogating her, though it didn't feel like an interrogation, just a casual conversation.

"My father was an accountant. He went to work for an insurance company there. They, my parents, I guess, thought it would be nice living near the water, the beach."

"Was it?"

She tried to think back, but it wasn't easy. The memories were laced with haziness and stress that seemed to cloud everything. "I can't really remember. The school I went to was difficult. The kids were mean. I was different, didn't have a Mississippi drawl. And other things."

"Yeah," he commented softly, "you don't blend in."

She raised an eyebrow at that. "What exactly does that mean?"

"It's not a criticism, Becca. You're unique, striking, and remarkably special. And I'm sure for people who weren't— Well, it rubbed them the wrong way."

Unarguably, she wasn't expecting that. Her face stung a bit with a blush at Gabriel's unvarnished compliments. "Okay, well, on my side of things, it was difficult, but at least we were past the psychiatrist thing."

"The psychiatrist?"

She sighed. How stupid to bring this up. "Yeah, about ten, I guess. I got dragged to a psychiatrist for complaining about voices I was hearing and bad dreams. Luckily, I got prescribed some tranquilizers and didn't get zapped with shock therapy or something like that."

"You were worried about that?"

She straightened up in his very relaxing desk chair. "I was worried about a lot of things. Anyway, I learned quickly to keep my mouth shut, especially about the waking dreams."

There was a pause before he inquired. "What did those look like, Becca?" He seemed content to let things unfold slowly.

"I don't know. Hallucinations, I guess, people moving in and out of the rooms of our house. That house, that little wood-frame house in Waveland, it was bad for that."

"Was it like Ellie?"

She breathed out deeply. "Not exactly. I mean Ellie had been around for a while. But the other one, the one I would see. She wasn't from that far back. We found out about her while living there from a neighbor."

"I'm not following. Found out what exactly, Becca?"

"There was a girl who lived there before us. She was a little older than me. She'd killed herself in our house."

"You have to watch auras, colors. Dark colors are indicative of problems, spiritual intransigence, muddling, and being stuck. Orange denotes confusion and, of course, reds, well real spiritual energy problems, danger, sometimes damage."

He was listening intently to Becca but was also watching. It was amazing as she talked, the shift in her aura, colors that mutated from blues, greens, and indigo into darker muddied shades and then finally orange, and alarmingly crimson bleeding in on the periphery, then yellow. What had Jean said about the color yellow in auras? Oh yes, intense energy-draining.

It took a moment for Gabriel to collect himself. He knew something was bothering Becca, something that was potentially hindering all the progress they'd made together, but he hadn't anticipated this, something with this kind of impact.

"Did you say there was a girl who killed herself in your house?"

It was quiet. He'd stopped seeing her aura. Something had closed off, perhaps inside of him, perhaps in the intensity of her distress. "Yeah, we'd been renting the house, and we found out after we signed a lease. The neighbor said it had happened maybe just over six months before we moved in. She, well, the girl, had cut her wrists. They found her in her bed, and it was too late."

He breathed in deeply. It felt painful. He was tapping into Becca, Becca's intense emotions, although it was not something he detected in her speech or manner. Actually, she seemed rather matter-of-fact in delivering the information, even detached, he might say.

"That must have been difficult for you, living in a house where something so disturbing happened."

She lightly tapped her feet, he noticed, not really nervously, though with distraction. Somehow, he doubted she would have even been aware of it if he pointed it out to her. "Yeah, I mean, at the time, I had no idea what was going on. That it had even happened."

Then she stopped, almost as though something had caught her up short. "Happened where Becca?" he asked, already certain of what she would say.

"I didn't know then, not until later. It was my bedroom where she had killed herself. I felt—"

She stopped, not finishing the sentence. He could feel it, though not inside himself. He could feel it as an observer, an analyst. The impact of this event had almost smothered her. It was the catalyst that had driven her so far over the edge of her sanity. "Did you see her, the girl, in the house?"

"No," she murmured, "not really. I don't think she was there, not like Ellie."

"I see," he said. But then he felt something, something distinctly that caused and still was causing tremendous fear. "What did you see?"

He was looking at her directly, but she had been focusing elsewhere as she spoke, focusing somewhere beyond him until now. Her eyes came to him, wide and questioning and, yes, unfortunately, more than fearful. "What do you mean?" she said shakily.

"Something is haunting you, Becca."

She stared at him almost accusatory, defensively, but truly all he could see was pain. "There was someone there, someone I would see in dreams, and sometimes not, in flashes, in passing in the house. It was—" but she hesitated and fell silent.

"Tell me," he said flatly.

"There was a man, a man who felt very evil."

She didn't know why she'd used that word. It wasn't a word she was in any way comfortable with or even believed in, but in this case— She stood up abruptly. It was too much. Talking about this was too much after everything else that had happened. "Look, I need a break."

Gabriel continued to look at her oddly. "This man, is he in your dreams? The nightmares you have."

She stared at him with irritation. Hadn't she just uttered the words — *I need a break*? "Yes, now I'm done, Gabriel." She walked out of the room and headed down the hallway.

She suddenly felt panicked, unbelievably claustrophobic, as though she had to get out, away. Severe irritation was crawling all over her skin. She headed toward the front door, but then as she put her hand out for the doorknob, she felt his hand close on hers. "Becca, you need to calm down."

She spun around, feeling as though she was ready to explode at him for no reason except that she felt like a volcano inside. "Look, I don't have to do anything. I told you I've had enough, and I have. Don't you get that?"

"Something is trying to control you."

She snatched her hand away from his, almost as though it was burning her. "Maybe, just maybe, that's a someone. I'm tired of being a little puppet being played with by you, experimented on."

"You can't think that's what I'm doing." He said very calmly, though she could detect some steel in his voice.

"Yes, Becca, do this, Becca, do that. Becca, quit your job. Becca, tell me this, divulge your deepest, most painful—" But then the words got jumbled up emotionally in her throat.

"It's all right," he said calmly.

"No, no, I can't take this. I don't want to dredge things up. I just want, I want."

"I know you want to be free. That's what I'm trying to do. Can't you see that? I want you free, free from everything that is causing you pain."

She put her hands on his chest and pushed against him forcefully, but he wouldn't budge. He wouldn't let her push him away. "Gabriel," she said in tears. "It's too much."

"I know," he said, pulling her close to him. "I know. We'll stop," he murmured. Then he pulled her right up against him and began to kiss her. Her head swam with confusion. Then she pulled on him more tightly. She needed this. She needed to forget. She kissed him back passionately, drowning her pain in the rage of emotion between them.

As he scooped her up in his arms and carried her to the couch, she heard him whisper so softly, "I love you, Becca," but then she let herself believe she'd imagined it.

Chapter Twenty-One

Thunderstorms

It bothered him. He left Becca asleep on his bed, pulling his clothing back on, t-shirt last, and heading to the kitchen. He heard the rumblings of an unexpected thunderstorm that had rolled in. He opened the door leading out onto the back patio. Standing outside under the overhang for a moment, he tried to soak in the energy from the storm, watching the heavy raindrops splashing on the wooden deck and wrought iron patio table.

It was like a cloud hanging over them, this thing, this new thing that evidently wasn't new to Becca at all. But it was to him, and it felt like a depressing energy clinging to them both now, hampering something indefinable.

"You know this world is filled with all manner of things, unseen mostly. If you could truly clear your mind and see what was there, the space all around you would be filled with all types of manifestations."

He'd studied for a year in Ireland, Dublin, with a teacher that Jean Rampart had referred him to. She'd told him succinctly, and he remembered, "If you're going to follow this path, Gabe, you must commit fully. Be willing to give your time, your energy, and your preconceived assumptions over. Be truly open to embrace a new world view."

Of course, there was hesitation to do it, but in the end, there was nowhere to go but forward. His new teacher's name was Garrett Buckley, a rather crusty psychologist who'd left traditional science behind to focus on parapsychology. This Irishman had rather easily and unabashedly violated all of Gabriel's expectations. Their classroom was the historic and mystical lands of Ireland which just happened to be quite packed with ghosts, poltergeists, and other varied supernatural entities.

"All this folklore you read about, don't think it's just stories, my young man. Stories are just an easy way to impart the truth, thinly veiled but widely consumed."

The thunder cracked in the sky, and the sheets of rain continued to fall more heavily. That was one thing he did love about the city, the sudden rise of a storm, a storm that blows through, rocking everything and then quickly passes. He heard the light footsteps behind him but didn't turn around. And then she was beside him, nuzzling up against him. "You're getting wet," she murmured.

"I know. I've always thought about screening in a porch out here but never got around to it."

"That would be nice," she said softly. He wrapped his arms around her and pulled her closer in.

"Yeah, I've been thinking," he said quietly.

"Okay, should I ask?"

"How would you feel about taking a trip with me?"

"A trip? That sounds nice. Where to?"

He hesitated, unsure if she was quite ready for this. "To the coast, the Gulf Coast."

Becca didn't say anything, just leaned back against him with an audible sigh.

She felt his arms tighten around her, but it did nothing to quell the drop she'd felt in her stomach at the mention of the Gulf Coast. She'd felt better when she'd gotten up.

She'd felt better after she and Gabriel had made love. It was as though there was hope in the world again as if the darkness she'd felt wrapped in after Ellie had crossed over had finally lifted. But she knew Gabriel, or at least she thought she did, and he wouldn't let unresolved things go.

"You know we can't always fix everything," she murmured.

"Referring to what?"

She took a quick breath, "My past is my past. Whatever lurks there can stay, and we can just move on."

"But what if it isn't staying there?"

She pulled away from him and walked deliberately out onto the deck. The rain was only a drizzle, but at the moment, she didn't care. She wouldn't care if she was getting fully drenched. Her arms were crossed protectively in front of her, and she stared out somewhere beyond the lovely little patio on Dumaine Street, wondering what kind of life she might have out there if she just walked away from this, all this, whatever it was. That was how much she didn't want to look back.

"Becca, I'm not trying to upset you." She could feel him standing just behind her in the rain.

"You could have fooled me," she muttered. "You should go inside. You're getting wet."

She felt his hands on her shoulders and him whispering into her hair. "You've come so far."

"You know I'm not your experiment. I came to you for help, and you've helped me."

Again, his arms wrapped around her, pulling her against him. "This really frightens you."

She shook her head. "I'm tired, tired of feeling pain, of being afraid. I don't want to look there. There's something awful, ugly," she whispered.

He turned her around slowly in his arms, then stared at her intently. The raindrops were dripping down his face a bit, and she couldn't help but smile. "Then we'll face it down together."

She reached up, tracing a drizzle of water that had come down the side of his cheek. "You're very wet."

He grimaced. "I know," then he softly kissed her. She remembered just then he'd said he loved her, and she wondered rather dismally if it was true.

There was something electrifying about traveling on Highway 90 along the Mississippi Gulf Coast. And the fact that it had taken them the balance of the week to agree on taking this excursion together did not dim the charge he felt being in such close proximity to the Gulf of Mexico.

"It's really a waste of time."

"Then let's just go on a holiday there."

"You know that house we lived in is probably not there any longer."

"Well, we can spend time in the area. If it's important, it will retain energies from whatever was there before."

"I can't stay in Waveland. I just can't, Gabriel. I don't know why it fills me with dread."

"Okay, let's stay in Biloxi. We can visit a casino while we're there."

And then she'd frowned, and it made him want to laugh. "Do you not realize how many truly miserable people spend an inordinate amount of time at casinos? My father would always say—" Then she stopped abruptly.

He'd touched her arm, seeing the upset look that had passed over her features. "What did he say, Becca?"

She crossed her arms in front of her as though trying to fend off any pain. "He said casinos weren't built from winners. They were built on the backs of people who lost."

He nodded, "Yes, I guess that's true. Your Dad, are you still in touch?"

"No, no, he and my Mom live near Tennessee, near my sister. It just seemed easier at some point to stop trying to hold those relationships together."

He impulsively pulled her into his arms. "I'm sorry. That must be hard."

"I don't know," she shook her head. "I know your birth family is supposed to be close, but they all just became like strangers to me." She shook her head impulsively, more to blot out her dark thoughts than anything else. "Anyway, no to the casinos."

"And no to Biloxi?"

She shrugged, and he knew at that moment he'd worn her down. Unfortunately, that fact didn't cheer him much. He'd prefer her to be fully on board with their plan. After all, it was just a scouting expedition, having no real idea what they might or might not find. "Biloxi is fine. We can find a decent seafood restaurant there and visit some crummy souvenir shops."

He nodded, "There's the spirit. At the very least, we'll have a nice little getaway," she smiled at him in a way that let him know with no deliberation how little her heart was in this.

"You have to get hold, Becky. If you continue to carry on this way, they'll take you away from us."

She remembered that she'd woken up screaming again, feeling as though she was being smothered by a masculine hand. Her mother had shaken her awake while her father lingered just outside the bedroom door with a disgruntled expression, clearly uninterested in entering. She remembered shaking uncontrollably, trying desperately to swallow the sobs of fear that were determined to explode out of her. She nodded, whispering, "Bad dream, sorry."

And her mother had patted her hands to calm her, but when she glanced at the doorway, she saw that her father was no longer there. It is a particularly virulent pain for a child to know they are not accepted or even wanted for who they are. It breeds the specters of low self-esteem and, at times, self-hatred. It did take her some time to climb out of that black hole, if she ever did, recognizing it was a weakness and failing on their part rather than having much of anything to do with her.

"What do you think about a walk on the beach later?" Gabriel asked with a slight lilt in his voice, pulling her away from dark memories.

"Sure," she said softly as his jeep continued to meander down Highway 90. It was more than clear Gabriel was enjoying this expedition, not haunted, as was his companion, by any painful recollections from the area.

Less than a quarter of an hour before, they'd passed through the small town of Waveland even before they'd reached the long stretch of highway running beside the beaches. In anticipation, Becca had deliberately shut herself off and did not raise her eyes from her phone that she was intently studying with feigned interest. Once during that brief interlude, she felt Gabriel softly pat her hand, but he didn't say anything, didn't prod her for engagement, clearly as though he accepted where she was in the matter. Then thankfully, they'd passed over the bridge, away from the bad memories heading deeper along the Gulf Coast.

The blue water around them sparkled under the sunlight as they drove towards Pass Christian. She took a deep breath, resolving to focus on what was positive instead of the shadows that threatened to overtake her.

Chapter Twenty-Two

As Real as You and I

She was sure they'd discussed where they'd be staying, though everything felt a bit scrambled just now. Gabriel thought an Airbnb would be easier on her than a hotel, possibly with less occupancy history. Becca recalled agreeing yet not completely agreeing. It wasn't necessarily the volume of people who had occupied a space as specifically what kind of people.

He'd looked at her a little blankly as she remembered, "Kind?"

She hesitated, how to meaningfully coalesce what she was thinking, "Yeah, like maybe people who are critically upset, are going through some great trauma like Ellie, or maybe even those whose energy is, well, shadowed if you know what I mean."

He frowned, "You mean like criminals."

"I suppose, but then again, there are all kinds of criminals, Gabriel. Most never get caught."

And then he had that insightful look on his face that she was so familiar with. He understood. "Well, hopefully, this place I booked will have none of that." And she'd smiled but still felt dread in the pit of her stomach. Wouldn't it be nice just to go away and have a lovely little holiday with her boyfriend? So odd and awkward, the word boyfriend felt ill-constructed for what he was to her. She couldn't define it, put a name to their relationship. There were so many levels. They'd become partners in this endeavor to ostensibly heal her psyche. Gabriel was her friend, her lover, her confidant. If she sat down and considered it, she was sure she could come up with such a myriad collection of descriptions. But she didn't want to, didn't want to examine it too closely lest it somehow evaporated. She was grateful for now, though she dreaded with the memories and insecurities of a young girl what was to come.

She was quiet. In fact, Gabriel would have to say that Becca had withdrawn inside herself, more so than he'd possibly ever seen her in their acquaintance. He was having second thoughts and third and fourth. Perhaps, it was selfish of him to have pushed this trip now, so soon.

It was just that he felt a shadow, a tangible shadow hanging over them, hanging over a bright future that he was beginning to envision.

It was that unsettled thing, as though a clock was ticking somewhere. Once they'd helped Ellie, it seemed as though some door had opened, and if they didn't quickly deal with whatever the problem might be, even the thought elicited an actual chill, it might deal with them.

As they pulled up on the street beside the collection of cottages where they'd be staying, he reached over and squeezed her hand. "It's going to be all right, Becca," he said softly.

She didn't answer for a moment but finally turned to face him. Her face was rather stoic, he thought, not warmed at all by what he'd said. And rather flatly, she responded, "You can't know that."

The duplex that Gabriel had rented was filled with light. It was a cozy little place with only two rooms, a large den/kitchen combo, and a bedroom with a queen-sized bed. It was decorated delicately with wicker furniture and walls, which had the slightest tinge of blue mixed with light gray. But what she liked most of all were all the windows, which, although covered with blinds, let the lovely sunlight flood in everywhere.

As she stood in the den and looked around, she felt herself relax and breathe in deeply, finally letting all the anxiety from the previous days sort of drip away from her. "What do you think?" Gabriel asked. "If it's a problem, we'll get another place."

She took a step forward, noting all the beachy accents from the seaside paintings on the walls to ceramic lamps constructed as nesting pelicans and seagulls taking flight. "No, it's lovely, Gabriel," she murmured, tentatively letting her feelings open up and lightly brush through the place to see if anything problematic was lurking. It was odd. Now that she'd been working with Gabriel for a while, she could intellectually separate what she was feeling from what she felt from the energy of others.

She could actively sense people who had been here before moving about the house. There was the older couple, in their eighties, who stayed in most of the time. There were also newlyweds who were in and out constantly, on the go, but boisterously happy. And then there was a family recently, four of them with two young children who slept on the sofa bed, squabbling constantly. And there were others, but nothing upsetting, nothing traumatic, just life, life filling the walls of this quiet little cottage.

"I think it will be fine." Then she looked over at Gabriel. She could tell how concerned he was about her, although there wasn't a trace of it on his face. She could just feel it, particularly on her skin, when she touched him. She grabbed his hand to get his attention. "I'm sorry I've been so out of sorts."

And then she did see it in his eyes. "I am trying to help you, Becca."

She nodded, smiling. "I know," but that oppressive feeling shadowing her made her wonder if that was even possible.

He'd lucked out with the duplex. It seemed quiet here, calming. In anticipation, he'd even packed white candles and some chunks of crystal quartz he used to boost energy to help out, but it didn't seem necessary.

Gabriel had even gone as far as bringing a bundle of sage he'd bought from The Waxing Moon Bookstore back home to cleanse the energy of the place if need be. But so far, all seemed quiet. Becca had seemed particularly tired after the trip, so she'd gone to lie down for a bit in the bedroom. He'd thought to join her, but something was bothering him that he couldn't quite put his finger on.

He stretched out on the sofa, briefly closing his eyes and trying to focus.

"Don't forget. Sleep is often a journey into the astral plane." He recalled that peculiar lilt of Garrett Buckley's Irish accent that, at times, he had to admit grated on him.

"So, you're saying all the outlandish things that I dream are real on some level?"

He'd narrowed his eyes ever so slightly. Garrett undeniably did not have the patience that his former mentor possessed. "You know, you can't take everything at face value. What you remember from your dreams are undeniably just translations for the sake of your human brain."

"Translations?"

"That's right."

"So, the big purple monster isn't real."

And then he'd frowned. Garrett had a bit of an impish face surrounded by a white beard and a full head of white hair. At times, Gabriel had wondered if the fellow himself was a descendant of some elves or fairies from the magical Hollow Hills or other enchanted realms of the country they were in. "Gabriel Sutton, I've been wondering why you're here. I can't yet tell if your heart is in it."

He remembered feeling somewhat perched in the curious position of being ostensibly chastised by an elf. "Good question," he said distractedly, wondering what the truth was. "I suppose I'm here because I've burnt the bridges to my old life. There is nowhere to go but forward, yet I must admit forward is daunting. It's unraveling everything I ever believed to be true, to be real and solid."

And then there seemed to be something akin to compassion that mutated into the older man's expression. He wasn't one to keep his emotions under wraps. "Yes, I remember that point. It can be scary, or it can be a great adventure. It's all in perception." Back then, they sat amid Garrett Buckley's rather cluttered office at Trinity College in Dublin where he taught psychology classes several evenings a week. Rather casually, he propped his feet up on his well-cluttered desk. "So, we're speaking of purple monsters from your dreams, young Gabriel. Well, it could be many things — a manifestation of negative thought energy that has coalesced into form, an astral shell composed of lower vibrational material in the process of deteriorating, a vitalized shell very similar to the former but animated by aspects of a lower mind, or even a Shade — a pitiable creature devoid of all spirituality yet more than convinced it is not and continues to resist its natural demise."

"You mean some sort of ghost."

"Ghost is a simplistic term. There are all sorts of entities, all sorts of ranges of existences that inhabit and wander the astral plane, a dimension precariously linked and near our own, and each I daresay, is individual. But your purple monster, did it seem malevolent?"

"It was chasing me."

"Ah, no doubt in search of energy to keep its existence viable. Did it reach you?"

He sighed. It was an actual dream but one he'd dredged up from a childhood nightmare. "Yes, it caught me once with its great claw that it dragged along my leg."

"Drew blood?"

"Yes, quite a bit, as I remember. It made continuing to run rather cumbersome, but I managed to do it."

"Yes, so the letting of blood surely represents a loss of energy. To the spiritual realms, the astral plane, and subsequent planes, blood is the equivalent of energy. So, whatever it was, and I find it difficult to classify it without closer inspection, it was a parasite of some sort. Perhaps a vampiric sort of creature or something more complicated."

"But you're saying it was real."

"Real, oh yes, as real as you and I."

Gabriel breathed deeply, reorienting himself in the present, away from the cozily cluttered office of Dr. Garrett Buckley in Dublin, back within the small Airbnb along Biloxi Beach. Part of him wanted to sleep, he did feel tired, but he also felt something disquieting pulling him. He closed his eyes, focusing his concentration on Becca. Traditionally, he couldn't travel astrally, but things undeniably seemed to have shifted for him since the episode with Ellie. He did believe a door had opened, and it seemed as though Becca was not the only one who had walked through it.

"It's clear that your psychic powers are profound, Gabriel, but strangely untapped. Perhaps it will only take the proper stimulus to ignite them."

He remembered he'd laughed at that comment by Garrett, thinking to himself that his role in this realm would never be as an active participant. Whether he wished it or not, that was what he believed.

But at this moment, this particular moment, he felt something quite to the contrary. He felt a tug, gentle, then a distinct pull that mutated into a violent yank.

Shaking off the profound disorientation, he found himself in the small bedroom where Becca was asleep. But she was not alone. The form he saw with her at first felt ill-defined, almost an amorphous blob of powerfully negative energy. Then, as he struggled to understand what he saw, slowly, it solidified from its ruddy, brick-reddish color into some sort of figure but still unsettled in its shape, see-through and gelatinous in places while solid in others. It stood beside her bed, reaching toward her with mushy blobs for appendages. "Stop," he called out from somewhere deep inside him before it made contact with her sleeping form.

Then slowly, nearly laboriously, it turned toward him, and he could make out a distorted face filled with rage. Then a voice from its depths, graveled but distinctly communicating in a language he did not understand.

Chapter Twenty-Three

The Shade

The place was unfamiliar, though it also felt as though she knew it well. Everything around her gleamed, the great pieces of furniture along the walls, dark heavy woods, topped with decorative marble slabs. Her feet stepped silently on the wooden floor of the foyer that merged into the hallway housing the grand staircase leading upstairs. She swayed, feeling insubstantial, her white shift brushing the top of her ankles and her bare feet rubbing against the highly polished surface beneath them.

And from outside, she could hear the roar of the storm thrash against the roof. Lights flickered on and off as the oil lamps responded to the weather. But as she turned, walking through an open doorway that she knew somehow was the parlor, most of it was couched in darkness, except for fluttering illumination from the open French doors running along the walls. As the lightning flickered, the room was starkly lit, then couched in darkness following a jarring clash of thunder.

When she could see, all was rich, decorated satin sofas, velvet chairs, ornate mirrors, paintings from that other time. But she couldn't help it. Her stomach flipped with nausea as the stench of decay reached her.

"Why am I here?" she whispered.

And then the shadows mutated, and she backed away.

The figure moved closer, a sizeable indistinguishable man towering over her. She recoiled in terror, stumbling into a round wooden table with an ornate vase atop it. She hit it so hard that she spun around as the vase crashed, splintering and dropping its bouquet of white roses over the dark floor.

Shaking, she turned back, and now the creature was directly in front of her, "Parce que je desire," he said huskily in a way that made her stomach wretch.

And then she felt something grab her, inexplicably, from underneath the table, a hand and a long arm attached, and then another that took hold of her gown and then her legs, yanking her to her knees. She struggled but was mute. No sound, no scream would come out. There were more hands, more arms, a countless number grabbing her and pulling her aggressively beneath the table into a gulf of darkness, hands over her mouth as she thrashed desperately in terror.

She fought, lashing out, flailing, but was helpless, dragged relentlessly into the darkness.

"Becca, Becca," she heard her name being called from some hollow place, some distant plane she couldn't reach nor respond to.

The hands on her arms were tight, and they shook her, but it wasn't as before, not so many, not the kind that burned her skin when they touched her flesh.

"Becca, wake up, Becca." She continued to fight, to strike out at anything to get away, to escape. She opened her eyes, and her blurry vision took in the form bent over her, sitting on the edge of the bed. She gasped in air as it felt as though her lungs had been entirely emptied.

She shoved him with all her might, backing away as far as she could get on the mattress. Gabriel was still staring at her with panic in his eyes. Then he held up his hands. "It's all right. It's just me."

She remained frozen, crouched against the white headboard, unmoving in terror. She didn't know if she could speak. Just moments before, everything had been paralyzed. "Gabriel," she whispered. "Oh, God."

And then he held out his arms for her, and she moved into them, his warmth reassuring as to where she was and what world she still existed within. He pulled her close against him. "It's all right," he said softly.

"I don't know. Was that a nightmare?"

"A bit more than that," he murmured against her hair.

She sipped a cup of tea on the light blue sofa in their home away from home, their lovely little duplex. But her eyes frantically sought Gabriel, desperately needing to see him, continuing to touch him —his arm, his hand, his very needed and reassuring presence. She could not remember this feeling, not since she was a child, just that feeling of terror that he was around the corner, beneath the bed, the bogeyman, a monster ready to pounce and drag her away from safety at any given moment.

It was entirely irrational, or was it?

He sat across from her on the sofa, lightly brushing her fingertips with his own. "How are you?"

She placed the mug on the glass coffee table in front of them. Not because she didn't want anymore but because her hand felt as though she were trembling. In fact, it felt as though she were shaking everywhere, all the way down to her soul. Now, whether this was true or not, she had no idea, only that this was how she felt.

"Horrible. Can we go back now? This isn't working."

He continued to entwine his fingers in hers. "I'm sorry."

She watched his face reflecting so many things, so very many things for Gabriel, who was usually more contained, more able to mask, well, more than he seemed able to at the moment. "Sorry? What does that mean exactly?"

"I'm sorry. I don't think I realized how serious this was. I didn't think that it would —"

She straightened up, feeling that there was so much more going on here than the standard nightmares she'd been struggling with since she was a teenager. "It-It, what does that mean?" He squeezed her hand, but he was not looking at her. Instead, he looked down at their hands, deeply and profoundly caught up in thought. "Gabriel, please tell me what you're talking about."

And then his eyes focused on her directly, and she had to admit powerfully. "I saw it, Becca, this thing. I can't call it a man. I can't even call it a spirit, but it was trying to attack you."

Her eyes widened with a deeper level of fear that she was surprised she was able to reach. "What does that mean, attack me?"

"I-I had an experience, an out-of-body experience, and I saw you asleep in the bedroom, and this thing, mostly a mass of negative energy, but also a convoluted sort of form, clearly was attempting to drain you of energy."

She stared at him blankly, trying to assimilate what he was saying. "You, wait a minute. I thought you said you didn't travel that way."

He shook his head. "It seems that may have changed. I-I tried to stop it. I yelled at it and startled it. And it had a man's face, and it spoke, but another language."

"What was it, Gabriel? A ghost?"

"I don't know. I don't understand, but what I felt was different, empty, almost an echo of something very old but alive in its way."

Again, she felt the heaviness in her chest and took a deep breath as though she could not get enough air. "I feel so weak."

"I'm sorry. It drained you. I'm sure of it. I wasn't prepared for such an aggressive attack so soon. Clearly, it became aware of you in the area."

"The area? You mean it lives around here."

"It seems very strong here. There must be a reason."

Her stomach flipped once again with nausea. She remembered this from the dream, from that place. "You said it felt me here. Why?"

Again, he squeezed her hand. "I know this is difficult for you. But this could be the same thing from long ago. It needs energy, and it's found a way to exploit you."

"Exploit me? My energy?"

"Yes, you lived a good deal of your life in a state of upset. You have unique and powerful energy, Becca. It used that to maintain its existence possibly. When someone reaches a level of negative emotion, they can be drained of energy much more easily. But all of this is a guess."

She stared at him almost without comprehension. "Like a parasite?"

"I suppose it began here, somewhere around this area."

She pulled away from him and stood up, walking across the room. She couldn't understand what he was telling her, yet it bothered her, haunted her, another thought. "The girl," she whispered, staring out the back sliding door onto a small patio outside their cottage.

He came behind her, putting his hand on her back. "Yes, it could be."

"Did that thing drive her to kill herself?"

"I don't know. Low energy can cause great instabilities of mind."

She took a quick breath as a host of despairing memories and emotions flooded her from those days, those teenage days in that house where she sometimes felt she could not take anymore. She felt his arms go around her waist and pull her against him. "What do we do, Gabriel? What do we do when we don't know what it is?"

"That's not completely true. I am certain that what we're encountering here is called a Shade."

Chapter Twenty-Four
All the Devils are Here

"So, what you're speaking of is what layman would term some sort of ghost, a person who has not moved onto the next level of evolvement, heaven if you will."

He remembered Garrett Buckley looking at him in that way that, despite all of Gabriel's years of education and post-graduate education in medical school, made him feel quite simplistic.

They'd just returned from a visit to Montpelier Hill in Dublin — though known by locals as the notorious setting of the Hellfire Club. It was the site in the early 1700s of a hunting lodge where the club convened, which just so happened to dabble in black magic, amoral behavior, and general debauchery. The rumors that abounded were that its members were Satanists and Devil-Worshippers. And Gabriel had been well-inclined to believe this as, even with his minimal psychic gifts, he felt he was being smothered by the density of the negative energy permeating the place.

They'd toured the grounds but hadn't stayed long as Garrett seemed to be even more profoundly affected than he was.

"What can be done about such a place?" he'd asked once they were heading back to the city.

"Nothing, I know it is a popular tourist destination, but it is quite toxic to those who visit it, whether they acknowledge it or not. I wanted you to see the power of events and how they can irrevocably scar the land."

And then he'd insisted they both go home, shower and change, then reconvene at his office in the city to discuss things. That was Garrett's teaching mode — visit a site, experience a particular phenomenon, and then discuss and analyze it later.

"Ghosts? Well, that's a generic rather non-precise term," Buckley had answered, taking what Gabriel could only describe as a swig of tea from his oversized mug. Clearly, the American rage for coffee had never entirely caught on here. "I guess we have to get down to basics," he'd muttered, and Gabriel knew that was his cue to lean back in his chair and settle in for a protracted bit of enlightenment.

"To start at the very beginning, to believe that death is the universal leveler is a bit moronic if one gives it thought. Think about physical existence and how many different levels of evolvement, mental capacity, and moral ambiguities you experience daily. And yet, we're all going to die, and that disappears? The loss of the physical body does nothing to erase who we are on this earth and the work we are meant to do. It simply just translates to the next plane. All the varieties of intelligence, personality, all of it, exist amongst the dead as they do amongst the living."

"No heaven, no hell, no Elysian Fields?"

"We create our hell here on earth and thus choose our existence in the hereafter. But it's not eternal hell. It's just experiences to learn and evolve from. There is a benevolence to the universe, to God, if you will. Ultimately, it is desired that we do better."

"Hell is empty, and all the devils are here," Gabriel murmured.

Garrett smiled, "Shakespeare, yes, some, I suppose. So, in any event, when one does die, a person crosses to the astral plane with a body composed of his spirit but also formed from matter that he has absorbed during his lifetime on earth. Those composed of a higher, positive, vibrational substance will travel with him, but those of a lower nature must remain."

"Lower, you say."

"Yes, there is an advantage to living an altruistic life aimed at higher aspirations of good and good service. It makes it easier traveling in the afterlife. Those who indulge in self-gratification of all sorts, which explore the lower passions, find their mind entwined with this matter. And extricating oneself can cause all sorts of situations."

"Such as?"

"Extended time on disturbing and lower planes of existence until this matter can be exorcised. I suppose that's where traditional images and tales of hell and purgatory come from. But it's not an eternal sentence, but a difficult one, nonetheless. Best to do your work while you're in the physical if you can."

"But what does this have to do with the Hellfire Club?"

"Yes, well, you asked about ghosts. There are ghosts, negative imprints of energy, and other beings, creatures in between, if you will."

Gabriel waited for further explanation, but Garrett had stopped, drinking his tea and seeming lost in thought. "Like what sorts of creatures?"

"Aberrations from this process of disentanglement from lower matter. When a person chooses a lower path, there are many consequences. When I say lower, I mean self-indulgent, selfish, deliberately hurting and exploiting others, greed, and all manner of things. When one lives life this way and reaches the astral plane, the mind is often too enmeshed in this lower vibrational matter. An actual tearing occurs for the spirit to disengage from this corrupted astral shell, and some of the individual's lower mind, as we call it, remains with the shell."

"Remains, so then what's left is still alive?"

He shrugged, "I suppose in a way. It often retains the appearance of the original person, his mannerisms, idiosyncrasies, perhaps memories, and fully believes it is still the physical individual but, of course, only now composed of their worst qualities."

He felt hard-pressed to envision such a thing. And yet, all the conflicting and dangerous energies he'd felt at Montpelier attest that something quite dark was happening there. "What happens to it?"

"If we're lucky, eventually, with lack of energy, it dissipates, causing no particular harm to those on the astral plane or the physical."

"What if we're not lucky?"

Garrett, he recalled, drew a deep breath at that point that some might interpret as a sigh. "Yes, well, some try to live on, exploit situations, gain energy however they might. Pull energy from those indulging in similar activities as they did during life, drain inexperienced mediums, or possibly find another way to draw energy to extend an existence they feel they need to protect."

"And you believe that is going on at the Hellfire Club?"

Garrett looked at him curiously. "At Montpelier? Perhaps, I sensed quite a cacophony of issues there. There may well be a few Shades still lurking at that place."

"Shades?"

"Yes, that's what they're called, these creatures that echo their former selves, Shades."

"Are you sure that's what we're dealing with?"

Gabriel was amazed at how well Becca was taking the rather enormous information dump he'd precariously laid at her feet over the last half hour. He'd covered a lot of ground — from his experiences studying with Garrett Buckley in Dublin to the actual nature of astral reality and postmortem existence to his suspicions about the terrifying creature dogging her dreams. "Of course, all I have to go on is my limited exposure to it, but it seems to check the boxes, though its form is somewhat deteriorated, so that's an encouraging sign."

She frowned, "In what respect?"

"Shades that are intact will resemble the person they were originally spawned from. This one, or what I saw in the bedroom with you, had the face of a man, but the rest of it was more of a tangled mass of negative energy, although it retained speech."

"French," she murmured. They were sitting next to each other on the small sofa at their Biloxi beachside cottage. And how he wished they were walking the beach instead of trying to figure out this mess.

"French? Why do you say that?"

"In the dream, the nightmare I was having, I heard it. It was there, but it looked like a man, I guess. Though it was so shadowy, it was hard to tell."

"I don't suppose you know what—"

She shook her head. "My high school French is shaky at best, and it happened too quickly. One minute that thing

187

was speaking, and the next, I was dragged under an end table by a thousand hands."

He reached over with concern and rubbed her shoulder comfortingly. "That sounds pretty horrible. Is there anything else you can say about the dream?"

She shrugged, and he knew that talking about this now was the last thing she wanted to do. "Let's see. It was storming outside, thunder and lightning. I was in a huge house. It looked like one of those old plantation houses."

"Really?"

"Yes, we toured quite a few in the area when I was young. I always hated it. Felt like I couldn't breathe there. No matter how beautiful they seemed on the surface."

He nodded, "That makes sense. A lot of abuse and suffering went on at those places. The slaves were treated inhumanely, like possessions. I'm surprised you could even tolerate being there."

"It wasn't as if I had much choice. But I did avoid them in later years."

"But the dream, you're sure it was a plantation house?"

"It felt the same, but intense, so intense."

He sighed, "And this Shade was there. Well, it's somewhere to start."

"What do you mean?"

"I mean, we need to see if there were any plantations of that sort in this area, particularly around Waveland."

She nodded, then silently put her head on his shoulder. Gabriel was more than sure that going back to Waveland caused more dread in Becca than perhaps anything.

Chapter Twenty-Five

The Pirate House

"You know, it's a little late to start on this."

She was pale. And for not the first time, Gabriel considered the option of bringing her back to New Orleans and somehow trying to piece things together at a distance. But something nagging in the back of his mind told him it was best to meet this particular challenge head-on. "It's only three. We can make a run by the Waveland public library and then get some dinner somewhere."

She looked at him pensively, then slowly sat on the sofa, facing forward. "There must be somewhere else we can go. I just — I can't face Waveland right now," she murmured.

Sitting next to her, he took her hand in his. It was cool to the touch, in fact bordering on cold. He tried to clear his mind and feel, feel exactly what was going on, but all he could sense was how tremendously low on energy she was. He put his arm around her, pulling her up against him. "Tell you what, I have another plan. There's a welcome center right here in Biloxi. Surely if there is or was some sort of plantation house in this area, they would know it."

"Maybe," she muttered, frowning a bit.

"I know this is hard."

"Sure, but then again, you don't have some sort of bizarre energy-sucking ghost preying on you."

He pulled her even closer because, on some level, he was afraid she was trying to pull away from him. "No, no, I don't, but I do know we're in this together." And then he picked up her hand and kissed it. "You have no idea how important you've become to me, how important your well-being is to me."

And then she turned to him, looking him straight in the eye. "I hate feeling this way."

"What way?"

"Can't you see it, Gabriel? The way I used to be, feel all the time, afraid, so afraid. Since we've been together, I've felt stronger than I ever have in my life. I felt, in some ways, like I could live again. But this terrifies me for some reason and makes me feel like I'm being dragged back to how it was before."

He nodded, "I know. I'm sorry, but I promise you will be okay. And we will get past this together."

He wasn't sure if she believed him, but at least he felt certain that she wanted to. "I'll hold you to it," she murmured.

And then he reached over, pulling her face to his and kissing her deeply. The one thing he knew without question was that he couldn't fail in this. Too much, way too much was at stake.

Her shoes clicked on the hard terrazzo floor of the Biloxi Visitors Center. She breathed in deeply, wandering a bit aimlessly around the collection of pamphlet racks near a great unlit stone fireplace in the main room of the building.

Admittedly, it was quite an imposing, classical-style building, white with columns and porches on both floors. She didn't remember ever coming here before. Then again, the structure had only been here since 2011. The truth was since she was a teenager, she may have visited the Gulf Coast only once or maybe twice, once connected to a school field trip and the other time just on the spur of the moment.

It was actually an odd memory that came floating back. After she'd left her job at the high school, she just started driving one day. She'd ended up going all the way to Waveland, down the street from where she'd once lived. She remembered just parking her car not far from her family's old house.

So strange that she'd almost completely forgotten it. She didn't remember feeling an aversion to the area back then. Though, she had felt numb, confused, and oddly compelled to sit there for close to an hour before she left.

Deliberately shaking herself back into the present, she noted again what an impressive building this was. On the outside, it was rife with traditional architecture, yet inside quite modern with offices and evidently an extensive museum deep into its complex.

Drawing a deep breath, she tried to calm her nerves. She glanced across the room where Gabriel was still at the desk talking to a clerk, evidently still trying to get information.

Closing her eyes, she worked to clear her mind. She really couldn't remember feeling this shaky since —

And then, *"Becky,"* just a whisper, *"are you lost?"*

Slowly, she opened her eyes, then caught her breath painfully. She was standing inside again, the foyer leading to that staircase. This building, the visitor center, had a staircase as well, but this was different. This was the other one, the one from the dream.

"Becky, where are you going?" That voice so soft, but it was taunting her.

She squeezed her eyes shut again, desperately trying to regain control, then abruptly felt someone grab her. Instinctively she yanked away, but he held firm. "Becca," she opened her eyes again, seeing Gabriel holding her arm. "Are you alright?"

Was she? She had no idea. "Just shaky," she murmured, not at all sure how to explain what had just happened.

She met his eyes and knew from his expression that he didn't believe her, but they would have to sort that out later. "Let's go. I have some potential suspects to talk to you about."

She stared through the plate glass window at the Silver Sails seafood restaurant out to the beachfront. Across the table, Gabriel stretched out his arm and touched her hand, pulling her attention back to him. "Tell me what's happening, Becca."

"I thought you were going to tell me what you found," she said evasively.

He nodded, "We'll get there, first you. I need to know what is happening with you."

She smiled a little sadly at him. Their so-called getaway wasn't really benefitting either of them. Gabriel looked so tired. There were dark shadows beneath his eyes, born probably of stress, maybe of worry. "Things are becoming confused."

He squeezed her hand, "Confused? What does that mean?"

She reached for an accurate description. "Things are bleeding into each other. While we were at the visitor's center, I had a vision, a sort of waking dream of that house from the nightmare, then a voice taunting me."

He let her hand go and leaned back in the chair. "This thing, it's getting very proactive."

She nodded silently. "What do we do?"

Then he looked at her with steel in his expression. "We find it, then put an end to this."

"How can you stop it?"

Garrett Buckley looked at him with a bit of surprise. They had opted to stop by a local pub in Dublin and have a drink before heading home for the evening. "Stop what, my boy? I'm afraid you've lost me. We've covered a lot of ground today."

"Oh, sorry, I guess that's true," Gabriel answered, sipping his beer. It was perfectly true. They'd covered poltergeists, multi-hauntings, and then, of course, the aimless ones, as Garrett had called them. "I understand that in the case of a lost spirit, they need to be encouraged to move on from the astral plane where they're stuck, but you talked about these other creatures, the Shades."

Garrett nodded slowly, looking at him intently. Of course, that wasn't unusual for him, always looking more deeply into Gabriel's questions than he anticipated. "You know, it doesn't serve to categorize anything as evil in this world. There is a purpose for everything in God's plan. For these aberrations, the Shades, the natural course of evolution is for their energy to dissipate and release their influence on the earthly plane."

"But what if they don't?"

"If they don't let go and allow the natural order of things to progress, well then, you do your best to cut off their food supply."

"Food?" he asked, somewhat bemused by the explanation.

"Energy, my boy. You find a way to cut off their energy."

It helped. The seafood platter that they'd decided to split was helping just about everything at the moment.

Becca was eating a stuffed crab that tasted heavenly in her estimation, but then again, maybe it was just all the stress. "So, what did you find?"

Gabriel, at present, was diving into a piece of fried catfish. "Am I crazy, or is this just really good?"

She laughed, "No, it is good. A much-needed reprieve, I think."

"Yeah, well, there are a few houses in the area, but none specifically in Waveland." He sipped his schooner of beer, and she had to smile. Such a handsome guy, and why were they out hunting ghosts again?

"So that's it? Nothing."

And then he frowned, and she knew that wasn't quite the case. "Not exactly. There was a place that used to be there, pretty much out on the beach in Waveland. It was a sort of plantation house built in the early 1800s but completely destroyed by Hurricane Camille."

She looked at him a little blankly, "Wait a minute. You're talking about the place that used to be on North Beach Blvd?"

"I think so. Apparently, it had a colorful past."

She leaned back in her chair. "I remember something about it from school. People around here were pretty proud of it."

He shrugged, "Like I said, it was colorful. Some even try to tie it to John Lafitte."

And then her eyes widened, "You're talking about the Pirate House."

He was watching her closely, apparently keenly interested in her reaction. "Yep, the lady at the visitor center said they used to smuggle slaves through a tunnel from the beach."

"Smuggle slaves?"

"Right, apparently back then, in the early days of the Louisiana Purchase, the slave trade was illegal in Louisiana. So, it was big business for the pirates. But, of course, all of that changed later on."

She nodded, "I remember that. Thomas Jefferson, of all people, had that clause put in the agreement. Still, you're saying this thing, entity—" She glanced around, suddenly aware of what she was saying in public but grateful that she saw no one at nearby tables who looked particularly interested in what they were discussing. In a bit of a lower voice, she continued, "You're saying this thing is connected to that house."

He shrugged, "It's possible. You said he was speaking French in the dream. That would fit. In the early days, the men connected with the place were French. The Spaniards called them French Corsairs."

She shook her head. "So, you're saying this guy is a pirate."

"It's possible, Becca. Bizarre as that might seem, it's entirely possible."

Chapter Twenty-Six

The Slaver's House

Traveling along Highway 90 at dusk, or as the locals liked to call it, Beach Blvd. felt oddly disquieting to her senses.

"You know, we could just put a pin in this until tomorrow."

Watching the water and nearly white sand buffering it from the land had an unreal quality. It made her feel as though she was slipping into some alternate world.

"I suppose. But it feels as though we should go there tonight. I can't explain it." To say Gabriel seemed surprised was an understatement. After all, she had been the one fighting this trip, this exploration, since it had begun. Then something had changed, shifted inside her.

This change had happened sometime during dinner at the Silver Sails restaurant when Gabriel informed her that her nightmares, in fact, all her childhood terrors, could be linked to someone who lived hundreds of years before her. "Do you want dessert?"

"So, you're telling me this is some sort of a ghost, possibly a pirate ghost that has been haunting this area that got attached to me, just because." And then she added absently, "Yes, do they have bread pudding?"

"Um," he picked up the dessert menu from the table and was perusing it, "I don't see it. They have all kinds of pie."

"Pecan?"

"Yep."

"I'll take that with coffee. "

"Okay," he muttered, putting down the menu. "It's like I told you, not exactly a ghost. It's called a Shade, a sort of animated astral shell devoid of its original spirit."

"Okay," she sighed deeply. "A Shade that's been—"

"Trying to sustain its existence."

She frowned, "Sounds like it's been doing a pretty good job. I mean, the Pirate House went back to the—"

"Early 1800s," he filled in.

It was undeniably getting a bit unnerving, being intercepted at every thought. "When did you get to be such an expert?"

He shrugged, "I found some articles online while you were in the restroom."

"I wasn't in there that long," she said a little shortly.

"I'm a fast reader."

"So, who is this, this pirate or Corsair guy?"

He shook his head dismissively. "Who? No idea. There were a lot of people at play back then. It was big business, the smuggling of slaves during the early years of the Louisiana Purchase, and a lot of profit to make off the suffering and torture of other human beings. A very shameful period in our history, slavery, as far as I'm concerned."

"And it evidently created monsters," she whispered.

"More than a few, I'd suspect," Gabriel said thoughtfully. "But we need to focus on getting its claws out of you, so to speak."

She nodded slowly, "Yeah, how did that happen?"

"Opportunity, I expect."

She hesitated, trying to soak in the big picture, "So, it's not really my fault?"

At that moment, Gabriel had looked at her with genuine surprise, truly taken aback at what she'd said. "What would make you say that, Becca? Of course not. None of this has ever been your fault. You're exceptionally gifted and, yes, vulnerable in some ways because of it. But we're working on that aspect."

She smiled softly, funny how he could send her self-esteem soaring with just a few words. She certainly liked looking at herself through his eyes. "I guess that somewhere along the way, I got into the habit of blaming myself for things. If I could be more this or more of that, none of this would be happening to me."

"I'm sorry for that," he said thoughtfully. "But it's as important as anything else that you shed those kinds of self-destructive thoughts; however, they were fostered on you. Any negativity leaves a vulnerability, a crack if you will, for creatures or even people to take advantage of."

She nodded slowly, truly allowing his advice to soak in. "I'm trying. I guess it's an old habit."

"Well, our society, our culture, is not very helpful to those who don't fit into the mold of what is considered normal. So, it's easy to fall into a pattern of self-incrimination for things we have no power over."

She smiled, "I'm glad I have you in my corner. You've helped me see things, see myself so differently."

"You should. You're amazing, Becca, so gifted," and then he added gently, "Lovely inside and out."

"It sounds like you're fond of me, Dr. Sutton."

And then he was gazing at her intently in a way that definitely made her feel warm inside. "More than fond, Ms. Wells, so dessert, then back to the cottage?"

"No, dessert, then let's take a ride."

"To where?"

"The Pirate House," she said.

Of course, they couldn't really go to The Pirate House. It wasn't there anymore. The best they could do was go to North Beach Road in Waveland, and for some reason, tonight, that was exactly what she wanted.

"You know, you've been through a lot today. You might want to let it be for a night."

Midway through her exceptionally sweet pie, Gabriel seemed to be getting cold feet. "Why? I thought you were gung-ho about getting this taken care of."

He took a sip of coffee before answering her, and she knew from experience that he was trying to think up a response. "The truth is I'm not completely sure about what we're dealing with. I mean that I'm even right about this, much less what the best tactic might be," he said flatly. "And I'm wondering if approaching with more caution might be the best course to take."

She took a sip of her coffee thoughtfully. This was not what she wanted to hear. She wanted a quick fix, a quick antidote, so she could put this behind her. "I'm just talking about a reconnaissance mission, gathering information."

"You're exhausted, Becca, low on energy. These encounters drain you tremendously." She liked and didn't like the concern in his eyes at the same time.

"Yeah, well," she said, trying to formulate the sudden hopefulness she felt about all of this. "I don't know how to explain it. I feel like doing this tonight, going there just to see, just to see if I can pick up something that will help. I've felt such an aversion, fear for so long, but now I want to do this."

He nodded, still looking bothered. "I know. I can feel that from you. But it's still my job to protect you."

"Okay, okay, quick trip. The minute either of us starts feeling it's a mistake, we turn back, okay."

He frowned and took a bite of his pie without answering, but she knew he was giving in, albeit reluctantly.

She felt she was sinking deeper into a sort of altered state the further they traveled down Highway 90 toward Waveland.

"So, there are a host of possibilities of who this wayward entity could be. From your description and the language he spoke in the dream, we can assume he was of French descent."

"Seems so," she replied, her eyes still glued on the fluctuating water of the Gulf of Mexico beyond the beachfront outside her car window.

"An Antoine or Antonio Peytavin was in the house when the Spanish seized it for slave trading. Others connected were his father Enrique, as well as other

Peytavins — Jean, Francis, and Duriblon, as well as associates Jean Blanque, Jean Reynaud, as well as other working-class pirates at the time."

"Working class pirates?" she murmured. "How in the world did you remember all those names?"

"Oh, yeah, I guess I never mentioned it. I have a bit of a photographic memory, not full-fledged, but enough to help significantly during medical school."

"I bet," she said. "But I have no idea who this could be."

"I know," he answered, "so much we simply don't know."

Once they crossed the bridge heading into Waveland, the light had dimmed significantly. She could actually mark a pronounced difference. She began to feel a curious sensation, two actually — a distinct pressure in both her forehead and in her chest.

"Feeling anything?" he asked.

"Yes," she said softly. Thus far, it wasn't painful, but definitely what she'd call a warning shot.

"Do you want to drive down your street to North Beach Road?"

"Yes," she replied. Strange how places had such unacknowledged power over you. Just heading down Whispering Pines again, she was reminded of her anxiety as a young girl. In fact, the memories brought waves of it, fear, anxiety, physical discomfort, sharp pains in places on her body, and then general physical aches. At times, it had felt as though her skin was hurting as it was beginning to do now. And she remembered, remembered the trips to the doctor who would prescribe tranquilizers, antidepressants. *"There is nothing physically wrong with her"* was always the diagnosis.

And then, just about a half block away from her old house, she felt something in her chest, like a physical punch knocking the breath out of her. "Gabriel, stop," she managed to get out breathlessly.

He pulled the car over to the side of the road, then took her hand in his. "What is it, Becca?"

She kept feeling it — panic, fear, flooding over her. "I don't know," she whispered. "I don't know. I feel like I can't breathe, like I'm drowning in it."

Gabriel grasped her hand more tightly, holding it securely and seeming to concentrate on her. "You're tapping in, tapping into all the pain and suffering here."

"Pain? What do you mean, from my house?"

"No, from the other one, the slaver's house. A tremendous negative imprint has been left on the area from it."

Chapter Twenty-Seven

Empty

"You're tapping in, tapping into all the pain and suffering here."

"Pain? What do you mean, from my house?"

"No, from the other one, the slaver's house. A tremendous negative imprint has been left on the area from it."

Becca drew in a deep breath which was no easy task, considering the sensation of breathlessness that she'd been battling. "Well, I guess that makes sense, though I don't remember feeling it to this magnitude when I lived here."

"People get numb to things if they're bombarded with it enough, and if your energy was as low as I'm sure it was, you probably couldn't sense it anymore."

Becca told her mind that she understood what Gabriel was telling her, but physically was another matter. This was nearly unbearable. Beyond feeling entirely out of breath, there was a strange pressure as though someone was actively pinning her down, particularly on her forehead and chest. And they hadn't even gotten close to where the actual Pirate House structure had been. "This seems more active than an imprint Gabriel. It feels—" She took another deep breath that almost felt like a desperate gasp, "so aggressive."

He was still holding her hand, but his eyes were closed as though he was concentrating. "Some places, some energy takes on an aggressive character as though actively defending themselves. They become a haven for those entities with a similar composition."

"In English," she muttered with more aggravation than she meant to. But the irritation felt like it was almost swallowing her alive.

He opened his eyes again, staring at her in the semi-darkness of the car. "It's possible it's still the imprint. It's just all the negative energy has mutated into something hostile."

"Okay," she whispered, "but again, this is not something I remember feeling from before."

"Well, I suppose it could have gotten worse being fed by other negativity in the area, but I would say again that maybe back then, you weren't capable of wholly understanding or sensing what you were dealing with."

"Maybe," she murmured. "But what now? How can we fix it?"

"I don't know that we can," he said softly.

Gabriel knew without a doubt that this was not what Becca wanted to hear. But what he felt reminded him undeniably of Montpelier in Dublin and the Hellfire Club. Too much had happened there to ever wholly eradicate the poison. But again, he didn't know that for sure because they hadn't even gotten close to the epicenter of the activity. "So, do you want to keep going?" he asked.

Becca's eyes widened a bit at that pronouncement. "Are you serious?"

"Maybe just a quick drive through the area. After all, how much worse could it be?"

She laughed impulsively beside him in the car. "Wow! I was expecting that you'd want to play it cautiously and go back immediately. But sure, let's see how bad it is."

He took his hand out of hers and put the car back into drive. "Now stay aware, Becca, and let me know exactly what you're feeling. I'm sure we'll both feel like hell later, but at least we'll have a better idea of what we're dealing with."

"If you say so," she murmured a little bit more light-heartedly than he'd expected.

Was he being reckless? Possibly, but maybe doing the unexpected was exactly what was needed here.

Once they'd driven by her old wood-frame house, the atmosphere momentarily lightened. Oddly, how it shifted, and she had no idea why. "It feels a little better," she said cautiously.

"Okay, well, I guess maybe that makes sense," he said hesitantly. "I'm sure there was quite a concentration of upset for you at your former home, draining, attacks, emotional upheaval, and residue from the trauma of that other girl, the suicide. Maybe you were tapping into some of that coming here again."

"Maybe," she murmured, actually beginning to suspect that Gabriel was as clueless about what was going on here as she was. As they twisted down, heading to the end of Whispering Pine Road, she began to feel other things, loneliness being the operative word, as they got closer to the beach. "This feels creepy."

"Desolate," he murmured. "Are you still feeling the irritation?" he asked.

Becca breathed in deeply, trying to analyze the strange fluctuations of emotion that continued to pass over her. "It's different. I don't know. I feel disconnected somehow."

He reached out, lightly touching her hand. "Just try to focus, separate yourself from what you're feeling." It helped. Just the contact from him made her feel markedly more grounded. It crossed her mind at that moment how the two of them had bonded into this sort of team that supported and bolstered each other in all sorts of ways.

"Separate?" she murmured with a bit of confusion.

"Yes, see if you can distinguish between what are your emotions and those you're picking up from the outside."

Again, she breathed in deeply, and it wasn't as difficult as it had been before, but there was a change, almost a density to the air. "Can you feel how heavy it's becoming, the actual atmosphere?"

"Yes," he answered. "We're getting ready to turn onto North Beach Road."

"Okay," she said. She braced herself as they took that sudden turn in the darkness. She turned to see the water, but all she could see beyond the beach was an inky blackness that sent a tendril of tangible fear down her spine. It occurred to her now, something that should have sifted in much earlier, that it probably hadn't been wise to come down here at nighttime.

"So, what do you think of pirates?"

There seemed to be hesitation in her freshman history class that day. But one dark-haired boy whose name eluded her in the memory did come out with an interesting comment. "You mean like Captain Jack Sparrow in the Pirates of the Caribbean?"

Several years back, she remembered sitting perched on the edge of her desk in the St. Jerome High School classroom. "Well, I was thinking of real pirates."

"Like Jean Lafitte?" This voice belonged to a petite brunette girl.

"Sure, like Jean Lafitte, but I wondered what you think of them. Are they swashbuckling antiheroes as portrayed in media, or were they criminals?"

And then, she did remember some grumbling and various answers thrown out in her direction. "Cool criminals" seemed to be the consensus.

"Cool, huh? Breaking the law, even back then, is cool?" She remembered laughing at that, recognizing at that moment how adaptable history seemed to be to the desires of its consumers and manufacturers.

And then there was some grumbling and young Jeffrey Guilbeaux threw out, "Well, they dressed cool."

She'd shrugged, "Okay, we'll give them that. But don't forget they were thieves, smugglers, and some were also slavers."

"But slavery was legal here," a young man piped up. He was a young black student named Greg Waverly.

"That's true, Greg, but only for a while and in some places. When it wasn't, the cool pirates took advantage, and of course, there was a market for white slavery as well."

That fact seemed to stun more than a few. As Becca recalled, she'd taken the air out of her Louisiana History class that day. And in the later days, Rebecca Wells fielded some complaints from parents who didn't like her take on history. It was probably then that she noted distinctly that history was fluid, relying largely on one's perspective.

"We're getting close."

Gabriel's voice abruptly yanked her out of her contemplations. She'd noted some large, sprawling houses sparsely situated along the side of the road opposite the beach. But not many, and she couldn't remember if that had been the case when she'd lived in the area so many years ago. "It's so dark."

"What are you feeling?" Gabriel murmured.

Again, the million-dollar question, her mind had drifted so oddly back to her teaching days that she felt strangely distanced from what they'd been doing. "I'm not sure. I feel like things have shut down a bit. I'm not picking up anything."

Except for silence, that was the curious thought that floated in. If this area was so toxic, shouldn't she feel it? And then, in a jolt, Gabriel slowed down, pulled the car to one side of the road, and then turned off the engine. "What is it?" she said because he was staring forward into the darkness.

"We're here," he replied quietly.

He thought it was him, the fact that he wasn't feeling much at Montpelier in Dublin that day. He and Garrett Buckley walked for a time outside the ruins of the grand stone hunting lodge on the hill purported to be one of the most haunted places in the area.

He remembered watching Garrett as he quietly perused the landscape. And Gabriel thought, not for the first time, that he was a wash with this psychic business. Because for him, it felt like—

"A vacuum."

A bit shocked, he turned to his companion. "What did you say?"

"I said it feels like a vacuum. That's what you're thinking."

"I-I don't know if I would have used that word, but yes, I guess that would be a good description. I'm just not picking up anything, any feelings at all."

"That's because it's been sucked dry of everything."

"Gabriel, are you sure this is the right place?" She leaned forward in the car, looking out her front window. Of course, she didn't expect to see anything here. There was no plantation house any longer, no actual Pirate House. But she had expected to feel something, given the cascade of events over the past few days.

"Positive," he said quietly.

"But, but I don't understand. I'm not feeling anything, not good, not bad, just—"

"Empty," he said with no emotion.

She looked at him oddly, "Yes, exactly, it feels empty, stripped of everything."

He nodded slowly, "Yes, I suppose that is what a parasite would do. Strip away all the energy."

Chapter Twenty-Eight
Subtle Signs

It was nearly a moonless sky, nearly that is because just the slightest sliver of a crescent moon cascaded across the dark water that was barely moving, as there was no breeze this night. But this wasn't a lake. It was the Gulf of Mexico, governed by deep currents underneath, so there could never be purely placid waters. She felt mesmerized as she watched the gentle waves lightly crash on the beach.

"Should we walk the field?" he asked, but she had her back to him, her back to that place that once had been so long ago and was now a vacant plot of land.

"Why didn't it collapse?"

"Collapse?" he asked with some puzzlement in his voice.

"The tunnel," she murmured. Of course, Becca fully recognized that she was making no sense. But it was the mood that had fallen over her the minute Gabriel had stopped the car, but no, maybe before even that. It had begun when they traveled down the twisted, turning Whispering Pines Road that led past her childhood home.

To say she didn't feel herself now was such a vast understatement.

"The tunnel," she repeated insistently with some irritation because he should know. He was supposed to know her better than anyone. Gabriel was closer to her than she had ever allowed anyone, ever.

"Oh, the tunnel from the Gulf to the house. Good question, sand around here would be unstable, but at some point, if you go deep enough, you should hit rock."

"Yes, rock, and then they could bring all these terrified souls into their brand new life of hell."

"Becca," he whispered, suddenly taking her arm. "You have to detach. You can't allow yourself to be drawn into this negativity."

"But that's the problem, period. I'm not feeling the negativity, the suffering, the horror, nothing. It's all a great cavern."

And then he was leaning against her, his arms wrapping around her waist from behind. "I don't think that's quite true, Becca. You might not feel what you expected, but you are feeling something. So, let's take a quick walk around, then get the hell out of here."

"Will that help?" she whispered distractedly.

"No idea," he answered.

"You know, it might not be obvious, but traces are always left, even at a very subtle level."

"Such as?" he asked Garrett Buckley with some aggravation. Because at that moment, they were standing near one of the most notorious satanic lodges in the world, and Gabriel felt as though he might as well have been in McDonald's on the corner of Veterans Blvd back home.

Garrett had stopped at Gabriel's dry response and looked at him with some perverse measure of satisfaction. "You have to read the subtleties that most people ignore.

For instance, there could be a heaviness in the atmosphere. Of course, some would disregard it as humidity, but it can also signal negative energy."

"Back home, it always feels like that. Louisiana is rife with humidity."

He nodded, "Acknowledged, but other signs as well — grass, foliage more brown than green, people more on edge, irritable, just as you are now, my friend."

"I—" Then he stopped. He was getting ready to reply with some sarcastic retort. But it was true. He was irritated, irritated inexplicably with—

"No particular cause you can attribute to it. And, of course, the negativity invites other emotions, perhaps even darker ones."

"Darker, you mean violent?"

"For some who hold a thin tether of control over themselves, yes, they undoubtedly can be incited to violence."

And at that moment, Gabriel remembered, he was staring at that old stone hunting lodge and, for the first time, feeling a genuine malevolence exuding from it.

Something was off and saying that seemed wholly ineffectual for what he was sensing. Becca appeared and, more than that felt remote to him. Something, or should he say someone, was getting to her. Gabriel had brought a flashlight from the car with them as they began a trek across the expansive plot of flat, freshly mowed grass. The field lay beyond the historical sign that marked the infamous *Pirate House*.

As they'd reached it, just on the side of the road, he'd shown the flashlight on the marker. It read,

According to local tradition, the "Pirate House." located here, was built as early as 1802 and was frequented by famed pirate Jean Lafitte and his associates. Later remodeled as a Greek revival structure, the house is believed to have had a secret tunnel. The house was damaged beyond repair during Hurricane Camille in 1969.

"I thought they weren't sure if Lafitte was even here," Becca had murmured hollowly.

"Better for tourism, I guess, if he had been," Gabriel commented dryly. The mention of the tunnel on the plaque bothered him as if it were something to be proud of. But he knew it probably meant little to nothing, and he was only feeling the subtle effects of negative energy that Garrett had spoken of — primarily, irritation that he must struggle to gain mastery over, irritation that would have him take exception to anything and everything and perceive antagonisms when there were probably none.

And beyond this, the moist grass they were tramping through was probably leaving its freshly cut pieces all over his tennis shoes, shoes that would have to be wiped down as all that living matter carried remnants of the negativity.

"Are you feeling anything?" Becca's voice shattering his petty and bewildering train of thought.

"Yes and no," he said as they trudged through the darkness. He was shining the flashlight ahead of them, but so much was crossing his mind — inhospitable insects on the lower end of the spectrum and snakes up near the top.

"Care to elaborate?"

"Nothing substantial, just a general agitation that seems to grow the further we go."

"Oh," she said quietly.

"And you?" he asked.

"It's not good, but I can't see anything."

And then, practically in the next breath, she stopped abruptly without warning. Becca just stood there, facing the empty field ahead of them. "Becca, what's wrong?"

She continued to stand there frozen, staring forward, then said softly. "It's him." But as Gabriel abruptly shone the flashlight ahead, all he could see was emptiness.

It had something to do with the clouded night sky overhead and the water in the distance. Strangely, the further they walked away from it, the louder the sound became in her ears — subtle but mesmerizing in its way. The sound of the water lapping against the wood was rhythmic, insistently against the wooden hull of the boat, no, the ship, and then the frantic rustling coming from beneath, as they hoisted the captives up to the main deck, bound, gagged, some still struggling against their bondage. And quickly, everything shifted in her mind, and they were in the cave where they docked the ship — the cave where they built the tunnel.

But it was so moist and small, narrow, it felt like a grave. Panic and horror flooded everywhere as they were all confident they were being led to death.

Becca kept moving, her feet not obeying her mind that had begun to scream to Gabriel. *Stop, go back.* But that Becca was somewhere else because her body continued to move forward mindlessly.

Hands were on her, grabbing, pulling her through the dark, moist tunnel made of rock and earth. The stench was horrifying as if something within was rotting.

"Gabriel," she gasped aloud, but he couldn't hear her because the sound never reached her lips.

The hands were harsh, violent, pulling and yanking, and there was laughter at their distress.

And then there were suddenly stairs, wooden stairs that painfully chaffed her bare feet. The cloth gag in her mouth felt as though it was choking her.

And then they stopped the ugly procession, grabbing her roughly and binding her hands into chains built into that cold, damp wall.

The light shone all around the empty field of grass. "Nothing here," Gabriel rasped. Of course, she must be having a vision, but his mind felt muddled, confused by it all.

He grabbed her arm and found it suddenly hot to his touch, as though a fever had taken her. "He's there, standing there," she moaned.

"Becca, listen to me. You need to back away."

She shook her head. "It's horrible, Gabriel, so cold. I can't breathe."

Gabriel pulled her back against him. So hot, her skin was so hot. "Back up, focus, back away," he repeated frantically.

And then suddenly she started sobbing, then screaming. In a panic to reach her, Gabriel shook her almost violently until she finally focused on him.

"Gabriel," she whispered brokenly, throwing herself into his arms. "I was there. I was one of them. I was one of the slaves they chained within the house. And he was there too."

He pulled her against him with determination. "It's all right, Becca. It's all right now."

Chapter Twenty-Nine
Surrender

There were so many possibilities. The fact that Becca was a powerful empath of extraordinary ability was incontrovertible. Gabriel had witnessed this almost from the very beginning of their acquaintance. That first day that she'd come to his house on Dumaine Street, she had connected so powerfully, though clearly unwillingly, with Ellie's lost spirit. He'd had real fears that she would drown right there in front of him and had taken extreme measures to ensure it didn't happen. And then there was the blond girl, Beth, and how powerfully Becca had become linked to her, feeling her emotions, becoming enmeshed in her despair until they were separated, ostensibly ripped apart.

But even with all of this, what had happened tonight, out in that field near the beach where that plantation house had once been, it seemed different somehow — the connection, oddly more intrinsic, personal. At least, that was what he was feeling.

As they drove back to Biloxi in the darkness, his mind was whirling, almost desperate to puzzle through a way forward. And beside him, Becca was largely silent, though not asleep. Even in the dim light, he could see her eyes wide open.

"Are you all right?' he asked for not the first time with genuine concern.

"It depends on what your parameters are?" she murmured. Well, that was good in any case, given what had happened that she could manage sarcasm.

"Let's see, breathing, hopefully calm, aware, not in a mindless panic."

He heard her sigh deeply from the dim light of the car. "Check to all, I guess. I am surprisingly calm, considering everything. And breathing seems to be okay. And also exhausted but unable to close my eyes."

"You'll have to sleep sometime."

"Sleep doesn't feel safe for some very obvious reasons. But what bothers me most is that we don't seem any better off."

"I don't know if that's true," he said softly. "We've gathered information."

"Have we?" she asked dubiously. But Gabriel was convinced they had and that everything that had happened gave them a foot in the door.

After a surprisingly restful and uneventful night, the following morning brought them both at least a little more energy, if not clarity. While Becca was showering, Gabriel tried to reassess everything, clear his mind, and hopefully, be open to any guidance that might filter in. At least, that was his hope.

"Sometimes you can't come at things logically, with reason. You might need to open yourself to other forms of help."

As he was sitting on the sofa finishing his morning cup of coffee in their little Biloxi Airbnb, this particular conversation he'd had long ago with Jean Rampart drifted in. Undeniably she'd been his first and perhaps most impactful mentor on the fantastical journey that his life had evolved into. He put his cup on the glass coffee table in front of him and leaned back, allowing the memory to cascade over him fully.

Back then, they'd been sitting on a yoga mat in her studio in Arkansas after a rather strenuous meditation she'd directed him through. She'd combined the mental process with positions of yoga. Gabriel had always thought he was in pretty good shape, but the contortions she'd walked him through proved otherwise.

"Well, the truth is that empirical evidence is something I've been taught to lean on heavily throughout my life, particularly in my education."

She'd smiled, "Yes, coming from your background, I'm sure it's more of a challenge for you than others to let go of their preconceptions enough to move forward in the field of metaphysics."

She wasn't mistaken. It wasn't as if this thought hadn't crossed his mind many times, but to hear it voiced was another matter. "But then again, I've always had a determined spirit. I don't take well to failure."

"That must be why the end of your marriage was so difficult for you."

He remembered he'd taken a deep breath because that comment oddly felt like a bit of a punch. Not because it wasn't true but because it was, at that point, wholly unacknowledged. "Yeah, maybe so. I've never really thought of it in those terms. But I suppose that could be true."

She nodded in acknowledgment. "Well, Gabe, those who come to a place where they want to know their world in all its glorious truth don't always find it an easy journey. In so many ways, we must unmake ourselves, stripping away the programming we've received through our culture before we can begin to see clearly."

He frowned, "Unmake ourselves? That sounds utterly painful."

"Yes, I suppose it can be. But it all depends on you and how hard you fight it. Understand that you might not always have the answers or be able to access them. You might need help, guidance, and at times access to wisdom that is not readily in your grasp."

"And not to be too simplistic, but how do I access this?"

Another smile that he could only describe as genuinely kind. "Well, we've started with meditation. It's important to recognize that the world you exist in is not just physical."

He leaned back on his hands, trying to absorb what she was telling him. "You mean energy."

"Energy is the beginning, Gabe. Recognize that we are not just this sleeve of flesh that you see when you look in the mirror. And that physical death is not the end of life, just a stage of it. Reality comprises all levels of existence, other dimensions, as well as other non-corporeal forms of life."

He listened, but at that point, admittedly, he still found it difficult to accept. "I think I understand."

And then she'd looked at him intently, though with comfort. "You're on a journey, a spiritual path Gabe. And at some point, you must decide whether you will surrender to it."

He leaned back on the pale blue sofa, clearing his mind, which was no easy task. As Jean had once told him, it begins with breathing — letting his focus entirely be on the physical act of breathing in and out.

"In reducing thought to a minimalistic level, you can begin to eliminate distractions to your meditation." — Jean's instruction had always been very concise, stripped down of extraneous language, which was helpful for his clinical mind.

"At the beginning, distractions from your ordinary mode of thinking will try to intrude but don't resist or embrace it. Just let them pass through and gently float away."

Gabriel continued to breathe deeply, letting his worries, thoughts, and any upset slowly dissipate from his mind. *"Once you achieve this level of calmness, let your intention crystallize."*

After taking one more breath, Gabriel, with focus, formed the need for guidance in his mind. This thought he didn't tether to words but rather a succinct image, an image of Becca in a total state of peacefulness and serenity. It was an easy image to summon because pretty much ever since they'd met, he'd begun focusing on this as the heart of his intent. More than anything, he wanted, no, at this point needed, her to be at peace, to be calm within, and to be in a state of acceptance of who she was.

"Remember, Gabe, at the core of our existence is acceptance, surrender if you will. We must learn to embrace, not reject, the spiritual path that we are on. We must learn to accept that our goal here in this physical existence is to grow, to learn, and to help others. We must find peace in that, acceptance."

As he focused intensely, he found a pull leading him from this place to somewhere else. He wasn't a traveler, so this experience was novel to him. Instinctively, he felt a bit reluctant but then felt a distant voice guiding him.

"Gabe, you must accept this next step in your evolution." It was different than before, not memory of Jean Rampart's voice but something new, something here and now. He knew without a doubt that she was guiding him from her new existence, and today, at this moment, he was still her student.

"Let go, Gabe."

"How can you give up so easily?" Had he really said that to her? He couldn't remember.

Cynthia shook her head. Though, he did remember seeing the pain in her eyes, and he'd been surprised that she still had that much feeling concerning him. He'd forgotten this. He'd forgotten so much. "Sometimes you can't force things," she'd said tearfully. "It's just better to let it go, to accept that whatever was is over now."

It truly had just taken him so long to get out of his own way. He remembered he'd felt angry. He'd felt cheated. And he'd felt as though he'd failed. But then, hadn't Jean said that failure sometimes is part of the path? Sometimes there is much more to learn from failure than success.

"Let go, Gabe," the words were repeated but differently now, in a different context. *"Let go."*

The pull was strong, insistent, bringing him elsewhere. He could still resist and fight it, but instead, he fought for acceptance. *"It will be harder for you than most to achieve that state of surrender. And that will make it much more powerful once you do."*

The swirl now felt as though it was encompassing all of him, his mind, his sight, his hearing. The roar of the waves and the endless night sky stretched over him. And when it finally all settled, he could see that he was standing on a sandy beach. He didn't know if he was pleased, but as he turned around, he could see the outline of the great house barely illuminated in the darkness — The Pirate House.

Chapter Thirty

Beyond the Darkness

"It's all right." His arms were around her in the darkness.

"I feel like I'm coming apart."

"Are you all right?" Before, they'd been riding back in the car. Her wrists still hurt where those heavy manacles had dug into her flesh, and her arms were roughly contorted over her head. But it wasn't really her flesh or her arms or her bones in her shoulders that had cracked and strained at the vicious yanks of the captors.

She shifted with agitation in the darkness of the car.

"Becca, listen to me. You need to back away."

That was before. They were still outside in that field, and all hell was cascading down on her. How had she survived? So much fear, so much terror. This must be what hell felt like.

"Back up, focus, back away." She'd heard his voice, clear, sharp, slicing through all that pain, all that hysteria. And then she felt him. He'd pulled her body against his, buffering her from that torturous pit she'd fallen into.

"I was there. I was one of them," Becca had whispered brokenly.

And he had held her fiercely, battling the demons erupting inside her. "It's all right, Becca. It's all right now." His voice, his words, his energy pulled her from the precipice — an inexplicable balm.

She didn't know how she walked into the cottage. Her legs felt like jelly, matching what was inside. She'd read, of course, about the horrors of slavery, but now she'd felt it, become part of it, terror seeping into her skin, being treated like nothing — like you had no soul. If everyone could feel what she had, they could never minimalize this suffering, this atrocity.

His arm was around her, guiding her out of the car. And she clung to Gabriel because if she hadn't, her legs might not hold her up, her knees might buckle, and she would sink gratefully to the ground.

"Becca, you have to stop all of this. You have to pretend at least to be normal, or you'll never survive in the world." Her mother's voice had been shaky. She'd been firm, trying to help in her way. Back then, there had only been two choices: she was normal or crazy. And if she was crazy, ultimately, they would lock her away somewhere where they, whoever they were, didn't have to deal with her, didn't have to see it.

His arm tightened around her. "Let's go inside," he'd whispered into her hair. And then she remembered what he'd shown her, what he'd taught her. She wasn't crazy. She was gifted. Her world had different boundaries, boundaries that didn't separate her and keep her distant from other people's suffering.

Gabriel had kept her close to him the rest of the evening. Making her tea, but not leaving her, having her next to him in the kitchen. He was afraid for her, afraid she might shatter somehow.

Then later, they sat quietly next to each other on the sofa. And then she'd remembered from the car.

"But what bothers me most is that we don't seem any better off," she'd said.

And he'd answered, "I don't know if that's true. We've gathered information."

"What information, Gabriel?" she asked abruptly because this was the first moment that this thought had occurred to her.

He squeezed the hand that he'd been holding. "Information?" he asked. Of course, the things she said this evening had been so random, so disconnected. He must have no idea what she was talking about.

"In the car, you said we've gathered information."

"Oh, yeah, let all of that rest tonight, Becca. You need to stop thinking about this for a little while."

"But I—"

"No," he said calmly, kissing her softly. "Tonight was traumatic for you. You need to give yourself a little time to recover." But she didn't want to stop. She wanted this over, dealt with, gone.

"I'm tired," she said abrasively.

"Then, let's go to bed," he answered.

She was too tired to shower. But she knew the negative energy they'd encountered was a problem, so she wiped her skin down with a cool cloth. It helped some, helped take away some of the agitation, leaving that pervasive feeling of just being sapped of energy.

Before they'd gotten into bed, he'd insisted she drink a glass of water. "I'm not really thirsty."

"It will help with energy," he'd answered. All evening, he'd been watching her closely. She'd felt it even when he wasn't in her line of sight. She'd felt his eyes on her intently, calmly watching every nuance, every flicker of emotion she displayed. She knew he was worried, but it seemed to go well beyond that.

Maybe he thought she was going to fall into a million pieces.

Maybe she would.

"It's all right." His arms were around her in the darkness.

"I feel like I'm coming apart."

Closer, he pulled her closer against him, and she could feel his warmth bleeding into her, covering her. "I'm here, Becca," he whispered, covering her mouth with his own. She trembled against his skin and genuinely sought to drown herself in his closeness.

"Gabriel," she murmured, feeling such healing, a balm in their intimacy. How was it possible to be so strengthened by another human being? Not just now, not just in intimate moments, but in so many others. "Hold me," she whispered against his mouth.

"I love you, Becca," he said softly as she felt his hands on her just before he began to make love to her. And she thought to echo what he'd said, but it was drowned out in the passion between them. But he must know. He must know what he meant to her.

Becca slowly dressed that morning after her shower, feeling persistent fatigue still clinging to her from the night before. Last night, Gabriel had held her much of the night, made love to her, and that intensely intimate time they'd spent had helped strengthen her, but it still felt like such a steep climb returning to normal, whatever exactly qualified as "normal" for her.

She'd never been like everyone else, never reached that plateau that her mother had encouraged her toward. Although, at times, she'd seemed to fake it well enough. But last night, on that beach, in that great empty field, she'd come undone. She felt, without understanding how or why, that she had been through a tremendous arduous battle and had suffered a somewhat decisive defeat. Of course, that must be nonsense, though it didn't stop her from feeling it strongly.

Once she'd dried her hair and dressed in a comfortable button-down shirt and jogging pants, she headed into the den. As she moved through the house, she noticed it seemed oddly quiet. She'd sensed something unusual, and once she'd gotten out of the shower, it only intensified as she made her way toward the den. So strange, how strong the energy felt even before she'd entered the room. As she crossed the threshold, she immediately saw Gabriel sitting on the sofa, but he was so still, leaning his head back as though he'd slipped into a light sleep. She opened her mouth to speak to him but then felt distinctly as though she shouldn't.

"It's all right, just wait," so odd. It was a voice, but a voice in her mind. Silently, she sank into the light wicker rocker across from the sofa and waited quietly, watching

him until he stirred after a few minutes, then opened his eyes, looking at her a bit disoriented.

"Becca," he said.

"Where were you?" she asked very softly.

Chapter Thirty-One

A Haunted House

"What does it feel like to travel in the astral state?"

"What does it feel like when you dream?"

That was often the nature of their sessions together, questions and answers. Even if they started somewhere intrinsically superficial, they would wind into profound territory, eventually. His questions, Jean's answers, then her questions, led him deeper into a tangent of thought.

"Everything's connected. Even if you can't perceive it immediately, you will find this is so."

It was a concept that she had banged into his head repeatedly. But then again, not all at once, he would find that she was right. There were always threads, threads connecting.

He had to consider her question before answering — the one about dreams. "It feels different at different times."

She nodded slowly, "Explain."

"Sometimes I dream, and it feels like regular life, though there are elements that seem extraordinary."

"Such as?"

"Oh, maybe creatures flying around that I don't recognize, colors that I don't see in everyday life, people I run into that I usually would not cross paths with."

"People?"

"Politicians, movie stars, I met Farrah Fawcett once."

He remembered that had made her smile. "Before or after her death?"

"Um, after, I think."

"And are you sure you didn't really meet her in your dream, her spirit?"

"I-uh, is that possible?"

"Of course it is. Haven't you ever met a relative in your dreams who has passed on, a grandparent or someone else?"

He had to consider. As a matter of course, he didn't usually remember dreams. He'd largely discounted them, made no effort to recall them. But some, some did persist in his memory. "Yeah, sure, I've seen my grandfather, uncles, all my grandparents."

They were sitting across from each other on a yoga mat, having gone through a cycle of light exercise before beginning their conversation. "And did it never occur to you that this was a contact, Gabe?"

He breathed out deeply, no sighed really, because the truth was his mind had never traveled in that direction. Dreams he'd always considered simply the realm of wishful thinking, imagination, though the truth was that they'd never genuinely fulfilled that particular function for him. "No, Jean, that thought has never occurred to me."

She nodded again, undaunted, it seemed. "So, let's return to your question about astral traveling. Like the dream experience, it can feel like many different things. And that is a good compass for you because, as it is, in dreams, we travel astrally — sometimes not very far. In some instances, dreams feel very similar to our perception of our physical reality. But in others, they feel completely different, an extraordinary experience as we venture out from our dimension into other realms of existence. Sometimes we feel as ourselves, with our body connected, and at other times not, more as moving, thinking energy.

"So, what's real?"

And then she laughed softly, "Why all of it, Gabe, all of it is real."

Thought felt unfocused, rather more expansive where he was standing.

"What do you think a haunted house looks like?"

"Hmm," he'd taken a moment to consider even though he was only ten. Anna was beside him, staring out the attic window of their Virginia wood-frame house. They peered into the pitch darkness of the night, darkness that was complete except for the lights of a few stray fireflies and the crescent moon overhead, occasionally peeking from beneath the quixotic cloud cover. "Well, I suppose it might be old."

"Does it have to be old?" she asked in all earnestness.

"I dunno, maybe not. But the one I can see in my mind is old. And it's dark all around it, like tonight. The house is white with pillars in front."

"Pillows? That's not scary."

He frowned. Anna was only a few years younger than him, though she could be vexing. "Pillars, you know, columns, like on the White House."

"Oh, okay, so what makes it haunted?"

"Well, there's a fog around it that seems to cling to it, even when it shouldn't be there."

"Where does it come from?"

"It comes from the sadness of the people trapped."

"The people or the ghosts?"

He considered because even at that age, he considered just about everything. "The ghosts, I guess. I mean, would you want to be trapped in an old house forever?"

"Is it a nice house?"

"No, not really, it creaks and is dusty, and there are spiders."

"I don't like spiders. But where would they go if they weren't ghosts?"

"Somewhere else, I guess, where everyone goes after they die."

"You mean heaven," Anna said softly in her most innocent voice.

"Hopefully, heaven."

"Well, not the other place. That would be terrible."

And then he sighed though he was only ten. "Yeah, terrible."

It felt as though he was still in his body as he refocused on where he'd found himself. He could feel a chilling breeze from the cold water of the Gulf tearing through him, and in the distance, he could indeed see that imposing pale house with columns and a heavy mist surrounding it in the darkness.

There was no electricity, though something kept it illuminated. He stared overhead and saw a nearly full moon spilling light into the sky. And more than that, he could feel it powerfully beneath his skin, a movement, an overwhelming typhoon of energy emanating from it.

He pulled his vision back to earth because it would have been so easy to feel pulled into its orbit and away. Away from the reason he'd come here.

It really did seem as though he was walking as he began his journey toward the house. Thinking had expanded, as his awareness encapsulated much more than his physical self could acknowledge.

What do you hope to accomplish?

There was that question from somewhere floating in the air — goals, achievable goals, as his analytical mind softly reminded him. He must find a way to help Becca. He must break this apparition's hold on her. He reminded himself and solidified those targets in his mind. Here, there was so much stimuli, so much thought. It would be easy to be distracted, to drift away with all the new discoveries.

So strange as he moved toward the house, it felt undeniably like trudging through some sort of muck. He looked down and could tangibly see his shoes had disappeared, becoming immersed in the unstable swampy surface. But it hadn't been that way when he and Becca had gone to the beach.

This wasn't physical. He reminded himself. It was symbolic.

He lumbered, actually, with effort, shuffled toward the house. It was illuminated from within. What sort of light would they have back then? Oil lamps, perhaps.

What he felt to be his body was heavy, weighed down the closer he got.

"What do you think a haunted house looks like?"

It looks like this one. He could answer his younger sister now. It looks and feels like this one. A structure that is no more yet still can dominate the landscape in its and nearby dimensions.

"It's negative energy you're feeling, Gabe." Jean Rampart's voice guided him. "There is a profound concentration of it here on this plane, so strong it's still bleeding into your plane of physical existence."

"What can I do?" he asked, as he'd just reached the front of the house and could either climb its decaying steps or turn back.

"Try to help," was her whisper.

"No one would want to go to the other place, would they?" young Anna had asked, or had she?

"We make our own hell." It had been the answer that he'd never voiced.

And in the next instant, the grand double doors at the entrance of the Pirate House creaked before they slowly glided open.

Gabriel Sutton took a deep breath before he ascended the front steps leading to the entrance.

Chapter Thirty-Two

Raveneau

As Gabriel crossed the threshold of the enormous house, so many thoughts rushed through his mind at once — his sessions with Jean, his experiences with Garrett, but mostly and primarily his relationship and the time he'd spent with Becca. And the thing that haunted him the most was that he hadn't told her explicitly that he loved her, was completely and irrevocably in love with her. Yes, in whispers, in deeds, in actions, but not in words — cold hard words in the light of day, not the throes of passion. He had not told her in starkness, in unambiguous clarity. That was important. And as he was journeying into possibly the mouth of hell, he knew that would be the one regret if, well, if things didn't go his way.

His tennis shoes still felt sloshy from the tread through the marshy grounds approaching the house. In fact, they felt chilled, as though the water had not been just thick and muddy but cold as well. His body was bathed in sweat, and he questioned, for not the first time, why he felt his body at all as he was in some sort of astral state, devoid of physical matter.

But as Jean had explained to him, the experiences of the astral state were as wide and varied as one could imagine. Wherever he found himself, whatever plane of existence, there was a tangibleness at hand. It felt bad — creepy, draining, and physically taxing.

"You can't stay here long." Jean's voice or just his wishful thinking, though at the moment Gabriel did choose to believe that she was with him.

He walked through the foyer — dark wood but sparse furniture except for a few long tables against the wall and ornate bronze mirrors on either side of the hallway. Crossing another threshold, he entered a room containing a massive staircase leading to the upper floors. On either side of him were double size doorways that led to parlors. It was a standard plantation house floorplan. He'd seen it before, with some variation in every house he'd ever toured—a staircase, an interior gallery upstairs, rooms on the right, rooms on the left. Downstairs was the same, parlors on the right and left, and kitchen in an exterior building often connected. Of course, some had more rooms and were more ornate, but all had French doors along their parlors to accommodate variations in weather. They were, at their heart, a utilitarian house.

But this one, for the moment, seemed to be abandoned. He moved sluggishly to the left of what he suspected was a mahogany staircase. Because it was difficult to see, the light was dim, shadowed, only supplied by flickering, inconsistent lamps. This parlor was a large one. His eyes scanned across a modest wallpaper and furniture sparsely spread here and there, some tables, some armchairs, one of those uncomfortable-looking satiny Rococo sofas, and a fluttering fireplace. As he drew a deep breath, there was a stab in his chest, a distinct pain.

"Why are you here?" The voice came from across the room, and an oversized wingback chair in the shadows that he hadn't even noticed when he entered.

He turned to its direction. "Who—" Then he stopped. Who or what exactly was he speaking to?

"Englishman, answer me," he spoke in a thick but guttural French accent.

He held his ground in the center of the room, not wanting to get much closer. "I've come to help." He said strongly because he was at a loss for what to say.

"Help what?" he or rather it responded. "I rule here. What is there to help?"

"Rule? What exactly?" he asked. He registered, for not the first time, the thick French accent this apparition was speaking with. Then why was he hearing him in English?

Thought transference, symbolic, remember.

"Did you bring her, the girl, with you?"

His heart sank. A Shade, remember, this is not an actual spirit. It only believes it is. "No, I've come alone."

And then the figure stood up, but Gabriel still could see little of him except that he was tall, tall, and broad. "You're of less use to me."

"I thought we could talk, find out what you want."

And then it started to laugh, a low rumbling laugh that made Gabriel remember this was the stuff of nightmares. "What I want is life."

Gabriel sighed deeply, feeling that pain in his heart escalate. Jean had told him that he could not remain here long. "Tell me your name."

"My name is Raveneau Surcouf."

He felt his head spin a bit. Not Peytavin or Lafitte, just one of the working class, not exactly what he expected. "Then you're just a corsair, a pirate."

And the towering specter began to move closer, and Gabriel shuddered as his face finally came into view, scarred, deformed as though a knife had slashed across it. "I rule here, and now you will die."

At those words, he felt himself fall until his knees cracked on a hard wooden floor, a floor where hands were reaching out, grabbing his legs, his shoulders, and trying to pull him beneath, beneath into the dark, dank tunnels that he knew held suffocating death.

His head spun as he struggled, then he was yanked back abruptly, viciously into his body. When he could finally open his eyes, he blurrily focused on Becca standing over him, staring at him.

"Where have you been?" she said with fear in her eyes.

His head still throbbed though the cup of hot tea and the aspirin Becca had given him were slowly helping. All in all, Gabriel felt he'd come out of his trip to hell pretty unscathed, except for his pride, which screamed that the whole business had been futile.

Becca was staring out the window, hands on her hips, clearly deep in concentration. "Raveneau Surcoaf? Are you sure he wasn't lying to you?"

He leaned back on the couch. "Hard to say. He was a thieving pirate. I suppose he could have been lying."

Then she looked over at him with a bit of a sarcastic frown. "You're pretty chipper, given what you've just been through."

"Yes, well, I'm a bit devastated. I had real hopes of putting things straight."

"All by yourself?"

He took another sip of hot tea, which, while burning his lips, felt somewhat comforting at the same time. "I've never said I didn't have delusions of grandeur."

"But really, Raveneau? A bit over the top," she murmured with distraction.

"I don't know. It might be standard for pirates. But this guy, he was big, towering, it seemed. I can't believe he actually looked like that. But then again, everything could have been symbolic."

She nodded, crossing her arms in front of her but still not approaching the sofa. "Well, my impressions of him were that he was always a hulking guy, sort of apish looking."

"Yes, not too polished, maybe a bit of a working-class pirate."

"And yet, he's the one who has stuck around."

"Or part of him has maybe, maybe a large part. A part that's not smart enough to move on."

"You said he was a Shade. Do Shades move on?"

He put the tea down on the coffee table, feeling completely drained but also having a distinct aversion to sleep. This journey made him feel distinctly vulnerable, as though a door had opened that Gabriel felt ill-equipped to navigate.

"You know, you could have told me what you were planning," she added softly.

Gabriel straightened up, a bit surprised, though, in doing so, it felt as though every bone in his body ached to high heaven. "It wasn't planned, Becca. It just kind of happened."

She nodded slowly, still looking unconvinced. "Something could have happened to you, Gabriel, something terrible."

"Now you know how I feel about you when you do all those extraordinary things that you do."

"But you're always with me. I-I wasn't there with you. I just can't stand the thought of —" Then she stopped abruptly.

He held out his hand to her, and she finally relented, coming to sit next to him on the sofa. Gabriel pulled her close against his side, wrapping his arm around her. "I just wish I'd been able to do more."

She shrugged, "Well, we've identified the culprit. But now, what do we do about him?"

"Yes, that is the question." He pulled her more tightly against him, so liking the feel of her warmth. "There is one thing, though, one regret I had when I found myself making this journey."

"What's that?" she murmured.

"That I hadn't told you something."

She was quiet beside him, waiting, then murmured, "Yes?"

"I love you, Becca. With all my heart and soul, I am completely and totally in love with you."

It was still for a moment, a long moment during which he wondered if she'd even respond. Then she reached out, taking his hand in hers. "I know that, Gabriel."

"You know?" That was not exactly the response he was expecting.

"I am an empath," she whispered with a soft smile in her voice.

"Well, I don't have your gift, so you have to tell me things."

"Like I love you too?"

The room around them felt more welcoming now, not harsh and difficult as it had been a few moments ago. Now it was beginning to seem as though hope was a distinct possibility. "Yes, like that," he answered.

"I do, Gabriel. I love you too."

And at her words, the fatigue seemed to lift, and he pulled her into his arms more closely, kissing her passionately and repeatedly until everything but the two of them faded away.

Chapter Thirty-Three

A Plan

She felt stronger. Being with him, close to him, literally in his arms, made the fear that had felt like a hallmark in her life fade away. The anxiety that had always been background noise in her existence was waning.

Becca felt understood.

She felt accepted wholly. And somehow, that had become a path to accepting herself.

Some might, she supposed, misinterpret this as a dependency. But it wasn't that, not at all. She was feeling strength within herself now, not a will-o'-the-wisp to be blown about by other's decisions, other's desires. Knowing who and what she was had made her feel strong within her core and capable of much.

"You're thinking a lot," Gabriel whispered into her hair. He was still holding her, but somehow, she believed he'd fallen asleep.

"I didn't know you were awake."

"Your intensity woke me up."

She wiggled a bit within his embrace. "It did not."

"Of course, it did. I felt you puzzling out all the world's problems. It shook my slumbers."

"You exaggerate," Becca murmured with lightness in her heart. How easy it would be to stay in this lovely bed in this lovely cottage indefinitely. And not face—

"Raveneau."

"What?" She stiffened just a bit as though cold water had been splashed across her lovely reverie.

"You're wondering how to defeat him."

And then she sighed deeply, audibly. "Is that what we're going to do? Defeat him? Is that even possible?"

Gabriel tightened his embrace, making her unconsciously relax again, or melt a bit might be a better description. "I'm not sure what's possible. It might be that all we can hope for is a measured victory."

"Measured victory? I can't begin to know what that looks like."

"Or maybe just a well-executed escape."

"Sounds like you're targeting your expectations rather low."

"No," Gabriel murmured before pulling her directly against his skin. "Not at all," he said huskily as he began to kiss her deeply.

It was midafternoon before things began again in earnest. They'd spent yesterday evening and most of the morning in bed together, determined it seemed to spend much-needed time away from the business at hand, the pirate business as it was.

But Gabriel didn't consider it wasted time. They needed to recharge, to solidify the bond between them that was only strengthening over time. It was confounding to him in some ways and astounding in others. He'd had a ringside seat to many relationships that, over time, just seemed to atrophy or at least erode into disarray. His marriage with Cynthia was a case in point. To say they didn't bring out the best in each other was such an understatement. Their being together was a detriment to each other, causing pain, causing negativity. Of course, he couldn't see it at the time. It was easy to cling to what was familiar, even if that familiar thing was poison to you.

But this, what was now between him and Becca, he never would have thought at the beginning that this relationship could grow as it had. When she first came to him for help, she was guarded, caustic in some ways. But over time, she'd come to trust him, let him in, and open doors for him that he never thought was possible. And he hoped in earnest and truly believed that he was doing the same for her. They genuinely complemented each other in so many unexpected ways.

And now, they would be putting all of this to the test.

"What is your plan?" she asked from the open kitchen across the room. That was the thing about this snug little cottage. Just about everything was in earshot.

He smiled, settling onto the sofa with his cup of tea. They'd had a late breakfast, sort of brunch, perfectly leisurely, which suited him just fine and, actually, suited his plan as well. They had to be in the right mental space for this endeavor — calm, relaxed, and positive. "You're sure I have one."

"I've never known you not to have some sort of plan."

He nodded, then patted the spot next to him on the sofa. "Come sit down, Becca."

Slowly, she drifted over to where he was, taking her time before settling in next to him. "You know I feel so good. I really don't want it to end."

He put his arm around her. The contact between them, especially skin to skin, was nothing short of electric, creating energy, he was convinced. "It's important to hold onto this feeling of peace and confidence. Thoughts, emotions are so much more powerful than you think."

"I'll try, Gabriel. But how does this help us?"

"I've been thinking, thinking about this entity."

"Raveneau?"

"Yes, but at its core, it's a lower life form. It's alive, but more in a rudimentary way like bacteria, a parasite needing certain things to maintain its existence."

"So, he's really not a ghost?"

He shook his head. "No, I wasn't picking up any sort of evolved sort of soul. He's a shadow, a shadow that has persisted by acquiring energy."

"Energy? Because he's a drainer."

He took her hand in his, holding it securely. "There are many types of drainers. But this thing, I believe, is an emotional drainer."

"Emotional? What does that mean?"

"The more upset someone is, the more they are controlled by negative emotion such as fear, anger, sadness, then they become vulnerable to this kind of draining."

She hesitated. "That girl, the one who killed herself, he, I mean it, was draining her."

"I believe so. It's a vicious cycle. What Raveneau can do is inspire fear, great upset which enables it to drain, feeding it, enabling it to continue to exist."

"And me?"

"It's clear you have a great well of natural energy, Becca. But being an empath with such profound abilities, you've also tapped into a lot of despair, upset."

"And it was able to drain me because of it?"

"Yes, where you lived was so close to that place, The Pirate House, where so much suffering occurred, compounding that with your sensitivities and the imprint in your house left by that unfortunate girl. Well, you can see why it is so reluctant to give up that link to you."

He could feel it through her skin as the realization hit her. And he could also feel a measure of panic accompanying it. "Becca," he murmured. "I must tell you it isn't just important you stay calm. It's essential."

She breathed sharply, "All right, Gabriel, I'll try, but all of this feels overwhelming."

"I know, but it doesn't have to be. There is power in understanding things."

"But how do we change all of this?"

"Well, we meet it head-on together."

That afternoon they went shopping, not for souvenirs that certainly would have pleased her more, but instead for clothing. Gabriel insisted they get comfortable light-colored, preferably white shirts and pants. She ended up with a loose cotton top and matching yoga pants, and he with a white t-shirt and white jogging pants. And then he insisted they wash them to rid them of any residual energy.

"But what if they shrink?" she'd asked.

"Heat, hot water, destroys energy. It's best," he'd explained.

Luckily, the clothing she'd bought was roomy. So, shrinkage didn't seem to be an issue. And then, there was another stop at a nearby department store for white candles, salt, and two glass bowls. "What are we cooking up?" she asked teasingly.

"Protection," he'd murmured. And she knew that voice, in fact, was quite familiar with it. Gabriel was in the zone, so to speak, determined, focused, and ready to get down to work.

It was around three in the afternoon when it became clear to her what was happening. They'd shifted some of the furniture in the den, and Gabriel had placed the white candles, bowls of water, and saucers of salt in opposite corners of the blue plush carpet in the den. He was forming a sort of circle with just enough room in the middle for—

He pointed to the center space, "Us."

"Us?" she repeated a little dubiously.

He nodded, "Yes, we're going back to the Pirate House together."

"And how exactly are we doing that?"

"Through meditation, but together."

"And you think that's possible, Gabriel?"

"I do. If we're calm, focused, and stick together. We can do this." He held out his hand for her. "I do believe we can do this, Becca."

She could see the resolve in his eyes, but the problem was that she didn't feel it. She felt dread in the pit of her stomach, the fear of those poor souls chained against the walls of that tunnel leading from the Gulf of Mexico to the Pirate House. "Even if we get there, what can we do?"

He pulled her into his arms. "Whatever we need to make sure this thing never bothers you again."

Chapter Thirty-Four

Obligations

Home, curious word — it's time to go home. Let's go Home. Where is your Home? These were the extraneous thoughts that continued to persist.

"Try to let everything go. Allow every thought to just leave your mind of its own accord." Gabe's voice was so strong and direct. But more than that, he held her hands in his. Sitting directly across from her, he faced her within the protected circle he'd constructed within their small bungalow. This was so different from the other journeys, astral journeys that she'd taken virtually alone.

Through the touch of their hands, she could feel a connection with him. Through his skin, she could feel his energy, his calm state of mind influencing her, strengthening her, calming her as well.

"Becca, remember where your home is." She straightened up with surprise at the sound of that particular voice, although her eyes continued to be closed.

"What is it?" Gabriel asked, immediately sensing the shift in her.

"I don't know, something filtered in," she said shakily. "It sounded like my mother's voice."

Again, she could feel through their connected hands. He was considering. "Try to stay focused. Let the thoughts, impressions flow through you, but try not to link to them."

She understood immediately what he was telling her. That was how this empathic thing worked. If she adhered herself to another's emotion, another's thought, it became complicated. "Okay, I'll try," she whispered.

"Becca, remember, you belong here," It pulled at her, her mother's voice, insisting that she be elsewhere. Now she could see it in her mind. That house, that painful house in Waveland, rose in a vision.

"Be careful," Gabriel instructed from somewhere a bit more distant now.

And the next moment, it came like a wave washing over her painfully. This was not the Pirate House, but it felt oddly and equally as caustic in this instant. It was becoming more concrete now, the small wood frame house they'd lived in for only two, or was it three years? Why would such a brief stretch of time feel so significant? "We need you here, Becca." Whispers, demands, tendrils were pulling at her.

"I can't," she murmured fearfully.

His hands squeezed hers, tightening, and she could feel his warmth seeping into her. "It's all right. It's all right to let go of some of the pain."

Her mother's face appeared in her mind, and she could feel a stab in her heart. "She was always so unhappy. And I felt. I felt—"

"Responsible for her," Gabriel articulated her thoughts smoothly.

She felt a bit stunned at the acknowledgment, remembering the feeling of sadness so often when she was near her. "I could always feel that pain with her, as though it was mine to bear."

"Try to breathe in deeply, Becca." She followed his instruction, still experiencing all that dormant, turbulent emotion digging at her. "Now let it go. Release the breath and the pain with it. Release it into the universe. You were a child. That was not yours to take on."

It wasn't easy. Oddly, it felt like a betrayal, yearning to be free of that disturbing emotion, but she did as he asked and felt some of the sadness she'd carried within leaving her. And she felt lighter for it. But then, out of nowhere, another sensation took hold abruptly. It felt distinct, as though tight cords had wrapped around her and were squeezing the breath out of her chest. "Gabriel," she whispered raggedly.

"I know. It's fighting this. Now follow my lead. Repeat after me. I am reclaiming my energy."

"I am reclaiming my energy," she murmured brokenly.

"I am severing all bonds that no longer serve me."

"I am severing all bonds that no longer serve me," she echoed.

"I walk the path of light and positivity and will no longer tolerate anything binding me to what is not of my higher good."

Slowly, she repeated his words and felt an acute release within her chest. Almost astonished, she whispered, "It's better."

"Good," Gabriel said. "Now imagine us both cloaked in pure white energy."

She concentrated, still feeling resistance somewhere, but she battled to hold onto that image in her mind. As she funneled her focus into this positive thought, into the vision of the two of them protected, the image of that old house swirled and drifted away. For the first time, possibly in her entire life, she felt release from those obligations which were not hers to bear. "It's better," she repeated softly.

"Good, try to hold onto that feeling," he directed.

"I'll try," she responded, and then she felt a distinct shift within him. It was more than clear that Gabriel was guiding this voyage. He was now targeting that place, that place where Raveneau still dwelled. "Gabriel, are you sure?" she questioned with concern. Despite the progress they'd made on the first leg of this journey, she was still fearful of what was to come.

"Yes, don't be afraid. We must strike while we have an advantage," she heard him whisper. And the last thought that traveled through her mind before it began was that she knew where Home was now. It was truly and completely with him.

Gabriel focused deeply on his connection with Becca. It was essential that they stay linked to one another through this journey. He had clearly witnessed her severing some of the energy bonds still binding her to that house in Waveland. They were energy bonds that had been exploited by the creature that still dwelled in the Pirate House.

It was becoming more evident that through a complete lack of understanding of her nature, Becca had been ostensibly used by others for energy. Linking with them through her empathic tendencies, she was then drained of energy by those going through their own pain and upset. There certainly was no problem aiding people by giving energy when needed, but to have it taken away without consent was another matter.

And while this thing, this shadow, they were entangled with was indeed such an offender, it was by no means the only one. Too many who possessed such draining abilities or acquired them through artificial means felt entitled to do so. It was as much a problem as individuals exploiting others through criminal means.

"Gabe, focus," he could feel Jean's voice somewhere in his mind, guiding him, just as she once did in their meditation sessions together.

It was true. At this vulnerable junction, it would be too easy to be swept up in a tangent counterproductive to their goals. In fact, for him, there was only one goal he had — freeing Becca from Raveneau's influence.

"Gabe," Becca's voice, stronger now, her hands still resting warmly in his. "I'm ready." Once again, he cleared his mind and focused his energy on their target.

"All right, let's go," he answered.

Chapter Thirty-Five

Playing His Hand

"You shouldn't go in there!"

Whispers were floating around her as they moved. Her vision had swirled into a mass of indecipherable color, but she still could feel Gabriel's hands holding hers.

"It isn't safe." Another whisper floating by from somewhere, but whose voice? She knew it but couldn't quite make it out. And then there was a rush of motion, almost like being abruptly yanked away to another place, and Gabriel, Gabriel's hands slipped away from her grasp.

"Wait," Becca tried to say, but it was muffled out in the storm, in the roar of a vicious storm.

For an instant, just an immovable second, she stood on the beach facing the ship, that magnificent, horrible ship tossing and leaping desperately in the turbulent waters off the shore. She remembered thinking, no praying, that the lightning would thrash it to pieces, and it would be swallowed into a grave in the watery depths. But then she felt the rope around her hands behind her being yanked tighter and an ugly voice rasping in her ears as her knees buckled. She collapsed onto the gritty wet sand. "Vous ne pouvez pas vous échapper. Tu es un esclave maintenant."

As she kneeled on the rough, abrasive surface, nausea rose in her stomach, and she vomited uncontrollably onto the cold hard beach. In response, she was jarringly kicked in the back with the toe of a heavy boot before she collapsed sideways into a jumble of pain everywhere.

"Gabriel," she called out in her mind, but there was nothing, no sense of him anywhere.

"You shouldn't go there," the whisper again as her eyes glossed over into blackness and into the swirl of the storm. She could hear it distantly, the rumble of the thunder, the waves crashing, but it began to recede into the background as something new moved to the forefront.

The brightness filled her vision, even though it was an overcast day. Her head was swimming with disorientation, and the emotions — terror, anger — still coursed through her combatively from what she had just experienced.

Becca found herself standing on the sidewalk, facing the house on Dumaine Street, Gabriel's house. As it all solidified, she felt utterly confused. This wasn't right, wasn't their goal at all. They were supposed to be headed to The Pirate House. Why was she here?

She looked around. She was alone, entirely alone. No one was walking the sidewalks, no cars driving by, nothing, no sound of birds rustling in the trees, just enveloping silence.

Becca stopped, steeling herself. Control and calm were the things that Gabriel had told her to focus on. She must not allow her emotions to take over.

"You mustn't go in there." It wasn't a whisper anymore. It was loud. It was concrete. "It isn't safe."

She turned to her side and could now see clearly who was speaking to her. It was Beth, Beth Wallace, the girl from St. Jerome High School where she had taught, the same girl she and Gabriel had tried to help but had just vanished. "Beth?' she asked with confusion. How could this be?

She looked at her with that same look of wide-eyed terror she remembered from her visions. "He's in there. It's not safe."

"Who's in there?" she asked.

"Him, that man, that thing," she whispered. Becca turned back to face the house on Dumaine Street and saw the door open. Gabriel was standing there dressed just as when they first met, smiling at her.

"It's all right, Rebecca. Everything's all right now. Come inside."

She turned to ask Beth to join them, but she was gone. Becca was standing alone again on the street. There was something, something in the back of her mind, but it was clouded now. Gabriel still stood there on the porch, smiling, waiting for her. Somehow everything must be all right now. So, she shakily headed up the steps toward him.

"You're not that powerful."

That thought permeated his mind as he stared down at the courtyard from the window of the St. Charles Avenue townhouse where they lived.

"You're not that powerful, Gabriel." That tangential thought had been repeated with a voice, in fact, his wife's voice.

He turned from the window, glancing across their den or, might he more aptly say, parlor the way it was decorated. She'd wanted traditional, antiquated New Orleans furniture, furniture it seemed from primarily a century before. Even the sofa had that oddly uncomfortable Chesterfield construction. "What did you say?" he asked directly.

"I said you're not that powerful, Gabe. You can't expect to save all your patients," she said lightly. Perhaps a bit too lightly in this instance, he thought.

"I didn't expect this," he murmured. "I thought Mr. Crawford's Addison's Disease was well-managed."

Cynthia stopped fluffing pillows for a moment on the Chesterfield and eyed him with what he could only term as an expression that lacked compassion. "You know, you're not God, Gabe. People die all the time."

Her cool demeanor and hard words seemed to take the air out of his chest a bit. He knew Cynthia had a practical streak, but he didn't remember her being on this level of unfeeling. But then again, he was confused. Was this a memory? Wasn't he, in fact, supposed to be doing something else?

And then she looked at him with a measure of disdain, "Come on, Gabe. Try to shake it off. We'll go out for lunch and forget all about it. There isn't anything else you can do for poor Mr. Crawford. He's well beyond your help now, not that it did him much good anyway." And she said that with a smile, artfully brushing her long black hair behind her shoulders.

And it was, undeniably, a bit too much. "I think you've overplayed your hand," he said quietly.

And then she stopped smiling, looking at him with a shrewd expression that, in all his memory, he had never seen on his ex-wife's face. "Did I? You know, it's probably having my attention split. My best efforts, you see, are needed elsewhere."

And then he felt a swirl of dizziness in his head, like a storm surrounding him, and Gabriel found himself against the wall of a very dank, damp cave with a low ceiling and both his hands manacled in chains over his head. The cold, clammy smell, or rather a stench, rose in his nostrils — the stench of decaying flesh, mold, and mud around him.

He concentrated firmly, controlling himself. This, all of this, was meant to inspire terror and panic in him. Clearly, clearly, something went wrong on their journey, their journey to the Pirate House. But Becca, he jerked, looking around frantically. Where was Becca?

"Upstairs," was the answer, though clothed in a thick French accent. Out of the shadows on one end of the cave, a figure moved out of the darkness. It was that man, the huge imposing dark-haired man he'd seen before. "Don't worry. She's being taken care of."

"I thought you didn't speak English."

He stopped in front of him, smiling with a smug, self-satisfied expression that Gabriel very much wanted to slap off his face if his hands had been free to do so. "I knew a smattering, and of course, the rest I can pull right out of your mind." He poked one of his stubby fingers right on the center of Gabriel's forehead, making his thoughts more clouded than they had been before. "As I said, you're not that powerful. You should have stayed away."

He took a breath, focusing on trying to track Becca. It was true. He felt her, felt her near through a connection that they had solidified during their relationship. She was near but caught in a fog, confusion. "What are you doing to her?"

"Doing? Nothing yet," and then he smiled again. That unshaven face looked like it had some strange scar from the end of one ear to his neck. Evidently, someone had taken a shot at cutting his throat but mangled the job — no doubt, regular pirate sort of fare. And then he laughed, and Gabriel almost gagged on the stink of his breath. He was so close to him. "You're worried about your woman, aren't you?"

"Let her go," he rasped. "You can keep me."

And then another guttural laugh. What? Did he practice this stuff to seem sinister? "You? Why would I want you? She's the one with the power, the real power. And she and I are old friends. Maybe I'll make her my woman."

Gabriel yanked on the heavy iron chains, which only served to send shots of pain through his wrists. "She'll see through you, just like I did."

And then something passed through those nearly black eyes that Gabriel felt even more than he saw, concern. "You know, little man, what you didn't realize was that I've always had this gift, this gift of foraging around another's mind and finding their weaknesses, finding them and making them come to life."

Raveneau walked away from him and ran his hand along the cold, clammy walls. "The ones we brought down here to keep until we sold them. I would fill their minds with torments of their homeland just to snatch it away again. Sometimes they would cry, and sometimes they would scream in pain."

Gabriel felt anger rising in him that he struggled to quell. This was what this thing wanted, so much uncontrolled emotion that he could then drain energy from him. This was, after all about getting as much energy from him and clearly from Becca. "Well, that's something to put on your resume," he said flatly.

"She felt it when she was here."

"Here," he said, suddenly feeling a flood of recognition—a past life. She must have had a past life as a slave. That would explain the bizarre link between them, the vulnerability within, a vulnerability that Raveneau had found a way to exploit. Then again, he steeled himself. His back and arms ached acutely from his bizarre contortion against the wall, illusion or not. "You won't win."

And then he shook his head, this thing, his longish stringy, black hair flipping about. "I've already won," he said with a flourish that Gabriel still felt seemed empty. Bravado, that was it, sheer bravado.

"We'll see," he murmured, marking his energy so that he could hopefully track him when he left.

And then Raveneau grinned again, "I'll give your woman your regards," he said with glee. And he melted once more into the shadows. Gabriel pushed down hard on his rage. He must think and think clearly. And then, after a few moments from another side of the cave, he heard a new voice. "I know where she is, Miss Wells."

Gabriel contorted his shoulders to face the sound. "Who is that?"

And then she walked, like Raveneau had, out of the darkness. And although he'd never actually seen her, he knew immediately who it was, could feel the energy. This wasn't an illusion. This was actually Beth Wallace. "Beth, where have you been?"

"Not far," she said shakily. "She's in trouble."

"I know. You said you know where she is."

She nodded slowly, fearfully. In fact, everything about this girl seemed to be permeating fear. "She's upstairs in a bedroom but thinks she's on Dumaine Street."

"Dumaine Street?"

"Yes, your house and she thinks she's with you, but it isn't—"

At that pronouncement, a sad, sick feeling came over him. "It's Raveneau," he said solemnly.

"Yes," she answered softly.

Chapter Thirty-Six

Severing Bonds

She was tired. In fact, beyond tired and relaxing here in Gabriel's den, on Gabriel's lovely couch, at present seemed too enticing to turn away.

"Just rest, Rebecca," Gabriel said, standing near the foot of the sofa.

"I am exhausted," she murmured, pulling the off-white throw around her. And cold, she was so very tired and cold.

"It might be best you sleep, my darling." She drew in a deep breath. It chaffed distantly. There were things floating around that she couldn't quite get a grasp of. Like outside, there was a girl talking to her, and what was it she had said again?

He sat down near her in a chair but hadn't touched her since she'd entered the house. And that was another thing, the house. Why couldn't she remember what had happened? The last thing she remembered was that they were attempting a meditation. But then something, what was it, something—

"It will come back in time, my darling. You're overwrought. You just need rest." He spoke in response to her concerns, her thoughts.

There was a pressure in her chest, in her head, and then that shivering feeling, that terrible shivering feeling—then, she knew. Becca sat up on the couch and stared at Gabriel. He was sitting in the rocking chair facing the sofa, staring at her placidly as though he hadn't a care in the world.

"Are you draining me?" she whispered.

"Rebecca, you're so tired. You have to rest, dearest."

She frowned. That was the very problem. "You're sloppy."

He stared at her a little blankly. "What did you say?"

"I said you're sloppy. Gabriel doesn't call me Rebecca, and he never calls me my darling or dearest."

And then a scowl crossed the very pleasant face she was so accustomed to. "Then he is a fool."

"Isn't that the pot calling the kettle black?"

Again, he stared at her blankly. "Are you daft woman?"

"No, I think we'll leave that distinction to you. Raveneau, I presume."

He stood up, still wearing Gabriel's face but looking non-to-pleased. "You have just signed your lover's death warrant."

She stood up, throwing the blanket off of her onto the floor. "What have you done with Gabriel?"

And the next moment, Becca felt a swirl go through her head. When it stopped, she found herself somewhere she'd never been before, in a bedroom, an antiquated bedroom filled with heavy wooden furniture and a great white wrought iron bed with a canopy. "Is this better to your liking?" The man standing near the doorway said.

She sighed deeply, feeling the rush of fatigue overtaking her again. It was clear that just being in his proximity was draining energy out of her. He moved closer, and she stepped backward against an end table with a marble top and a ceramic pitcher of water that sloshed against her back. Whatever this was, illusion or not, it felt real enough.

And he, Raveneau, was playing the part of the pirate to the hilt with all the clothing, red satin shirt, sword and dagger at his waist, thigh-high brown boots, and a dark gray jacket atop it all. To her, he looked like he had stepped straight off a float at Mardi Gras. But still, that face she remembered, a puddy-like Neanderthal face. How could he be orchestrating this?

"You should be more hospitable, mon amour."

"Mon amour, are you kidding me? What do you think this is some cheap romance novel?"

Again, a hostile expression crossed his face, but something else, confusion. And what felt amazing to Becca was that she didn't feel afraid, not at all. In fact, she oddly felt like she was in the driver's seat.

"You know, I could kill you with the snap of my fingers and your lover," he rasped with exaggerated menace.

"But you haven't done it yet. Instead, you're trying to get as much energy as possible out of us first."

"You don't understand, little one. I know you," he said in a creepy voice that seemed to ring a bell somehow.

And then it flooded her mind, the beach, the man shoving her to the ground, dragging her back to the bowels of that horrible house. Of course, it was him. It had to be. "But I do," she said softly. "And I'm still not afraid of you."

Then suddenly, as if on cue, the door to the bedroom flung open, and Gabriel and Beth came barreling into the room. "Becca, are you all right?" Gabriel said, her Gabriel because she could feel it was him just being in his proximity. But then she looked around the room, recognizing the truth. Raveneau had vanished.

Becca flew into Gabriel's arms, not questioning the tangible nature of this reality that they'd found themselves in. "Are you all right," he whispered into her ear again.

"I don't know. I really, really don't know." And then her eyes focused on the quiet figure standing in front of the open door. "Beth," she murmured. "I don't understand how you're here."

"She's been shadowing you," Gabriel explained, a little out of breath. "Ever since your attempt to help her the first time at your townhouse, she's been in the vicinity, attached to you, it seems."

"I knew you were in trouble," Beth said haltingly. "I could see him following you, stalking you. He didn't pay attention to me. I wasn't important enough to be of consequence."

Gabriel turned to her. "You're much more important than you realize, Beth. You may very well have saved us all."

"But he escaped. He's gotten away," Becca said with exasperation.

"Not really," Gabriel said. "You see, he or it is bound to this place, and I think I know why — energy bonds, bonds the real Raveneau created while he was alive. This shadow of him still seems to be tapping into them. The way he had an avenue to you, Becca, he may very well have an avenue to others."

"Past lives? The slaves."

"Yes, he tortured them and then fed off of their energy. He used this ability to create illusions to do so."

"Where did he get it?"

"Hard to say, might be a natural ability or cultivated with low-level magic. But while they were under his control, he planted scenarios in their minds that caused great anguish. So symbolically, many are still chained in that dark tunnel."

She nodded as an image rose in her mind of that place, that place and all the suffering inflicted upon the prisoners there. "It's so horrible there, Gabriel."

"Yes, I've seen it firsthand," he grimaced. "Maybe, just maybe, we can help relieve some of that suffering, just a little bit."

"How can we do that? It was so long ago."

"Time isn't linear, Becca. It's all happening at once. The present informs and influences both the future and the past." And then, again, he turned to Beth, who had been silently listening. "We're going to need your help."

She nodded, looking at Becca with wide eyes but with, at least, she hoped, at least a tiny measure less fear.

She knew the way. Becca didn't want to examine too deeply why she knew a door downstairs in a cellar connected to that long winding tunnel. From there, the tunnel led to the caves near the Gulf of Mexico, where the ships had brought the captives. Gabriel went first, grabbing an illuminated oil lamp he found sitting on a downstairs table.

"I don't understand," she'd said to him. "Is this place even real?"

"In a sense, it's been created by Raveneau, his reality, where he's been existing, so to speak. So, it adheres to his rules."

"Then where is he?"

"Good question," he murmured. "Let's get going."

The three of them began their trek through the darkness. Initially, the tunnel was just that, a cramped, winding passage with dirt walls and floors that, after a while, became more stone. She wondered how long it had taken the pirates to construct this passage. As they moved forward, Beth followed them silently. Undeniably, Becca knew there was something different about her since their last encounter, but she couldn't pinpoint exactly what it was. Her senses were simply on overload from all the bizarre vibrations she was experiencing.

And then they turned a bend, and for her, it was like being punched. She extended her hand to the wall to stop herself from falling to her knees. Gabriel stopped as well, holding up the lantern. "Is this it?" he asked.

She breathed in deeply, but all she could smell was that awful stench of mold that seemed to permeate her lungs. "I can barely breathe."

Gabriel reached out, holding her arm. "I know this is hard, Becca." But the truth was that just the contact with him felt strengthening.

"What can we even do here?" she asked, staring down the tunnel at the empty manacles along the walls.

"Come on," he whispered, pulling her along. They walked a few more yards and then stopped. Gabriel turned, facing her, and then put their hands together. Though it was odd, he made no motion to include Beth. It was just the two of them. "Remember the ceremony we did to release you from bonds not for your higher good."

She nodded slowly, "Yes, I remember."

He closed his eyes and began. "For all who have been victimized here, we ask that their bonds be broken."

She closed her eyes and repeated what he'd said. Gabriel continued. "For them, we are severing all bonds that do not serve them. We ask that they are released from the influence of those who do not walk in the light of positivity. We ask that they be released from the control of those not seeking their higher good."

Becca could feel something within her, a change, a shift, and a distinct lifting of the atmosphere around them. She felt him tighten his hands in hers, and then she opened her eyes. He turned from her to Beth, who was still quietly waiting for them, somewhat blocking the entrance back to the house.

"What am I to do?" she asked quietly.

"Good question," Gabriel said a bit pointedly, and then Beth smiled back at them slowly, insidiously, and her heart sank because she knew.

"You know there are a million souls out there to take from. You've done nothing here."

Gabriel shrugged, "Maybe, maybe not. We'll see."

And the next moment, it was Raveneau staring at them, standing exactly where Beth had been. And he spoke to her directly, "You'll never really be free of me."

She took a deep breath and said slowly and emphatically, "Of course, I will."

She looked at Gabriel, and he nodded. Becca closed her eyes, feeling a distinct pull, a yank to somewhere else. And when she finally opened her eyes again, she was sitting on the carpet of the den in the Biloxi cottage, still holding Gabriel's hands.

Chapter Thirty-Seven

The Days Ahead

Her head was still spinning, and the room, in some ways, felt insubstantial, as though things had not quite solidified. But almost the very first thing that Gabriel did once he opened his eyes was haul Becca directly into his arms, pulling her right over his lap into a fierce embrace. "Thank God," he whispered, "thank God, you're all right."

And at that moment that seemed to blot out all others, she wrapped her arms around him with all the strength she had. "Let's go home," she said emphatically but feeling intently that she was indeed already there.

Before leaving the Gulf Coast behind, she and Gabriel made one last journey to the grounds where The Pirate House had once stood. Bringing a combination of herbs and crystals that she was only superficially privy to, they both walked the grounds, performing one last ceremony in an attempt to cleanse the area.

"Do you really think this will work?" she asked.

"I don't know. I hope it will help as the ritual we did in the cave. Even if we can't fully purge the area, maybe we can eliminate some of the negative energy in some small measure."

The cool wind blew in her face as they walked the perimeter of where the structure used to be. There was no doubt the area still felt problematic, heavy with imprints of negative events that had taken place over so many years, but maybe, and perhaps she was indulging her newly born optimistic nature, it felt a tad bit lighter here.

"I don't feel him."

Gabriel stopped momentarily, gazing out to the waters of The Gulf of Mexico in the distance. "Yes, well, don't focus on him. All we can hope is that he has moved on and may one day evolve as well, into something of a more benign nature."

She smiled, taking his hand, "And is that even possible?"

"Anything, anything is possible, my love."

Becca worried that the house on Dumaine Street would feel strange to her after the illusion that Raveneau had created when he'd impersonated Gabriel. But oddly enough, it didn't feel strange at all. It only felt comforting. She didn't delude herself into thinking that all her difficulties had passed or that her connection with that thing in Waveland was gone forever, although she hoped that was the case. She believed life had to be lived moment by moment, relishing what was good and learning from everything else. At least, that was the mindset that she would strive for.

"When did you know that it wasn't Beth?"

Gabriel was sitting on the sofa reading a book two nights after they'd returned to Dumaine Street. She hadn't asked him this before. In fact, there was much about the whole sequence of events that she hadn't asked him. Part of her wanted everything to be simple for a while and not open up that beastly can of worms.

He looked at her intently. "You mean, once Raveneau had taken her place?"

"Yes," she said quietly.

"Initially, I believe it was Beth. She came down into the tunnel where I was being held and helped me escape. But once we came into the bedroom, and Raveneau simply disappeared, then something changed. She felt different, not as vulnerable and fearful as she had seemed. Then I put it together."

She nodded, taking his hand. "He had a problem with subtlety."

"Yes, not giving great attention to detail. And how did you figure out, well—" and then he stopped. It seemed that Gabriel also had issues with revisiting these events.

"When he was posing as you?"

"Yes," he said a bit begrudgingly.

"Well, he kept calling me Rebecca and my darling, which you never do. And he didn't seem to want to touch me. Not like you at all. You're always touching me."

He frowned a bit. "I suppose he was afraid if he did, you'd figure it out. And as for touching you," he reached over and pulled her against him. "I'm afraid I can't help myself."

She smiled as he bent over to kiss her. "That's fine. But never call me my darling, or I'll have to get an exorcist."

He nodded, "That's a promise," and then kissed her again, making her forget, well, just about everything.

About two weeks after their return from the Gulf Coast, what Becca had been anticipating for some time finally happened. She and Gabriel had spent many quiet days recovering from their ordeal, which he explained had drained so much energy from them. They would spend days resting quite a bit, taking long walks outside along the Bayou St. John, in City Park, or in the many other beautiful spots in a city they both loved. And Becca learned something essential during this quiet time. She learned that not only could she be happy, but she could be peaceful as well.

Then one morning, when she was resting in their bed while Gabriel was working on his book in his office, she saw Beth Wallace standing in the corner of the room. Becca sat up slowly, not initially sure that this was not a dream. But then she realized that it was not.

"Are you all right?" she asked her.

The girl was quiet, watching her with very wide eyes, not so unlike those early times in her townhouse, which seemed like a million years ago. "I'm sorry I left you two in that house with him. He scared me so much."

Becca sat up, feeling much turbulence still within this soul. "It's all right. You helped Gabriel, Beth, and you warned me about him. That means so much."

She said quietly, "I've been watching you. You seem happy now, Miss Wells."

"I am Beth. I'd like you to be too."

She nodded slowly, "It feels like I will be leaving soon. I mean, I feel like I can now."

"That's wonderful. There are so many amazing things for you out there. You just need to let go and not be afraid."

"I wanted to say goodbye," she said a little tentatively.

"Yes, well, it's not really goodbye. We'll see each other again someday."

And then the girl smiled, and Becca remembered how lovely her smile was.

"I saw Beth," she said to Gabriel later that day.

He turned around, looking at her with some concern, "Are you sure—"

"Yes, it was her. I felt her energy. She's decided to move on, cross over."

He took her hand, and she realized at that moment that Gabriel taking her hand must be one of the best things in the world. "That's wonderful," his eyes lighting up. And Becca realized how soppily she was in love with this man. What in the world was she going to do with this?

"There is something I wanted to talk to you about, Becca," he said, standing up from his office chair and taking her other hand. "I've had an offer to go to Ireland to do a lecture at a University in Dublin concerning the work of a mentor I once had who was from the area, Garrett Buckley. And I thought, maybe, we could spend some time in Ireland doing research for another book."

She smiled softly, "Don't you think you should finish this one first?"

"Yes, undeniably, and maybe you could help me with that and the writing and investigations for the next one. We could work as a team."

"Ireland, huh? That doesn't sound too bad."

"And one more thing," he said, looking at her speculatively. "Before we go, I thought maybe we could get married."

A circle of warmth seemed to wrap around her heart in that instant. Was this possible for her life to become so wonderful so quickly? "Is that a proposal?" She asked with some amusement.

And then Gabriel smiled at her with that twinkle in his eye that she remembered, remembered from the very first day they met. "Maybe, but I think I can do better."

And one day, not too far in the future, beneath one of the great oak trees in City Park, he did just that.

About Author

Evelyn Klebert (1965 to present) is an author from the grand old city of New Orleans. She's written numerous acclaimed books: paranormal novels, collections of supernatural short stories, and esoteric poetry collections. She is an avid reader and student of esoteric studies intent on examining the "big questions" in life as are her characters. *Treading on Borrowed Time, one of her novels,* is a love story set in New Orleans which explores the issue of past lives, karmic obligations, as well as other dimensional beings. One of her most recent short story collections, *Travels into the Breach: Accounts of a Reclusive Mystic*, follows the exploits of a supernatural detective who specializes in psychic attacks.

Dragonflies - Journeys into the Paranormal
6 x 9 Softcover 120 pages
ISBN 978-1-88756-072-6

A powerful wizard, love-crossed ghosts, a mysterious dark warrior, and an enigmatic time traveler -- a mystical wordsmith entices you into the world of the paranormal with a collection of inspired stories. Each tale takes the journey of the dragonfly imbued with the momentum and energy of change, following a winding path that ultimately will lead you to find the truth buried beneath perception.

Gravier's Bookshop
A New Orleans Paranormal Mystery (#1)
6 x 9 Softcover 190 pages
ISBN 978-1-61342-288-5

Caroline Breslin always knew that she would have to live her life differently. Being an extremely sensitive and gifted empath in a family full of psychics has led her to a somewhat cautious existence. But she is determined to strike out on her own, moving out of the protection of her Prytania Street home. And all is going well, except, of course, if you don't count the neighbor upstairs in her apartment building, who may or may not be a dark witch, and the increasing flow of malevolent energy that seems to be directed just her way. All of that and trying to make ends meet seems a bit much for this rather inexperienced New Orleans girl. The last thing Caroline wants to do is run back to her family for help, even though she is painfully in over her head. What she really needs is a knight in shining armor or maybe just that guy that keeps haunting her dreams.

Max Gravier had no intention of becoming a recluse, but after his wife's death, it seems his life is heading in that direction. He spends his time running Gravier's Bookshop on Magazine Street and occasionally, on the quiet, helps the police solve a crime with his psychic sensitivities. That is until he answers Caroline Breslin's call, a cry for help out of his dreams that draws him rather unexpectedly into a fierce battle for a young woman's soul. Join them and the whole Breslin family psychic clan in this first installment of The New Orleans Paranormal Mystery Series, where you'll travel into a new world just a few steps into the turbulent realm of the unseen.

The Hotel Mandolin
A New Orleans Paranormal Mystery (#2)
6 x 9 Softcover 138 pages
ISBN 978-1-61342-290-8

Peril is wrapped up in the most enticing of disguises in *The Hotel Mandolin*, the second installment of The New Orleans Paranormal Mystery series. It's opulent, classic, and one of the most renowned hotels nestled deep in New Orleans' famous business district, but something is amiss at The Hotel Mandolin. PI Peter Norfleet is calling out the big guns to help him investigate a recent suicide at the famous establishment — his good friend Max Gravier, a formidable psychic, and his girlfriend, Caroline Breslin, a talented empath. But none of them can seem to scratch the surface of this puzzle, no one except Cassie Breslin, Caroline's clairvoyant mother, who has somehow tapped into an unexpected connection with a tragic ghost from the turn of the century. And the more she uncovers, the more dangerous and malevolent the mystery becomes.

The House at Pritchard Place
A New Orleans Paranormal Mystery (#3)
6 x 9 Softcover 136 pages
ISBN 978-1613422922

Nothing is really wrong with the old Warrick House on Dante St., except that there most certainly is. Nothing is exactly wrong with its new mysterious owner except that Elise is sure something doesn't add up. It isn't obvious, but sometimes the most dangerous things aren't. In the third installment of The New Orleans Paranormal Mystery series, with the help of her very psychic sister and her children, the Breslin clan, Elise Ashford is about to embark on a wild rescue mission straight into another dimension that will land her squarely somewhere she doesn't expect, right back into her past. She'll land full circle; in a childhood home whose memory still haunts her to this day — The House at Pritchard Place.

A Quiet Moment
6 x 9 Softcover 295 pages
ISBN 978-1-61342-326-4

Jacob Wyss is caught in a rut, in fact, on the verge of being engulfed by it. After an excruciating and disillusioning divorce, his life as an artist in a sleepy-college town at the foot of the Appalachian mountains has become quiet, routine, and maddening in its predictability. One wintry day, his deep restlessness drives him out in precarious conditions to a largely empty bookstore nearly devoid of another living soul, nearly.

Aimee Marston isn't like everyone else. On the surface, she lives a sedate life working as a feature writer for a small local newspaper in addition to several other editorial jobs to help make ends meet. But just beneath, her existence is largely not her own. She is a sensitive, an empathic psychic, guided by her calling to use her gifts to help others. Unfortunately, as a result, her secretiveness has made her defensive and protective of herself, preventing her from having much of a life.

A psychic call for help sends Aimee out on a freezing January morning, where her destiny and Jacob's collide, spiraling both their lives onto an unexpected and often disturbing track. Two lonely souls connect, not by accident, but by design. Theirs is the intersection of two spiritual paths, two lovers who must struggle to overcome the phantoms of a past life, as well as the challenges of their own inner demons to carve out an extraordinary future together.

Treading on Borrowed Time
6 x 9 Softcover 198 pages
ISBN 978-1-61342-214-4

For Julia Moreau, life seems complicated. Emerging from a failed marriage and managing a lifetime of diabetes, she lives alone in her childhood home, where she communicates with the spirit of her Great Aunt Lilia. But Julia doesn't have a clue what complicated is until she is thrust into being the key chess piece in a match between two powerful men of extraordinary abilities on the wild hunt for a mystical creature hidden in the heart of New Orleans' French Quarter. Will Julia lose her soul to the karma of a devastating past life or her heart to the love of a man driven by dark forces? What is clear is that whichever way she turns, she is *Treading on Borrowed Time*.

Sanctuary of Echoes
6 x 9 Softcover 338 pages
ISBN 978-1-61342-211-3

Ghosts unacknowledged do not sleep.

Corey Knight has resigned herself to a quiet, reclusive life spent living out the rest of her days in her childhood home on the fringes of New Orleans' French Quarter. But the unexpected specter of her deceased father plunges her into a mad quest for a missing supernatural weapon unearthed long ago. And unfortunately, her only ally is a lost love she once betrayed.

Iain Shaw returns to New Orleans, a city he abandoned a decade before while fleeing a devastating past. Here, he is forced to confront it again in the visage of the woman he once adored - one that he is now determined to get back at any cost.

Follow them both in a wild paranormal tale of discovery and redemption as they confront and unearth the echoes of a buried and unyielding truth that once tore them irreparably apart.

Dragonflies - Journeys into the Paranormal
6 x 9 Softcover 120 pages
ISBN 978-1-88756-072-6

A powerful wizard, love-crossed ghosts, a mysterious dark warrior, and an enigmatic time traveler -- a mystical wordsmith entices you into the world of the paranormal with a collection of inspired stories. Each tale takes the journey of the dragonfly imbued with the momentum and energy of change, following a winding path that will ultimately lead you to find the truth buried beneath perception.

A Ghost of a Chance
6 x 9 Softcover 174 pages
ISBN 978-1-88756-050-4

Jack Brennan, an ambitious high-powered attorney, dies, only to find himself constrained to a peculiar afterlife as an earth-bound spirit trapped in an old Virginia farmhouse with a very much living, reclusive writer of campy vampire novels. Hallie Barkly recovering from a painful and disillusioning divorce, has forged a career and exorcised her demons by writing under the pseudonym of Sebastian Winters. Their lives intersect, and two unconventional lovers are brought together under insurmountable circumstances. Together they must battle an unseen force hell-bent on possessing Hallie's life and bridge death itself to make possible what cannot be - to find a chance.

Breaking Through the Pale
6 x 9 Softcover 92 pages
ISBN 978-1-88756-045-0

Journey with metaphysical author Evelyn Klebert into a collection of short stories that travel beyond the pale into the unpredictable realm of the paranormal.

In "A Grey Mourning," a disillusioned man encounters a mysterious being on the foggy streets of New Orleans. "Contact" is a tale of automatic writing, when a young artist establishes communication with a spirit guide, and the victim of a car crash unravels the true nature of her existence in "Dancing on the Threshold." The final tale is called "Isolation," in which a confused and disoriented woman finds herself in an old, quaint house where she must piece together the mystical implications *surrounding her predicament.*

Explanations
6 x 9 Softcover 82 pages
ISBN 978-1-93493-515-6

In this, her second poetry collection, Evelyn Klebert takes us down the intricate path of a personal journey. Life, with its particular struggles, pitfalls, and ultimately triumphs, clearly begins to mirror a universal path, the quest for answers that we all ultimately pursue. In this reflective, esoteric collection, we can all explore and seek some of life's elemental mysteries and, hopefully, when all is said and done, emerge with some *Explanations.*

The Witches' Own
6 x 9 Softcover 124 pages
ISBN 978-1-61342-058-4

On the surface, things seem quiet and serene in the picturesque coastal village of Kilmarnock, Virginia. But something unseen roams its lush forests as the past and present collide, and the unthinkable begins to wreak its vengeance. Young Lucy Bonner is executed for witchcraft in the town's distant and brutal past. Her death triggers an unholy chain of events that grasp at the restless heart of novelist Peter McQuade, spurring him towards a quest to uncover the dark and terrifying truth.

The Left Palm
And Other Halloween Tales of the Supernatural
6 x 9 Softcover 104 pages
ISBN 978-1-93493-556-9

Halloween is the time of year when that veil between worlds is thinned, and you can just catch a quick glimpse into the realm of the unknowable. In this collection of short stories, Evelyn Klebert takes you to a place where ordinary life splinters into the sphere of the paranormal.

The journey begins with one woman's unstoppable quest for vengeance against a supernatural creature in "Wolves" and continues in an old historical graveyard where a horrifying discovery is uncovered in "Emma

Fallon." In "The Soul Shredder," a psychiatrist's unusual patient opens his eyes to a disturbing new view of reality, while in "Wildflowers," a woman strikes up a supernatural friendship with impossible implications. And in "The Left Palm," a fortuneteller in the French Quarter receives a most unexpected and terrifying customer.

White Harbor Road
And Other Tales of Paranormal Romance
6 x 9 Softcover 130 pages
ISBN 978-1-61342-066-9

A psychic soul mate, a time traveler, a horror writer, and an enigmatic stranger take a selection of resilient, life-battered heroines to a place of paranormal healing and transformation. In this collection of short stories, White Harbor Road is the last stop where life's burdens and hardships evolve into something unexpected.

The Broken Vow
Vol. I of The Clandestine Exploits of a Werewolf
6 x 9 Softcover 140 pages
ISBN 978-1-61342-133-8

In the heart of every man, there is a history. In the heart of every monster, there is a story. In this first installment of *The Clandestine Exploits of a Werewolf,*

Ethan Garraint is on a vendetta that begins in the heart of the Pyrenees with the fall of Montségur and leads him to the streets of New Orleans nearly five hundred years later. But the person he chases isn't really a man anymore, and Ethan has been a werewolf for almost a millennium. With the aid of a gifted seer, he is on a blood hunt that will culminate in a journey that crosses the line between heaven and earth and ends somewhere in between.

Travels into the Breach: Accounts of a Reclusive Mystic
6 x 9 Softcover 176 pages
ISBN 978-1-61342-323-3

At first glance, his life seems quiet, serene, and even uneventful. Malachi McKellan, a 65 five-year-old widower and author of esoteric books, lives largely as a recluse in a house situated just off the banks of Bayou St. John in New Orleans. But unbeknownst to most, he is also a bit of a detective, a specific kind of detective whose specialty is psychic attacks. Alongside his lifelong companion and spirit guide Simon Tull, a nineteenth century, twenty something English gent, Malachi battles the unseen, and is an unacknowledged hero to the most vulnerable - most of the population who have no idea what is really happening beneath the surface of the world in which they live.

In this collection of adventures, Malachi McKellan and Simon Tull wage war against the most insidious elements of the paranormal. In "The Three," Malachi and Simon come to the aid of a young woman being victimized by a group of dark witches. An old apartment building is the scene of an unimaginable battle against monstrous forces in "The Lost Soul." Malachi and Simon find themselves strategizing against a psychic vampire in "Obsession," and "The Hotel" turns back time to the 1980s where Malachi confronts a demonic spirit. In "Between," a past life is revisited as Malachi attempts to rescue a beloved sister from committing her existence to vengeance, and "The Wedding" takes a personal turn when Malachi must confront painful truths while endeavoring to protect his niece from a potentially devastating union. Travel into the Breach with a pair of paranormal warriors who choose to confront overwhelming forces on a battlefield unsuspected by most.

Considerations
6 x 9 Softcover 68 pages
ISBN 978-1-88756-062-7

Sometimes the struggle to understand the meaning and complexities of living comes down to a single moment of introspection or a fleeting yet meaningful reflection. This collection of poetry by Evelyn Klebert takes you down a winding path of self-discovery where the resolution may not always be absolute, but the journey is indeed unforgettable. It is a wide and varied map of inspired poetry for your examination and consideration.

Appointment with the Unknown: The Hotel Stories
6 x 9 Softcover 151 pages
ISBN 978-1613423608

A hotel, for most, represents a normal place, a predictable realm of commonality. One might even go as far to say a safe space, the reliable where nothing particularly unusual is expected to happen. Or is it? Dimensional traveling, spirit guides, mystical storms, and soul mates separated by time are only a few elements dotting this supernatural landscape. Drop into a collection of romantic paranormal stories where that place of commonality is only the threshold, the jumping-off point, for extraordinary adventures into the unknown.

The Tethering: A Portent of Crows
6 x 9 Softcover 201 pages
ISBN 978-1613425992

Deborah Brandt's beloved Aunt Gena always told her that she was special, a bit different, and would have to live her life, unlike other people. Of course, this she disregarded as the ramblings of her lovely but notably eccentric aunt. Although there were the things that Aunt Gena said that seemed true — like Deborah being sensitive to energy shifts, having potentially psychic impressions, and dreaming of a spirit guide — none of it could be real. But the most ridiculous thing that her Aunt Gena told her before she died was that someone special was out there for her. She said that he was an extraordinary man who was not only her perfect match but someone who she would learn from so that they could help the world in difficult times. How ridiculous! It sounds like a fairy tale, and no such person exists.

Daniel Wren is unique. He has been raised and trained from a young age to hone his psychic gifts. He lives in a world unimagined by most. And he has been waiting for years to contact his counterpart, soulmate, if you will. But the problem is that she is painfully unaware of the type of life that he lives and the life she would be entering into if they came together.

His dilemma becomes how best to proceed. How can he win her over and move forward before outside forces take that decision away from him?

The Lady in the Blue Dress Paperback
6 x 9 Softcover 214 pages
ISBN 978-1613426005

When she was a child, Mika Devalieur was introduced to her grandmother's most precious possession — a priceless and mysterious painting that she simply called The Lady in the Blue Dress. Upon Adele St. Clair's death, the painting is left in the care of her granddaughter with only one stipulation. Mika must hand over the family heirloom to a total stranger. Mika Devalieur desperately wants to deny her beloved grandmother's last request, but she can't. Torn between her Gran's last wishes and her desire to hold onto the Lady, she ultimately journeys to rural Virginia, where an enigmatic man shows her that this painting is only the beginning.

What quickly becomes clear is that James Clairmont knows much more about her and the Lady than he is letting on. He begins to slowly unravel a powerful supernatural connection that spans three generations of her family. Mika finds herself desperate to uncover the entire truth before she falls in love with a man filled with so many secrets — secrets about him, about her, and most especially about The Lady in the Blue Dress. (First published on Kindle Vella, episodes 1-23.)

Visit Evelyn's website at:
www.evelynklebert.com

Cornerstone Book Publishers
www.cornerstonepublishers.com